KU-181-998

I GAVE HIM MY BEST SHOT

By the same author

Because Abe Died, Book Guild Publishing 2013

I GAVE HIM MY BEST SHOT

June Felton

Book Guild Publishing

First published in Great Britain in 2015 by
The Book Guild Ltd
9 Priory Business Park
Wistow Road
Leics LE8 0RX

Copyright © June Felton 2015

The right of June Felton to be identified as the author of
this work has been asserted by her in accordance with the
Copyright, Designs and Patents Act 1988.

All rights reserved. No part of this publication may be reproduced,
transmitted, or stored in a retrieval system, in any form
or by any means, without permission in writing from the publisher,
nor be otherwise circulated in any form of binding or cover other than
that in which it is published and without a similar condition being
imposed on the subsequent purchaser.

All characters in this publication are fictitious and any resemblance to
real people, alive or dead, is purely coincidental.

Typesetting in Garamond by
Ellipsis Digital Ltd, Glasgow

Printed and bound in Great Britain by
CPI Group (UK) Ltd, Croydon, CR0 4YY

A catalogue record for this book is available from
The British Library.

ISBN 978 1 910508 52 7

To Anton

Contents

CONTENTS

1

I Gave Him My Best Shot – June 1992

It might have been the sound of a car backfiring that startled her. Lying on a lounger in the garden, worrying that she had left Max alone in the house to wait for Barney, their autistic son, and feeling a presence near her, she opened her eyes. There, silhouetted against the sun, looming large, was Barney. His arms dangled at his side, and he held a small gun in his right hand. It made no sense. Hearing groans coming from the house, Anna leapt up and ran inside. Barney followed slowly behind.

'What have you done?'

'I gave him my best shot,' Barney replied. 'You told Madellaine that you wanted to be shot of him.'

'Oh my God!' Her heart pounding, her legs trembling, she rushed to see her husband Max sitting up against the wall with blood oozing from his shoulder, staining his white shirt.

For the past twelve years, Anna had devoted her life to Barney. It was unimaginable that his naivety could have caused this calamity.

'I told you he's fucking mad! Call an ambulance,' Max groaned through clenched teeth. 'For God's sake, take the gun away… get him out of here.'

Anna, consumed with panic, approached Barney gently and held out her hand.

'Can I have the gun, please, Barney?' Her voice was more pleading than threatening.

'Have I done something wrong?' Barney asked, handing Anna the gun.

Anna rushed back into the kitchen to dial 999 and in a

tremulous voice said 'My husband has been shot.' The operator seemed to waste a lot of time with questions before telling Anna to stay where she was and that an ambulance and the police would be with her shortly.

Kneeling beside Max, she unbuttoned his shirt to examine the wound. Fortunately the wound was in the right shoulder, well above his heart. Anna carefully mopped up the blood with a tea towel she grabbed from the kitchen. Grim-faced, pallid and in pain, Max sat clutching his right shoulder. Neither of them said a word. They could never have imagined that after being married for twenty-three years, each would now feel like a stranger to the other.

Now twelve years old, Barney seemed to control the whole family with his demands and rages, but Anna, believing in the power of perseverance and of love, had been blind to the effect that her preoccupation with Barney had had on her older son, Oska, on her husband Max and on herself. She was consumed by Barney's idiosyncratic behaviour and had no other thought beyond looking after him, while Barney – having no other thought than to maintain his singular world – was oblivious of the life his mother had given up.

Six minutes later the ambulance arrived.

The medical team gave Max an injection for the pain and reassured him that they were taking him to Accident & Emergency.

'At which hospital?' Anna asked.

She thought she heard them say The Royal Free, which was a few miles away from their home in north west London. She was too distraught to say anything to Max as she watched him being lifted onto a stretcher. His penetrating look of accusation added to her agony.

As the ambulance drove away, it was as if time stood still. Her thoughts went back to the events of the last six days. The trigger for it all had been when Max's personal assistant Dinah had phoned Anna to say that she and Max were deeply in love; they had been for years. Anna, shocked to the core of her being, and in an eruption of fury at his deceit, could not stop her emotions from spiralling out of control. Enraged, she had screamed at Max to pack his bags and leave immediately. She could not see further than Max's betrayal of their marriage – it was the only thing that mattered. She had no thought of how Barney and Oska would be affected at the sight of their mother exploding in a frenzy of hatred for their father.

Anna hardly noticed the unmarked car pull up and a man and woman walk towards her. Showing his police identity card, the man introduced himself.

'Good morning. I'm Sergeant Murray and this is my colleague, Constable Grahame, from Victim Support. May we come in?' Neither was dressed in uniform.

Anna burst into tears. The words 'Victim Support' confirmed her lifetime of suffering. All those years she hadn't allowed herself to think of herself as a victim. She loved Barney and couldn't blame him. What else could she have done but take care of him? All those arguments between Max and her came down to 'we can't let that child run our life'. And now Max had proved his point. Suddenly realising that Barney might have to be sent away, she collapsed onto one of the wooden chairs around the oak table in the kitchen.

'Could you tell us what happened?' Sergeant Murray asked calmly.

'I must go to Barney.' Anna's first thought was to protect her son. He would never survive questioning, nor cope with being taken to a strange place.

'It was an accident,' she added. 'My autistic son fired the gun by mistake. He didn't know what he was doing. He doesn't always understand language.'

'Where is he, and where is the gun?'

Anna took the gun out of the kitchen drawer and handed it over. 'This gun belongs to my older son Oska; he has a licence.' She watched Sergeant Murray put on a pair of latex gloves, then drop the gun into a sealed plastic bag. In trying to sound rational, she heard her own quivering voice and felt defeated. 'I must find Barney. I think he's in the garden. He doesn't understand what's happened.' Anna's trembling and pallor reinforced the officer's gentle approach.

Her mind slipped back, trying to recall what happened. She remembered calling Barney to hurry up, because Max was waiting for him. She had then left Max in the hall and gone through the kitchen and out onto the terrace. It was a perfect summer day, with blue skies and hardly a leaf moving on the trees. She'd walked under the canopy of blue wisteria hanging over the terrace and stretched out on a lounger outside the kitchen door. She'd looked up at the wax-like magnolia, its dark green leaves climbing up the weathered wall to the drawing room, forming a square with the opposite wall of the dining room. In her mind she would draw shapes of the intricate petals of magnolia surrounding their delicate yellow stamens; her years at art college had instilled the habit of drawing images in her head.

'Mrs Elliott? Mrs Elliott, I'm sorry. I realise this is very distressing for you but we will have to question him,' Sergeant Murray insisted.

'Can I help? You see, Barney has never left me. He suffers from autism. He won't respond to strangers and he could have a tantrum. He had an epileptic fit a few days ago. I'll go and get him.' Anna went out into the garden to find Barney repeatedly rocking backwards and forwards, a habitual sign of high anxiety. Suddenly she noticed how much he had filled out; he had become overweight and ungainly. Anna knew she had to protect him.

'Barney, these people want to ask you some questions. You must listen carefully and please tell them everything. Let's go inside.'

Sitting around the kitchen table, Barney remembered his lunch. 'I have to have my hamburger and chips! Max said he would take me to a restaurant.'

'Max is in hospital. He's not well because you shot him with Oska's gun.'

'Is Max dead? Will you take me to the restaurant? I'm hungry.'

Anna, knowing Barney's strange response would help the policeman understand the problem, relaxed a little but her thoughts still leapt from one thing to another. She thought of Max, needing to know the extent of his injury. She thought of Oska, and blamed him for not locking away his gun. She struggled to understand how a casual remark that she couldn't even remember making could have such devastating consequences.

'Barney, did you use the gun to shoot your father?' Sergeant Murray asked.

'I gave him my best shot,' Barney insisted.

'Why did you shoot your father?'

'We all wanted to get shot of him, he is unreliable, he should have come home, we are tired of waiting for him. He kept his promise about coming today but it was too long for me to wait. I've waited one hundred and fifty-six hours and forty minutes. And Anna cries every night. She is also very upset because Max did something he shouldn't have, but I don't know what it is so I can't put it right. Rob, my friend who lives next door, also says he can't make things better and he understands how I feel. He says you just have to wait for the right time.'

Tears welled up in Anna's eyes as she contemplated Barney's innocence, and wondered whether anybody else would understand. Yet beyond that she realised that shooting his father, whatever his intention, had plucked Barney out of the privacy and protection of his home into a new and dangerous world of police, social workers, psychologists and lawyers.

'Did anybody tell you to shoot your father?' The kindly manner in which Sergeant Murray asked the question was a relief to Anna.

'If I tell you, can I have my hamburger and chips?'

'Of course.'

The Victim Support officer made a telephone call.

'No cheese, just ketchup,' Barney cautioned her.

'Can you tell me if anybody told you to shoot your father?' Sergeant Murray repeated.

'I heard Anna tell Madellaine she knew she wasn't being rational but she was so upset she wanted Max out of the house, she couldn't bear to look at him and wanted to get shot of him.'

Sergeant Murray turned to Anna. 'I understand your dilemma. I don't think it's appropriate to take Barney to the station for an interview at this stage, but an accidental shooting is a serious matter and has to be fully investigated, reported and recorded.'

Automatically Anna asked them if they would like a cup of tea. The Victim Support officer offered to make it. Anna flopped into a chair and held her head in her hands and, paralysed by the pain of what was happening, her mind went blank.

Fifteen minutes later the doorbell rang and the hamburger and chips arrived. After lifting the hamburger out of the cardboard box, Barney turned it upside down, then sideways, and opened the bun to examine the tomato sauce. Satisfied, he sat down at the kitchen table. Absorbed in his meal, he delicately lifted each chip into his mouth, indicating that he had had enough questioning for now.

The police sergeant suggested he phone the hospital to enquire about Max.

'You are both being so kind, I can't tell you how much your support is helping me cope.'

'Thank you. We're just doing our job,' Sergeant Murray said.

After replacing the phone he turned to Anna. 'Good news about your husband. He has returned from the theatre; the bullet was successfully removed.'

'Thank you, I've been so worried about my husband, I'll phone the hospital later.' Anna's mind now spun to Oska, who had gone out for the day, needing to relax in the middle of his A-level exams. Four years older than Barney, Oska played a vital part in helping Anna with his younger brother. Now caught in the middle of a terrible row between his mother and father, Oska thought that Anna was being lied to by Dinah, his father's personal assistant, who he had never liked. Anna, desperately needing to contact Oska, ransacked her phonebook to find his friend's phone number. Fortunately Oska was still there. She heard someone call, 'Oska, it's your mother'. Anna hadn't thought through how to tell Oska and when he said, 'Hello mum, what's up?' she detected his slight irritation at being disturbed.

Her voice faltered. 'Please come home.'

'Why, what's wrong?' Oska insisted.

'There's been an accident. Barney has shot Max with your gun. He's alive, and it will be all right, but please come home now.' She struggled to get the words out, her wavering voice barely audible.

'What! My gun is locked away. Oh my God, I'm coming…'

Anna thought of Oska, the perfect first child. He had her generous spirit and Max adored him. But Barney's behaviour when he arrived four years later, was hard to understand. Anna recalled thinking the second child was supposed to be easier but even as an infant Barney, with his inexplicable crying, seemed to control the whole family.

Ten minutes later Anna heard Oska's car screech to a standstill outside the house and the front door was pushed open. Oska ran into the kitchen. Unlike Barney, Oska had Anna's fine features and large brown eyes. At five foot six he was slim but well toned from his stints at the gym. Dressed in a navy T-shirt that hung loosely over well-cut blue jeans, he had natural good taste. First kissing his mother, he then shook hands with the policeman. 'What's happened?' Oska asked. 'How is Dad?'

'We've spoken to the hospital and he'll be alright' Anna replied.

'Your brother seems to have got hold of your gun and used it.' Sergeant Murray looked directly at Oska, waiting for an explanation.

'I have a licence to hold a gun. I belong to the Hendon Rifle and Pistol Club and have held a licence for six months. I've no idea how Barney found it; it's locked away in its cupboard and I carry the key on my keyring.' Oska fumbled for his keyring. 'See, here it is.'

Sergeant Murray examined the key and asked if they might examine the cupboard now.

'Of course, I don't understand how Barney found my gun.' Sergeant Murray followed Oska upstairs.

Anna got up to give Barney his Diet Coke before he asked for it, then flopping back onto a chair realized that she had relied too much on Oska to help her with Barney. She thought too of Max, whose needs had also always been subjugated to Barney's.

Anna felt responsible for all that had happened. Why had she ever thought she could solve Barney's problems? Max was far more realistic. How often had she rejected Max's attempts even to talk about Barney going into a sheltered community? She had been convinced that he would improve at home. An overpowering sadness combined with a sense of relief washed over her as she no longer blamed Max for his opinion, which she had attributed to his lack of caring. He had understood more than she had allowed herself to admit. Even though it had been clear Barney was getting more difficult, she couldn't reject him. She had adapted to his behaviour for so long that she'd forgotten there was any alternative. Now she felt desperately alone, aware that she had done harm to the three most precious people in her life. When did it all go wrong? Where had she missed the signs? Max wanted Barney to live in a protected environment, but she didn't know of any nor had she made any effort to find out. It was not in her nature to give up, whereas it was in Max's to escape. Her determination had given her strength but now she wondered whether she could cope without Max.

Anna's anguish turned to another fear. She had coped with Barney for almost thirteen years and had managed to hide the bizarre elements of her life from others. Now all that was at an end; she would have to face lawyers, social workers, psychologists and possibly even newspapers. She had shielded Barney and herself in the privacy of her home, secure in the knowledge that no one could judge her; her pain and her shame was private. Only Madellaine, her friend and neighbour, freely entered her home, offering her help in a crisis. Perhaps Madellaine would now have to be a witness to those words 'I'd like to get shot of him'. If so, she could rely on Madellaine to give a good account of Barney, as she had often experienced his tantrums. Anna recalled the moment when Barney became frightened of Madellaine, the day he decided to scream, 'Mad-Elaine must go away.' They had both laughed and thought

Barney imaginative, never dreaming that his phobias would dominate his behaviour. She was often amused by Barney's phonetic interpretation of language, fascinated by the way he made up new words. How was she going to explain to a judge that Barney attached different meanings to language? In the past, Anna had attributed his unique ability to hidden genius and remained intrigued with what she saw as a fertile imagination. She recalled the time when he was five years old and had called their carpet a floor blanket.

Oska and Sergeant Murray came down the stairs.

'I told you, mum,' Oska burst out. 'I always keep my gun cupboard key on me. My gun is still in the cupboard – so where did Barney find this gun?'

'That is what we must find out,' said Sergeant Murray. He handed Oska a pair of latex gloves, before allowing him to carefully examine the gun Barney had used.

'I've never seen this gun before,' Oska declared, emphatically.

'I'm afraid I must now question Barney,' Sergeant Murray said, looking at Anna.

'Perhaps it would be better if I questioned him,' Oska suggested.

Sergeant Murray took out a note pad and pencil while Oska called Barney in from the playroom.

'Barney, where did you get this gun? It's all right, nothing will happen to you if you tell me.'

'I can't.'

'Why?' Oska pleaded.

'Because I've made a promise and if I break my promise, someone will break my neck. I know a neck isn't the same as a promise but they can both be broken.'

'Nobody will break your neck. I won't let them. Sergeant Murray won't let them, nor will mum and dad.'

Barney, unable to maintain eye contact, rocked backwards and forwards under the scrutiny of Sergeant Murray. Anna felt unnerved, as if she and Barney were inextricably bound in each other's anxiety. Her thoughts went back to that traumatic phone call that had started it all. Anna did not want to believe Dinah but she had sounded so convincing, especially whilst, sobbing desperately, she told Anna that Max had insisted on her having an abortion – because their child might be autistic. Anna wanted to die with the pain of hearing it all; why would Dinah, a trusted family friend, want to destroy the family? Shocked to the core that Max could have lied to her, cheated on her she did not for a moment stop to think that Dinah might not have been telling the truth.

2

Max's Awakening – 1992

As Max came round from the anaesthetic, the last thing he remembered was going home to take Barney out for the day. Being uncomfortable about using his own front door key, he had rung the bell.

'Barney's upstairs, he'll be down in a minute,' Anna had told Max in a detached voice, emphasising her cold disaffection.

'Come down Barney, Max is here,' Anna shouted then turned to Max, 'What time will you be back?'

'I'll see how it goes – I'll phone you.' His half-hearted reply barely concealed his resistance to the outing as Anna left to go into the garden.

He was counting the minutes; how he would spend one hour maximum in a restaurant where he could be sure of getting Barney's routine hamburger without cheese but with chips drowned in tomato sauce, followed by vanilla ice cream and Diet Coke. Then, watching him slowly eat one chip at a time, he would be aware of people looking at Barney, who would never look up from his plate or say one word until he had finished. At least he could rely on him not to make a mess. After eating, their conversation would be made up of a series of contrived questions and answers leading Barney into monologue. Max wondered how Anna coped. After lunch, they would go for a walk in the park, then onto the bookshop where Barney could spend a good hour looking for something that, complementing his latest obsession, would be added to his collection of objects that had meaning only to him.

Max recalled hearing Barney walking around his bedroom, a sign of his heightened anxiety, reminding him how these outings usually left him with a deadening feeling. Barney would talk endlessly about his obsessive interest leaving him with both an overwhelming desire to return him to Anna, and with a crushing guilt at his own inability to cope. He worried how Barney would greet him after not seeing him or having any contact for six days. He recalled how he'd waited hesitantly in the hall, as if needing permission to come into his own home. Looking around he'd admired the way Anna had had the vision to enhance the Georgian proportions of the square hall by painting everything white. White walls, white cornices, white marble floor, and the rosewood chiffonier with the green marble top under the large Adam mirror. He remembered how Anna had told him that the secret was to make every white a slightly different tone in order to give the interior movement and depth as the light bounced off the different surfaces. The hall was strewn with five, richly-coloured Persian rugs; four leading off the central rug, each directed towards the four doors to the dining room, the lounge, the playroom and kitchen.

Max had looked at himself in the mirror as he plucked up courage to do his duty, seeing as if for the first time his tense poorly-shaven face and thin pursed lips. Diminished by his sense of failure, he seemed to have lost his six foot two bearing. He had tried to look his best in neutral-coloured casuals. His straight, dark hair, lately streaked with grey and in need of a trim, fell across his forehead. His bloodshot eyes hardly focused as he waited for Barney's heavy footsteps.

Lying in hospital Max reflected that all he had tried to do was not to upset the balance, the harmony, in the family. They had managed because each of them played their part in containing Barney's idiosyncrasies. His one damn stupid mistake – and Dinah's malign interference – had destroyed the love and trust essential to their functioning. It had broken Anna's hold on reality. He couldn't believe that they had come to such a low point in their marriage and that Anna had shown no sign of wanting to repair it.

Perhaps he shouldn't have left when Anna had lost all sense of proportion. Her distress had frightened him and he thought that if he went away as she demanded, she would calm down. He should have realised that after twelve years of continually working day and night to take care of Barney, combined with her commitment to design a new fashion collection each season for their business, she had become totally exhausted. He now realised that he should have stood his ground with Anna and protested that Dinah was a liar – and much more. He knew he was guilty of damaging the one person he loved in life and was deeply upset that Oska and Barney had witnessed the mayhem.

Max reflected sadly how Anna had let herself go. That wonderful head of curly hair the colour of rich nutmeg was now mostly grey and tied back in an elastic band, making her appear much older than her forty-five years. Her heart-shaped face with its sharp jaw line and pale skin accentuating her beautiful brown eyes and rosebud mouth was still there, but hidden behind a mask of tension built up of years of total dedication and consequent exhaustion.

He thought he must at least phone Anna and try to talk to her, even at the risk of another rejection. He reached out to the hospital phone at the side of his bed.

Anna rushed into the hall to answer the phone.

'Anna? How are you? We must talk, I must come home,' Max insisted. There was a momentary silence on the other side of the line and he heard Anna taking a deep breath.

'You always said Barney could read people's minds,' Max went on. 'Well, he certainly read mine. I've been contemplating suicide all week. The only reason I didn't finish the job and kill myself was because I didn't know what would happen to you and the boys. In a way I felt some sort of relief when Barney shot me.' Max broke down and in a voice she could hardly make out, pleaded: 'I need to tell you my side of the story… Even a criminal gets to defend himself. You never gave me a chance. I think after all these years, I deserve better than that.'

A tear slid down her cheek. 'Oh Max, I'm so sorry. I was so upset. You had just come home with the amazing news that Barney had been accepted at Highlands. It's a fantastic opportunity and a dream come true: Barney would go to a normal school and at last everybody would value him as I do. Then to hear what Dinah told me was so upsetting I couldn't think – even now I can't think clearly. When can you come home?'

'As soon as they release me from hospital. My things are at a bed-and-breakfast off Russell Square.'

'I thought you were staying with Dinah.'

Max contained a surge of anger; her words momentarily left him stunned.

'Absolutely not! Why would you possibly think that? I really don't think I should come home until you trust me. We can't risk going through another trauma. I'm terribly worried about Barney.'

'Oh! There is so much I don't understand. It's a total nightmare with the police. Barney could be sent away, we need a good lawyer. I don't know what to do.'

'I'll come home as soon as they discharge me. In the meantime, phone up Charles Devon, he's an excellent lawyer and is working on a few matters connected to Dinah.' Anna felt a warm glow sweep over her. 'I love you,' she said.

'We'll do this together.' Max was relieved, the conversation had gone better than he'd expected.

Anna felt that she could function again. The past six days since she had insisted that Max leave their home made her realise how much she needed him. How could she ever have been so stupid as to let one row over one misdeed, no matter how terrible, destroy their family? She had let her obsessive belief in fidelity and trust distort any mature judgement.

Anna regretted not giving Max a chance to tell his side of the story. How could she have believed that Max would abandon the family? Her reaction and everything that followed had destabilised Barney; she doubted whether he would ever recover from the trauma and so would lose his place at Hillside.

She recalled how Oska tried to protect Barney by taking him into the playroom and putting on an Elvis film. Oska had told her how Barney couldn't be distracted and had paced up and down the room holding his hands over his ears frantically repeating, 'Dinah must Die-now, Die-now, Die-now Dinah, Die now Dinah.'

She had been so overwhelmed by events that she had left Oska to take charge of Barney.

Whilst it was in Oska's nature to be kind, she had expected too much of him. Perhaps her overpowering pre-occupation with Barney had given Max and Oska no choice but to support her but this time she'd gone too far. She felt Oska's anger, and now realising how much she had taken his supportive role for granted, saw she was at fault.

Whilst Anna couldn't recall her exact words when she told Madellaine that she 'wanted to get shot of Max', she knew that Barney had overheard and that had led to him shooting Max. A few inches lower and he would have killed his father. Anna didn't know how she was going to protect Barney from the consequences. She wept again, recalling how Barney had told the police sergeant he was pleased Max was alive and still had a heart, because if his heart wasn't broken it meant that he could still love him. Her thoughts went on and on, round and round.

Oska insisted he believed that Barney's sudden obsession with killing was due to his friendship with Rob, Madellaine's son. Both Max and Oska had warned her but her need for some respite had made her welcome Rob into their home. Anna also suspected that Oska was jealous of Rob. She wondered whether Rob's anger towards his own father, who had walked out on his family, had influenced Barney.

All these thoughts but added to her confusion.

3

Pondicherry – 1970

Lying in her all-white bedroom, on the white silk eiderdown, Anna sank into a comforting reverie. She thought back to the time when, as an accomplished and productive dress designer, she had helped Max build up their successful business. She had only had to look at a piece of material to plan the design in her mind. Her collections were fluid and flattering to any size and their luxurious fabrics and fine detailing demanded respect. She was surprised when she had won the Designer of the Year Award at The Fashion College. She had worked quietly believing that every stitch mattered and whereas most of the other fashion students were designing dramatic styles in vibrant colours, creating dynamic impressions at the expense of detail, she had used the best materials she could afford in muted colours that blended in with the soft light of England. It made sense to use her prize money to research into fabrics, silk and bead embroidery, and that gave her the confidence she might not have had, helped too by the head of the fashion course at the prize giving ceremony saying, 'We expect great things from you, Anna'.

She thought of how free she had felt travelling around India on her own. It was 1970, everybody seemed to be going to India and Pondicherry was a favoured goal. A former French colony, Pondicherry had become part of an independent India in 1954. It was full of crumbling cathedrals, its leafy boulevards bordered by narrow streets lined with painted houses that made you feel as if you were in the South of France. Its long coastline with wide beaches and warm seas provided the perfect combination of French and Indian culture. But that was not why she was in Pondicherry.

She had gone there to buy luxurious materials to inspire her fashion design career. It was still the swinging sixties and London was ready for new ideas in fashion. Anna saw the possibilities.

She recalled the day she first met Max in one of the silk shops hidden in the back streets. Out of the corner of her eye she was aware of him watching her drape the silks and scrunch up sections to check for creasing. Wanting to hold a piece of silk to the light, she backed towards the door and bumped into him.

'Sorry, I've got a bit carried away in this treasure trove.'

'My pleasure,' Max stepped aside. 'You seem to know a lot about it,' he ventured.

'Beginner's enthusiasm. I'm a dress designer, so I'm kind of doing research.'

'Well it must be my lucky day! I want to import fabrics to London,' Max responded.

'Really!' Anna thought this was just a ploy but instinctively trusted him.

At just over five-foot three, she looked up at Max. Her curly chestnut hair under a straw hat framed her face and brown eyes. Her petite frame was swathed in a white cotton kaftan top over white baggy trousers, exposing slim ankles and dainty feet in brown leather sandals. She was weighed down by a large multi-striped fabric bag, into which she was stuffing sample cuttings from the vast collection of silks.

'Could you spare the time to have tea? I spotted a little place on the corner'.

They stopped at La Maison Rose, a café meriting its French name. And that was the beginning. Max was the kind of man who was always on the lookout. He would try never to let an opportunity slip by and prided himself on his good judgement. Perhaps he was just lucky in being at the right place at the right time – and recognising his luck.

His chance meeting with Anna proved his point. Two people far away from their familiar surroundings enjoyed each other's company. Max told her how surprised he was when he detected her

London accent as she negotiated with the salesman in the Silk Plaza in Nehru Street, and freely admitted that she knew much more than he about the quality and weight of the silks.

They sat in the tea room for almost three hours, talking. She learned that Max had been to Pondicherry in his gap year between school and university and loved India. Subsequently he had graduated with a degree in Economics at Sussex University and when his father unexpectedly died leaving him a modest sum of money, he thought of going into business or, he said more convincingly, was looking for an excuse to return to India. In his gap year he had stayed with a family in Pondicherry working part-time in their silk shop to help pay his way, learning about silks, bead embroidery and hand-woven textiles. It had been one of the happiest times in his life. With that nostalgic memory coupled with his entrepreneurial skills, he decided to research a few ideas that had been germinating over the past few months.

Inspired by the colours of nature and a love of textiles and crafts, Max totally agreed with Anna that Western fashion could become more adventurous. He felt that his idea to import silks and cottons of the right hue would go down well in London. Beyond that, their mutual interest in Indian fabrics and how to transform them into Western fashion engaged them for two weeks in India and changed both their lives.

Anna found his enthusiasm contagious but recalled telling him that his ideas were too vague and then promptly provided the detail. She agreed that London was ready for the rich fabrics of the East but finding an appropriate design for their use would determine the market.

Max smiled excitedly. 'Do you have any ideas?'

Anna talked as though the ideas flowed without her really thinking. 'I take my orders from the material. We are looking at the luxury end of the market. Wedding outfits, special events, galas, opening nights, Academy awards, that sort of thing.'

'That's very specialised, I was thinking more bread and butter.'

'Just look at the material, it practically decides for itself and if you put in all the work why not use the best?' Anna asserted.

'I like the way you think. Will you have dinner with me this evening – every evening?' he added.

The way their ideas bounced off each other felt so natural. Their chance meeting must have been fated. Anna firmly believed that if you want something strongly enough, it will happen. Her determination, natural energy and her compulsion to complete a task once undertaken brought results.

Anna proved her point when she designed her own wedding dress, selecting an off-white silk with sprays of hand-embroidered pastel flowers. She still had the dress hanging in a cotton bag in the wardrobe. Its simplicity set the bar for her first collection.

It was a golden time when she and Max combined their skills and built up their unique business. Anna relied on Max to negotiate the prices of the fabrics she chose and to manage the business, while she understood what the material could do, often announcing as she fingered the latest import, 'Good material behaves itself'. Soon they were selling their exclusive dress collection under their 'Anna' label in London and New York.

It seemed the perfect marriage of a fashion graduate and an economics graduate. Max could make decisions and act on them, which gave Anna the confidence to create her designs. If she hesitated over a fabric, it was because she had to envisage the whole design in her mind before purchasing it. Max would say, 'It's beautiful, I'm sure you'll think of something, let's just take a chance'. They made a good team. She, a designer's designer with great attention to detail, would spend hours looking for the right button or the exact colour silk to enhance the seam. She prided herself on the inside of the garment looking every bit as good as the outside. In her mind she couldn't let go of an idea until she had every detail in place and only then would she cut out the toile to begin the long process to create the finished garment.

She remembered arguing with Max: 'We can't afford to take a chance – the first collection must be perfect'. She was prepared to wait and look around for the right piece of material. Max replied that he should be grateful for the way she was looking after his money.

As a young girl, Anna had determined that a life of purpose was better than transient pleasures. It wasn't something she could explain, it was just part of her nature. Now, twenty-three years later, she looked round the bedroom thinking of all they had created together. And in just one hour in a mad rage she had almost destroyed it all.

Shattering her introspection, the telephone rang, she stretched out to take the receiver from the bedside cabinet.

'The surgeon has just seen me and says I can go home tomorrow morning. Anna, I love you and I always will.' Max sounded tired.

She believed him. She was too proud and still a little suspicious to believe everything would go back to normal, but knew she had to try. Nor could she entirely blame him; she only had to look in the mirror to see what she had become. For in focusing on Barney she had neglected Max and perhaps driven him to his thoughtless action. Dinah was there, ready and waiting, as she not so innocently sat in the office plotting her move into Max's life. She should have seen it happening in the early days when she had spent more time in the business. It was ironic that she had interviewed Dinah for the post of Max's PA/secretary and preferred her to the other applicants because she had looked dowdy and trustworthy. Nowadays, Dinah was hardly recognisable. She had dyed her hair a reddish copper colour, and her sharp bob and brownish-toned lipstick made an immediate impression with her brown almond-shaped eyes, framed by red spectacles perched on her nose.

4
Breaking Point – 1992

The thought of Max coming home lightened Anna's mood. She stopped herself from going downstairs to the playroom where Oska and Barney were watching another Elvis Presley film.

She recalled the time when Max had come back from one of his buying trips to India; he couldn't wait to open his suitcase to lift out a crumpled packet that he handed to Barney. 'Open it, Barney,' he'd urged excitedly. Barney took his time while they all gawped. Out fell a pair of blue suede shoes. She couldn't tell who was more excited, Max, Barney or Oska, who rushed to play Elvis singing 'Blue Suede Shoes'. It was a happy moment when Anna knew that Max loved Barney. Her heart softened towards Max, easing her bitterness and the thought that perhaps something good might come out of this terrible time.

There were other happy moments that she forced herself to bring to mind. After five years of marriage they felt blessed when Oska, their first child, proved to be the perfect little boy. Max didn't mind Anna bringing him to the office and he would break away from what he was doing to give Oska a hug and let him finger the magazines or help himself to a biscuit. They were delighted when Anna fell pregnant again. Anna had hoped for a girl to dress in her own designs and share her creativity. She believed few men could have the same intuitive understanding but was grateful for Max's business skills. She had little patience for the administrative side of their business but endless patience for the detail of working on her designs.

They moved to a spacious home in South Hampstead. Anna

recalled how a week before his fourth birthday Oska was aware of the imminent arrival of the baby, and she had hoped that the detailed planning of Oska's birthday party would compensate for the displacement he might feel when the baby arrived. Oska seemed to have caught his parent's excitement. He constantly asked questions, welcoming the fact that he would have someone to play with and promising to help look after the baby. There was every reason for optimism, and the preparations for their new arrival involved the whole family. Oska enjoyed choosing toys for the baby and Anna rewarded him with a toy for himself. He participated in arranging the nursery and Anna engaged him in all sorts of conversations to prepare him for what some books described as a traumatic supplanting of his unique position.

When Anna first saw Barney she suppressed a passing disappointment, having set her heart on having a girl. But the moment she held him, he seemed perfect. She was mesmerised by the way he opened his brown eyes as she stroked his velvet skin. It was re-assuring to see that Oska wanted a brother. Oska was petite like her but Barney, at eight-and–a-half pounds, was the image of Max.

She couldn't have known what it meant when she held Barney across her shoulder to comfort him and he would scream and stiffen his little body. At three months old he seemed to have a mind of his own. Another worrying sign was his persistent crying as she put him to her breast. She knew he was hungry but he would interrupt each gulp of milk by turning his head away and screaming. Each feed became a nightmare for both of them. It was as if whenever she made contact his body would radiate with anxiety; he seemed to be more content when he was left alone in his cot. Her suspicion that there was something wrong with Barney grew and never left her. She tried to conceal this fear and couldn't explain her feelings but knew she was right. Anna hesitated to discuss this with Max who was working day and night in their business, which had expanded too rapidly, and Barney's constant demands interrupted her work, which only added to Max's problems.

At times Anna consoled herself that Barney was different to Oska, that a baby simply went through different phases in its development. She also experienced many lovely moments with Barney as she stood over his cot watching him sleep.

As time went on, Barney's behaviour gained a hold on Max. He wouldn't believe that nothing could be done. By nature Max was a problem solver and he had proved this in their business. He saw much of Barney's behaviour as simply naughty, believing it could be changed by not giving into his bizarre demands but by forcing him to behave rationally. When Barney screamed for his special toy from which he would not be parted, Max would take it away, telling him if he behaved and stopped screaming, he could have it. Max would also insist that Barney look at him instead of turning his head away when spoken to. When none of this worked, meals became a nightmare for all of them as Barney collapsed screaming on the floor. Max gave up, finding it easier to go to work where his efforts brought results and, being away from home, helped him to forget the growing problems with Barney. And so the slow change in family relationships evolved. Max, who had been a loving husband and devoted father, would take Oska out at weekends, leaving Anna to cope with Barney.

It was when Oska started complaining about Barney's persistent screaming that Anna could no longer deny Barney's problems. In 1983 little was known about autism and she struggled to get help. Her GP had advised that she should relax, for it was often the case that a baby reacted to an over-anxious mother.

Barney was almost four years old, not toilet trained, and speaking only a few words when Anna applied to get him into a nursery school. He hadn't been at the nursery school a week when the head indicated that there were problems. She told Anna that Barney would neither join in any group activity nor would he play appropriately with the toys. During playtime, ignoring the other children he would run round and round the edge of the garden on his own. Anna saw this for herself when she would come to take him home. She recalled standing at the entrance to the nursery watching the children sitting attentively in a circle patiently waiting to be collected, while Barney sat alone in the sandpit pouring sand from one container to another, mesmerised by the falling grains.

The day came when the head of the nursery told her they could no longer cope with Barney. Even though Anna had anticipated this possibility, the rejection cut deep. She begged the head to let Barney attend the nursery school for two hours a day and this was agreed on condition that Anna bring him after all the other children had settled and pick him up early.

Anna felt she had wasted time. Why hadn't she acted sooner? Why hadn't her GP referred Barney to an expert? After years of unremitting anxiety Anna at last had an appointment with a paediatrician. At first Barney flitted on tiptoe around the consulting room, one hand clenching a ball of damp tissues and the other holding a small wooden dog he called Hoppy, which they had given him for his first birthday and from which he would never be parted. Then he crawled around the room repetitively pushing Hoppy backwards and forwards.

Dr Bishop looked directly at Anna while Barney, seemingly oblivious, climbed under his desk.

'Have you heard of the condition autism?' Anna nodded. She had read books and articles, and had also been subjected to the scrutiny of family and friends who had stopped short of telling her what she feared.

'I believe your son is autistic although of course we will have to do a few tests to assess the degree of his problem. I'll write to your local authority education department, who will assess him for attendance at a special school.'

Anna was mortified by Dr Bishop's harsh statement, considering they had only been in his room for thirty minutes. With anger mounting she had the overwhelming desire to sweep Barney into her arms and rush home. She thanked him, hardly listening to his suggestion that he see Barney in three months' time. She called for Barney to come out from under the desk and, embarrassed further by his lack of response, was forced to crawl under the desk to pull him out.

She recalled sobbing, carrying Barney stiff as a board on her shoulder, she walked to her car. Thus began her long journey into another reality. She placed Barney on his chair in the kitchen and prepared a slice of bread with Marmite, careful to take the slice from his special bread tin that nobody but she was allowed to touch. Then she spread the Marmite at the required thickness and cut it into equal-sized squares to avoid another of his tantrums. Barney quickly settled into the familiar routine. She sat at the kitchen table looking at his anxious face, his forlorn eyes avoiding her gaze whilst gripping his toy. Anna thought about him covering his ears with his hands if he found any noise intrusive. His thin mouth would hardly ever break into a smile or make utterances unless he was deprived of his special objects or he found himself in a new situation. She worried too that he walked rather stiffly without moving his arms, tentatively watching the world from inside a world of his own.

Max came through the door. 'Sorry I'm late but we just closed the deal with Liberty's.'

'Barney's autistic,' she blurted out in a quivering voice. Max looked at her puffy face which, filled with tension, had lost its softness. Traces of lines forming around her soft lips had aged her. Max sat down. He had got used to her swollen eyes and her endless descriptions of Barney's behaviour, but today he listened as she justified her fears.

5

The Search For Help – 1984

'I've always known that Barney wasn't normal. Why didn't anybody listen to me? We could have got treatment earlier – that is, if there is any treatment. I feel so let down, when I think of our GP telling me that there wasn't anything wrong with Barney and intimating I was over-anxious and if I relaxed Barney would settle down.' Anna sobbed.

'If we know what's wrong with Barney, surely that's good. We can get the right treatment. For God's sake, he's only four,' Max said.

It was the first time she had felt that Max was engaged in the immense problem that was Barney, and she wanted to keep him involved.

'You're right, he's our child and we won't give up, these doctors don't know everything.'

Turning directly to Max, she said, 'No one must know until we get proper treatment. No one understands – and we must protect Barney.'

This was the moment she knew that her family was different and that she would protect Barney and be his link to the world. She felt diminished, and decided that she should avoid their friends. She remembered Madellaine, her next-door neighbour, commenting that she found Barney's behaviour fascinating. She now realised she had been trying to tell her something, and had felt disinclined to further their friendship. She'd felt compelled to join Barney in his retreat from the world and decided that her new life suited her. In some way it was a full life as she succumbed to Barney's world of rituals, phobias and obsessions. Without realising it she had exchanged her industry and focus as a designer for a deeper commitment to Barney. He had become her project and her purpose. In the mornings after Max had dropped Oska off at school, she felt safe, alone in the house with Barney.

The day after the consultation, Anna looked through their photo albums. Perhaps there were some clues in those early pictures of Barney. There was one taken on his second birthday, Barney's face blank as Oska stepped in to blow out the candles. She recalled how Oska had taken over the presents and opened them for Barney and joined in singing 'Happy Birthday' while Barney seemed oblivious to what was going on. Why hadn't she noticed this before?

At the time she had thought that Oska was asserting his right for attention but she now realised that he had held the party together and saved her the embarrassment she now felt. Other photos showed Barney's disinterest in his surroundings. There was not one photograph of him smiling.

All she could think of was that she had never left him or sent him away, unlike Max who had tried to love Barney but perhaps knew better than she that the sacrifice of living with Barney might eventually destroy them all. Max was adamant that Oska also had rights and shouldn't have his childhood dominated by Barney's ever-present needs.

Oska, an intelligent and imaginative child, soon found his own entertainment. He enjoyed dismantling toys and then putting them together again. He was fascinated by mechanical toys, making model aeroplanes, cars and guns and spent hours placing his toy soldiers in battle lines. His interest in military warfare and armaments seemed a rational outlet and on joining a local cadet unit he found like-minded friends. Anna and Max both agreed that Oska's pursuits, even though his school reports were disappointing, were a sign of his intelligence and motivation and were proud of his knowledge of military history.

The balance in the family shifted, at first for practical considerations, as the emotional divide split the family into pairs. Anna attended to Barney and Max took Oska out. It was difficult to go out as a family even to the park where one of Barney's tantrums would become a spectacle to embarrass them all.

At first Anna approached the meetings and appointments with the educational psychologist, social worker and a local authority psychiatrist with enthusiasm. She co-operated fully, read articles on autism, was never late for an appointment, and always took her notes detailing all Barney's idiosyncratic behaviour. Even so, she had expected a more compassionate approach from Dawn Atkin the social worker who had come to her home first to interview her.

'What do you do?' Dawn Atkin asked, surveying the luxurious room with its abstract paintings, its Corbusier chaise longue, Charles Eames chairs and Cassini settees surrounding the central, square Persian rug. The high ceiling was perfectly in proportion to the large windows that looked out onto a tulip tree in bloom in the garden.

'I'm a dress designer. Well, not so much nowadays,' said Anna, watching Barney climb up the back of the white leather chaise longue and slide down on his bottom. The social worker moved as if to leap up to stop the chair from tipping over.

'Don't worry, he is quite safe. He has perfect balance and knows exactly how far to go,' said Anna, not wanting to miss an opportunity to praise Barney.

Dawn Atkin gave what Anna thought was a condescending smile as she made her notes, having bombarded Anna with multiple choice questions – an exercise in ticking boxes rather than allowing Anna to put them into context. Anna rapidly began to resent her.

'Is he toilet trained?'

'He's only four. Is he supposed to be?' Anna blurted out defensively as Barney repetitively pushed his toy dog backwards and forwards, seemingly detached from everything. Dawn Atkin added to her discomfort by not answering. Anna felt intimidated and trapped. It was as if she was being propelled into an examination that she was bound to fail; more than an intrusion, it was an invasion eating into the sanctity of their private family life.

Perhaps it was a feeling she had developed as a child when she was too ashamed to take her friends home because her mother, who suffered from multiple sclerosis, was confined to a wheelchair.

Dawn Atkin seemed robotic and unaware of the intensity of Anna's desperation. Anna expected kindness and support instead of a question and answer session. She felt her entire life was threatened by having to expose details of her family, details she hadn't even had time to consider since Barney's birth and which had no place in the public domain. She had succeeded as a dress designer but failed as a mother – a realisation that cut deep into her sense of self.

'Can Barney stay at the nursery school?' Anna asked, more to stave off any more questions.

'An educational psychologist will be contacting you after visiting the nursery school next week to observe Barney.'

'I don't exactly know why I am talking to you. I thought you were here to help me with Barney?'

'We need to know the background and circumstances of each family. I appreciate that you are very motivated to get the best for Barney and I will pass on this information to the consultant paediatrician who, together with the educational psychologist, will find a placement for Barney.'

'Do you know of a school, and how long all this will take?' Anna could hardly suppress her irritation.

'You only saw the consultant paediatrician two months ago so I don't think we are doing too badly.' Dawn Atkin stood up, indicating the end of her visit.

Anna led her out through the hall and opened the Georgian front door.

'We'll be in touch,' the social worker said, as Anna closed the door behind her.

Each meeting seemed to draw Anna into another world. All she could do was to co-operate with the investigations, because she could not deny Barney's behaviour was odd. There were so many things that didn't make sense, such as his long silences interrupted by strange hand signals requesting tissues, which he sucked until he could make them into a damp ball to hold in his hand. She knew that if she deprived Barney of any one of his special objects, even for a second, he would collapse into a heap. It was as if she held his life in her hands and, rapidly becoming familiar with his needs, kept her handbag full of his current special objects at the ready to ameliorate his ever-present anxiety.

As time passed, Barney began to control the entire household. If the phone rang, Barney screamed, 'No phone! No talking!' If he heard the toilet being flushed, he'd collapse on the floor, fear written over his face and scream, 'No toilet! No water!' Anna dreaded Max being around during one of Barney's tantrums. She worried that he might over-react and traumatise Barney. She recalled the day when Max shouted at him: 'I will not have you say NO. I'm tired of your noes. You are not the kingpin in this house, so just stop saying NO! DO YOU UNDERSTAND?' Anna recalled how she had wanted to scream 'Leave him alone', but knew better than to argue with Max over Barney.

The next day Barney came to her with a pencil and paper indicating that he wanted her to draw a nose shape. After a confusing start she drew a large nose shape that delighted Barney who insisted that she cut it out and attach it to a string. He jumped up and down twiddling the shape. Eventually she made a more robust nose shape out of cardboard which Barney twiddled and repeatedly said 'Barney's nose'. She told Max that Barney needed to be in control of his 'noes'.

'What are you talking about?' demanded Max, barely concealing his irritation.

'It's Barney's way of saying NO! NO! NO! to protect himself from your reprimand when you say "No, Barney". He calls his shape "Barney's nose".'

Anna felt Barney's presence as if it were a current radiating through her. When Barney was upset so was she, and step-by-step she slid into an increasingly intense relationship as she gradually succumbed to colluding with his bizarre world. There were so many other odd behaviours, so many tears, so many messages that he signified with gestures or one or two words for what he wanted as she desperately turned the house upside down to find a missing piece of puzzle or some crumpled damp tissue.

Anna no longer contacted her friends; only her next-door neighbour Madellaine Walker with her seven-year-old son Rob were allowed to drop in uninvited, and Rob would also help by entertaining Barney. He was more amused than put-out by Barney's compulsive requests. Apart from shopping, Anna rarely went out and was pleased when Max suggested they convert the attic into a large studio, so that she could continue her work as a designer. At least she had help in the house and Barney did settle at night. She did a lot of thinking while she watched him aimlessly running in the garden or repetitiously doing jigsaw puzzles in the playroom. She couldn't help thinking that he was brilliant; he seemed to know more than he was letting on.

She read him his books endlessly, again and again, and although he never uttered a word, he knew them by heart. If she mistakenly left a word out, he would leap up in front of her, circling his arms like windmills until she went back and corrected her mistake. He not only had his favourite books but his favourite page. He would bring the book to her, find the page with the image in seconds and visually fixating on it would calm down. There were so many things she didn't understand, but she was certain of his intelligence. His memory was just one example. Once taken on a journey he memorised the route and would scream if she deviated from it.

She continued to meet many professionals, each with their own assessment. It was just a matter of finding the right environment for him. And so began the long search for his next school.

Nine months of uncertainty and desperation had passed. Barney was still attending the nursery school for two hours a day. One morning when she stopped by to fetch Barney, the head of the nursery school came over to her.

'I think Barney is extremely intelligent. You know what he did?' Anna's face relaxed into a rare smile.

'When we came in this morning, the bookcase in the book corner had collapsed and all the books were strewn on the floor. Well, I couldn't believe it when Barney arrived. He went straight to the book corner and put every book back in exactly the right order.'

'I think he has a photographic memory,' Anna replied, wondering why the head didn't suggest he stay at the nursery for an extra hour. Anna knew Barney was special and she alone would prove it.

Barney's fifth birthday was a small family gathering. Oska once again saved the day by singing 'Happy Birthday', ending with three cheers and 'hip hip hoorah'. Max's widowed mother and his brother Harold had come up from Sussex. They bought Barney a present of a soft grey hippo, and he must have made some connection with the hip hip hoorah because from then on Barney would not be parted from Hoorah Hippo and the whole family accepted it as an essential part of his being.

One dark February morning, Anna was wondering whether it was worth the effort of putting layers of clothes on Barney, just for two hours at the nursery. But Barney was used to the routine and it seemed easier to go than to face an upset. Just as she was leaving, the phone rang. She thought she recognised the voice but couldn't quite place it.

'Mrs Elliott, I'm pleased I caught you, this is Dawn Atkin the social worker. Do you remember, I came to visit you nine months ago? It's about Barney.'

'Oh yes.' Anna waited.

'I think I've found a nursery for Barney. It's all a bit of luck really. This is probably quite unprofessional but I couldn't stand by and not do anything. I was having dinner with some friends last night and a woman whose name is Molly Mandel was talking about a small unit for pre-school autistic children. Apparently she runs it in a building next to her home. There are only five children in the unit and a one-to-one staff ratio. It sounds just the place for Barney. She seems very unconventional in her approach but her dedication and enthusiasm make sense to me. She also believes that the family should be involved. There was something about her that impressed me. I know it all seems a little unusual but sometimes we have to take a leap outside the box. If you are interested we can go and see the Peeling Onions Unit on Thursday morning.'

'I am very, very interested but don't I need a referral from the local authority?'

'Yes you do if we want a place, but there's nothing to stop you looking yourself and, quite separately, I am also interested, as the local authority needs to know about every placement available for children. So I just thought it would be a good idea to combine our visit as I will be going in any case.'

'Thank you so much for thinking of Barney,' Anna said excitedly.

'I must rush now. I'll pick you up around ten.'

'Can I bring Barney with me?'

'I don't see why not, he also has to like it,' Dawn replied.

Anna felt elated as she strapped Barney into his car seat. A small, personalised place was just what she wanted. Anna felt ashamed of her previous resentment towards Dawn Atkin. She had been wrong about her but she had felt so angry with all the professionals who had seemed so matter-of-fact towards her. Perhaps she had only imagined their disinterest, seeing them only as functionaries without feeling.

Almost five years of living with Barney had altered her perception. She was depressed, had lost interest in her appearance, found no joy in life and couldn't remember the last time she had laughed. Living in a strait jacket dictated by Barney's endless routines, her own interests and desires were curtailed. It was as if her life had come to a standstill. The thought that Barney might go to a new school provided hope; deep down she believed Barney understood more and was capable of achieving more than he disclosed. She noticed how clever he could be when he wanted to avoid an activity, creating elaborate actions to delay or resist it such as spinning around or walking backwards away from an interaction. She recalled how Barney, even as an infant, would crawl up and down the cot and sit in the far corner, rather than come towards her when she held out her arms to pick him up. She was just beginning to get the hang of his devious ways. It wasn't surprising that she had mistrusted Dawn Atkin – in her frame of mind, the whole world seemed against her.

Max was right when he had complained that hardly would he open his mouth to talk about a new idea when she would become resistant to it. And they hadn't been away for two years.

'For God's sake, we need a holiday, I need a holiday, you definitely need a holiday and why shouldn't Oska do something normal? And if I may say, I think even Barney might manage a bucket and spade on a beach in Florida. Anything would be better than February in England.'

'I agree,' she said, even though she was terrified at the prospect of leaving the safety of their home.

'Are you sure?' Max asked.

'I had some good news. There's a possibility of a place for Barney at a small specialised unit and I'm going to see it on Thursday.'

'That's marvellous.'

'Can Barney go to a real school?' Oska piped up.

'We'll know later but it sounds like just the place I want for Barney.'

Max saw her face soften. It gave him hope of improvement . . . perhaps she might even be more creative with her designs.

6

Peeling Onions – 1986

Barney seemed surprisingly relaxed holding onto Hoorah Hippo, who today was but a shadow of his former self. Anna would never forget the lesson learned when she had prised Hoorah Hippo away from Barney while he was asleep. She quickly washed Hippo, dried him and placed him back. Instantly Barney recognised the change in Hippo's structure, smell and feel – all so vital to his need for sameness. He touched Hippo and screamed in desperation as he collapsed on the floor, shouting 'Hoorah Hippo, Hoorah Hippo'. She had tried to besmirch Hippo again with Marmite, tomato sauce and butter, hoping to regain its special smell, but Hippo's new thin, lumpy body was beyond repair. Barney threw him away and mourned for him for days. It was only when Max came to the rescue and suggested they go to Hamleys toy shop that he calmed down. Barney scoured the entire store but couldn't find a replacement. When they came home Barney picked up Hoorah Hippo and finally the whole household relaxed.

Molly Mandel had phoned Anna to confirm their appointment and asked her to bring some of Barney's favourite food and anything else he needed for reassurance. Molly explained that there should be a link between home and Peeling Onions so that Barney wouldn't be confronted with a totally unfamiliar environment. She also stipulated that she expected all mothers to participate whenever possible in the programmes at Peeling Onions. There was an open house policy, Anna could visit whenever she wished, and fathers and siblings were also welcome. She added everyone was on first name terms to lessen formality and to facilitate a non-threatening culture.

There were no more than five children in the unit and a one to one staff ratio and also extra staff to support mothers. It would take time to get know Barney. Whilst every child may be autistic, each one was different as all children are different. Barney would have his individual programme and the needs of each family are considered as part of an integrated programme.

Anna was ecstatic. It was obvious Molly not only understood the sensitivity of autistic children, but also the mother's needs. Anna knew she had at last found the right person and place for Barney.

The morning of the meeting came. Anna and Barney were standing in the hall waiting when Dawn Atkin rang the bell.

'You look very smart today, Barney.' Anna smiled, pleased that Dawn had spoken to Barney. So often he was ignored, even by the head of the nursery school who Anna thought should know better than to talk over Barney's head about him. Anna was putting so much hope into the visit that she couldn't imagine being disappointed. She even liked the name of the autistic unit: Peeling Onions. It aptly described the layers of the autistic child's mind, combined with the tears the families regularly shed.

The Peeling Onions Unit was situated in a quiet, leafy street off Kilburn High Street. Parking outside a Victorian house they saw a wooden side door with a painting of a half-peeled onion with its transparent golden leaves. They stepped through the doorway onto a York-stone courtyard bordered with potted plants. Ahead, they saw a large picture window with some children and adults sitting at small tables. Molly Mandel came out to greet them.

'You managed to find us easily. Come in,' she said warmly. Molly was an energetic forty-year-old, who moved with purpose and agility. Her long dark hair was tied back in a ponytail, her complexion fresh, her slim figure dressed in blue jeans and a red polo neck sweater.

'I am so pleased you came. Barney, would you like to see some lovely toys?' Molly took Barney by the hand as if the expectation of his co-operation was a foregone conclusion. Anna was amazed to see Barney sit down at an empty table in the large playroom, away from the other children, who were engaged at their own tables with a teacher sitting by each of them. Molly pulled out two small chairs for Anna and Dawn.

'What does Barney like doing?' Molly asked Anna.

'I think his favourite is jigsaw puzzles and books,' Anna replied, having already decided that Peeling Onions was the place for Barney.

'Well, we will all have to go into the puzzle room. We call it the "Quiet Room".' They followed Molly and Barney into a small room, its shelves neatly stacked with box after box of jigsaw puzzles, and sat on small wooden nursery chairs.

'Would you like to choose a puzzle, Barney?' Hardly had Molly finished speaking when Barney leapt up from his chair, rushed to the shelves and pulling every puzzle down made a huge pile of mixed-up pieces of jigsaw on the floor.

'I'm so sorry,' Anna apologised, and rushed to clear up the empty boxes.

'It's all right,' Molly said calmly. 'Barney has an awful lot of work to do. If I put all the boxes in a line, do you think you can help me put back the puzzles?' Molly got up and lined up all the different boxes with their lids displaying the pictures of each puzzle.

Anna, Dawn and Molly sat quietly watching Barney as he rapidly sorted out all the different pieces and completed all the puzzles. Replacing the lids, he then returned each box to its place on the shelves.

'Well, I think you should have a break now, Barney. That was very good work.'

Molly asked Anna if she had brought a snack. They were joined by another teacher who helped Barney settle with his snack, while Anna, Dawn and Molly went into Molly's office to talk.

'He is a lovely little boy,' Molly said with a large smile across her face. Anna had never experienced such relief and sheer delight. Molly explained there was a mother's group every Wednesday morning for two hours when the mothers had time for themselves to discuss any problems and she hoped Anna would participate.

She explained that by sharing problems and experiences with the other mothers, not only did each mother gain perspective but was also supported emotionally by new understandings. There were also many activities and outings for the children.

Anna was enthralled. 'Do you have a place for Barney?' she asked.

'We will have a place in two months' time and in the meantime we would like you to bring Barney in on odd days so that he can get used to the environment. We call it the integration programme and find it is very reassuring for both you as a family and our staff to get to know each other.'

When they returned, they found Barney settled next to the teacher who was reading one of Barney's favourite books. Barney seemed reluctant to leave when Anna called him.

At home Anna felt renewed. For the first time she believed that Barney had a chance. Dawn Atkin had helped them hugely and she assured Anna that she would get going with the referral procedure from the local education authority.

Barney was calm for the rest of the day and Anna assumed it was because he missed his two-hour stint at the nursery school. There was a knock on the door.

'Hello Rob, what are you doing home?' Anna asked.

'It's half day today so I thought I'd visit Barney,' Rob replied.

Barney, his hands flapping with excitement, rushed forward and taking Rob's hand, led him into the playroom.

'Would you like a sandwich or something, Rob?' Anna asked.

'No thanks, I've just had lunch,' Rob shouted from the play-room.

Anna was usually pleased to see Rob, who would drop in from time to time. He was Madellaine's only child and Anna supposed he felt lonely, so all in all it seemed like a good arrangement. Rob would entertain Barney playing with toy cars, and she would be able to get on with the cooking as well as work on a few ideas for a dress design.

Anna heard the familiar bang of the front door closing. Max

walked into the studio, pleased to see Anna at the drawing board. 'Lovely lines', he said, peering over her shoulder.

'You're home early.'

'I couldn't wait to find out what happened at the new nursery.'

'Oh Max, it's a dream come true, we couldn't have imagined that such a place existed.'

'Will they take Barney?' questioned Max, doubtfully.

'Yes, Molly really likes him.' Max listened as Anna relayed the whole experience.

'I'll go and say hello to Barney,' Max said. 'I see Rob is here again. You'd think he would prefer to play with Oska. After all, he is nearer to his age. It doesn't seem natural for a seven-year-old to be so interested in a four-year-old.'

'Oska doesn't like Rob. Besides, it's quite a break for me when Rob entertains Barney. What's the problem?' Anna asked.

'No problem, we're just lucky to have good neighbours. You get on well with Madellaine and Rob entertains Barney. It's a pity her husband walked out – perhaps I would have got on well with him too!' Max's joke affected Anna.

'Really Max, you have no idea how devastated poor Madellaine feels. She comes in almost every day and weeps in the kitchen. It's not enough that Doug left her but he went off with her best friend. And it has also affected Rob, who won't talk to his father.'

'Well at least he has principles. But why is he home from school so early?'

'He has a half day.'

'That reminds me, I could pick Oska up from school later.'

'He'll love that.' Anna couldn't remember being so happy. It was as if the black dog sitting on her shoulders had gone and she could think of work again.

Later, Max and Oska came in smiling. Oska ran into the studio. 'Guess what?'

Anna turned to see Oska with a large smile on his face and Max standing behind him looking a little nervous.

'We are going to Disneyworld at half term,' Oska announced.

'That's wonderful,' Anna replied but her mind spun around, worrying about the application forms for Peeling Onions and how Barney would cope with the long flight and being away from home.

7

Orlando

Max had organised everything. All Anna had to do was to pack but she didn't know how she was going to manage with Barney. For a start he wasn't toilet-trained and changing a large five-year old in an aeroplane toilet wasn't going to be easy; even at home Barney struggled against the procedure. Then besides all the necessary changes of clothing, he would not go anywhere without his special toys, jigsaw puzzles, books and plastic containers for all his latest food fads, and of course Hurrah Hippo, all far in excess of the hand-luggage allowance. And, as of a few days ago, Barney had decided that he would only eat white foods. They had to be soft, like macaroni cheese, cheesecake, rice with cheese sauce and vanilla ice cream, and everything had to be cut into small pieces before he would even look at the plate. If confronted with anything dark, like meat, chocolate or Marmite – a previous favourite – Barney would throw a tantrum. In Orlando, it would mean Anna, in addition to scrutinising every plate, would have to carry around her own supply of food.

Oska was so excited about the trip that Anna could hardly complain. She began to look forward to the holiday, and to starting the integration programme at Peeling Onions when they returned. Her confidence in the venture increased when without prompting, Max spent more time with Barney, leaving her to spend time with Oska. Barney seemed calmer under Max's influence and had stopped repetitively flicking his fingers. Anna wondered if perhaps the GP had not been so wrong when he suggested that Barney's behaviour might be a reaction to her.

On the plane Anna was comforted to see Max relax with Barney fast asleep on his lap. Perhaps Max found it difficult to accept Barney because he saw him as an imperfect image of himself. Often when she tried to explain some of Barney's behaviour, Max would look at her as if she was mad. Her latest attempt was to suggest that Barney's anxiety about toilet-training was the reason why he would only eat white food.

'Did he tell you that?' Max asked, in bewildered disbelief.

'No, but I just know these things. It's obvious to me as I try to toilet-train him and he shows extreme fear when I have to change his nappy,' Anna explained.

Unlike Anna, Max was not a natural worrier. He saw problems in black and white, which is why he had found it so hard to deal with Barney. She liked to think in the abstract. She always had to have a concept in mind when designing a dress, ever-sensitive as to whether the material dictated a soft, flowing look and the need to accentuate one or other aspect of the female form. Anna recalled an Italian teacher at college who, while she was contemplating a piece of material, would say: 'Anna, when it's cutted, it's cutted, but you still have to make the first cut.' There were times when Anna was unsure of her own talent. The easier the ideas came to her, the less she trusted them. She and Max were opposites and complemented each other, giving each other a combined strength that more than doubled the sum of the parts.

Landing in Orlando, standing in line waiting for a taxi, Anna welcomed the warm weather, her eyes adjusting to the bright light as she admired the planted gardens outside the airport. Large bushes of pink and white bougainvillea and the scent of frangipani trees filled the humid air. It was nine o'clock in the evening, London time, both boys had behaved well during the long flight and Anna was beginning to have more confidence in the holiday. As they piled into the taxi Barney was beginning to flag. Max picked him up onto his lap and he fell asleep.

As the taxi pulled up under a covered portico at the entrance to their hotel, Mickey Mouse was waiting to greet them. The inside lobby under the triple height ceiling had been decorated and furnished to show the ambiance of Africa. Oska was now fully alert and excited, amazed by all he saw. He wanted to rush off and explore but knew he was needed to help with Barney. Max and Anna caught each other's smile, feeling Barney's amazement as he looked at the brightly-painted, oversized figures from his nursery books. Anna felt bombarded by the sheer abundance of earth-coloured patchwork carpets, carved wooden couches, cages full of multi-coloured birds and towers made of differently-shaped, coloured African pots. In the background the sound system recorded the chatter, the shrieks, the roars and many of the sounds of Africa. Max led them to a sitting area where he placed sleepy Barney on a couch, while Anna and Oska sat on the matching wooden chairs.

'Stay here while I check in,' Max said, and went off.

Anna surveyed the multi-faceted scenes of Africa and smiled to herself. It had only taken five minutes for her to adapt to the plastic rocks as she suspended her reality and decided that the whole place was imaginative and enthralling. She looked at Barney now motionless in his sleep, Hoorah Hippo tucked under his chin.

Max returned with an enormous grin. 'I've scored the "King of the Jungle" suite. Let's go.'

'How did you do that and how much does it cost?' Anna asked.

'Not a penny, or should I say a cent, extra. I told them that I had an autistic son and he gets upset easily by noise and this was our holiday of a lifetime.'

'I'm beginning to think it will be.' Anna held onto Hurrah Hippo, Max carried Barney and Oska pushed his small trolley case, followed by the porter with their luggage.

'Wow,' Oska shouted as they entered the suite. He looked at the huge lounge with a generous, carved wooden sofa and two carved African chairs, all with large cushions in terracotta, yellow ochre, orange and brown, the earthy tones of Africa. The lounge led onto a bedroom with a magnificent, carved wooden bed covered in an African patchwork, and an en-suite bathroom. Through a door was another bedroom with twin beds and its own en-suite bathroom. Glass doors opened onto a balcony looking across grassland with trees and shrubs, where two live giraffes were taking a stately stroll across the savannah.

Max put Barney down onto one of the beds in the children's room and tipped the porter, who was demonstrating how to work the TV and air conditioning.

'Max,' Anna enthused. 'You've been marvellous; everything has fallen into place. It's as if we've landed in some fairy tale. Life just seems to fall into a good pattern with you. I don't know how you do it.'

'I wave my magic wand!' Max gestured with his hand.

Oska came in from the balcony. 'There's deer and a lake with beautiful white birds with pink feet.'

'Flamingos – their legs are pink because they eat shrimp,' Anna said, suddenly noticing that Oska looked very tired. 'Oska, I think you should have a quick shower and go to bed.'

'I'm hungry,' he protested.

Max looked at the room service menu, a large book covered in leopard print faux suede.

'There's hamburger and chips, pizza with five different toppings and chips, fish fingers and chips, vanilla ice cream. What do you feel like, Oska?' he asked.

'Is that all they have?' Anna thought of Barney and his food fads.

'Sure, that's just the children's menu.' Max was keen to get the children settled so that he and Anna could have time alone together. It had been a long time since Anna had been free to relax and staying in the suite with the children next door gave them the privacy they needed. He could see that Anna was beginning to be her old self. He couldn't recall her smiling so much or making light of Barney's behaviour. He felt as though they were beginning to recapture some of the earlier togetherness that had faded since Barney was born.

They woke up next morning to find Oska cutting up the leftover food from last night and disguising it with tomato ketchup for

Barney, who was hungry. It was nine o'clock. Anna felt secure and content in a way that she couldn't have imagined. Max had been so patient and gentle that she could do no other than respond.

'Oska, thank you for looking after Barney. Put on the TV while Max and I get dressed. We are going to have a wonderful day.' Her enthusiasm was infectious.

Max added: 'First, a real American breakfast in the Monkey Tree Restaurant, then the Jungle Adventure. There is so much to do. Come on, Barney, I'll dress you.'

Barney left his plate of food and ran towards Max. Anna couldn't believe how amenable Barney had become.

'Mom, come quick!' Oska usually called Anna 'mom' when something unusual happened. Anna ran into the children's bathroom and saw Barney sitting on the toilet and performing. She had tried for a year and he'd refused to even go near a toilet.

Anna didn't know whether to clap. She didn't want to frighten Barney but she had to acknowledge his supreme leap. 'Well, I think that Barney deserves a present. After breakfast we will go into the hotel shop and you can choose whatever you like, Barney.'

Barney spoke softly in a monotone. 'Oska sits on the toilet; Max sits on the toilet; Anna sits on the toilet, Barney sits on the toilet.'

Anna thought how little she understood. She had read books on autism, and yet only bits seemed to describe Barney's behaviour. There was no clear cause or treatment. It was like being blind making your way through a minefield. Only through living with Barney had she come to understand a fraction of what was going on in his mind and she was certain that there was an awful lot more. She wasn't going to give up on him. She also realised that Max in his own way understood Barney on another level that was just as relevant, and that she should have more trust in Max's judgement. She would never have contemplated taking Barney on a holiday if Max hadn't suggested it, let alone taking Barney to a strange place or changing his routine. Yet Max had demonstrated that Barney could not only survive but could make progress.

At the Monkey Tree Restaurant, Barney was eating three waffles with loads of cream when a large figure of Mickey Mouse appeared at the table. Anna thought Barney would scream and was surprised when he accepted a balloon from Mickey Mouse. Oska laughed generously; he always seemed pleased with Barney's achievements.

After breakfast, Barney had not forgotten the promise to go to the shop. The hotel shop was filled with a thousand-and-one things and Barney rushed around scouring the shelves, moving objects around. She dreaded having to explain to the staff that he was autistic but fortunately nobody seemed to be too bothered. 'After all', she told Max, 'this place is designed by adults who understand the minds of children, and – more importantly – turns adults into children again.'

'Perhaps we shouldn't have grown up. I can't remember being so happy,' Max said. After about ten minutes Barney presented Anna with a keyring attached to a tiny metal hippo.

'We've got off lightly,' said Max until he saw Oska coming towards him holding a khaki safari hat and a pair of binoculars. He relented. 'OK, but this isn't going to be a daily occurrence.'

'I need to see the giraffes and birds from the balcony,' Oska protested. While Anna was delighted at Oska's choice and his interest in nature, Max was pleased to get out of the brightly-lit gift shop which, in spite of the air conditioning, felt oppressive.

'Let's go and find out how to get tickets for the Jungle Adventure.' He took Barney's hand and Oska and Anna followed.

At the dock Max boarded the boat and lifted Barney onto his knee. He asked one of the theme park helpers who were all easily identified in their bright green T-shirts and khaki shorts.

'Please could you tell me what happens on the adventure as my son is autistic and I have to be sure he won't be frightened?'

'Do you think this is a good idea?' Anna intervened.

'Oh please, Max, I want to go,' Oska pleaded.

'I'll wait here with Barney,' Anna suggested.

Max, suddenly realising that once on the boat there was no way off until the end of the tour, passed Barney back to Anna.

'We'll look at the birds, Barney,' Anna said with relief, having found out that not only did the boat go through tunnels with a simulated area of white water rafting but life-sized roaring tigers and lions leapt out from the riverbanks – and if that wasn't frightening enough there were rangers in a gun battle, capturing ivory hunters. She realised the experience would have been too much for her and was pleased to use Barney as an excuse.

Half an hour later the boat returned; Anna saw Oska waving to her. He couldn't wait to tell her about the wonderful adventure. Max smiled. 'Only in America,' he said.

8

The White Balloon — 1986

They took the shuttle bus to another part of the park for Barney to see Mickey Mouse, Donald Duck and many of the other Disney characters parading up and down, greeting and meeting children.

As they got off the bus, there was Yogi Bear handing out honey buns to everyone. Barney looked but wouldn't take one. Anna knew why, but stopped herself from making any reference to Barney's phobia of dark foods.

Stopping off at the Magic Kingdom they were greeted by Cinderella and Prince Charming. Then suddenly Barney ran off after a Mickey Mouse. Anna ran to him and Barney secured another balloon from Mickey. In the distance Anna saw another Mickey Mouse standing by a tree and hoped Barney hadn't seen him.

They stopped at an ice cream stand and Barney consumed a tub of vanilla ice cream.

'I could do with a swim and cool drink on the balcony and Barney and Oska can watch the animals from our balcony', Max suggested.

Anna noticed the shuttle bus stop nearby and, their energy flagging, they went and stood in line.

Back in their hotel suite Oska was keen to get onto the balcony to use his binoculars. Anna took Barney into the bathroom. Without prompting, Barney took off his trousers and climbed onto the toilet. Anna, controlling her surprise, behaved as though it was nothing out of the ordinary. She felt that Barney didn't want her to comment on his action and if she did he might regress. It occurred to her in some inexplicable way that she and Barney shared many anxieties and that she couldn't confidently separate her emotions from his.

The following day, Anna was surprised when Barney came to her saying, 'Want to see Mickey Mouse, let's go to Mickey Mouse.'

'Max, I know it's a bit hard on Oska and you to go back to the Magic Kingdom again, but Barney hardly ever makes a constructive request and I feel we should respond to it. If we reward him for wanting normal enjoyment perhaps it will lessen his bizarre demands,' Anna asserted.

'I don't mind,' Oska interrupted.

'Well if Oska doesn't mind, it's OK. I just didn't want Oska to think the holiday is all about Barney,' Max said, also feeling that Barney was making progress.

'Can I go to The Lion King show? It's next to Cinderella's castle,' Oska asked, revealing his hidden agenda.

'What a good idea – now everybody will be happy!' Anna smiled.

After breakfast they stood in line for the shuttle bus. 'Can we sit in front?' Oska asked, empowered by the thought that he suddenly had rights.

'Of course,' Max responded as Oska rushed ahead to the front seats.

The bus was full of families; children laughing, parents smiling. Anna couldn't remember ever being amongst such a happy group. The atmosphere of expectant pleasure was contagious and for the first time she felt like a normal family. She turned to Max.

'Isn't it remarkable that everybody including the staff seem to smile all the time and the place is so clean. If only the world could be managed by Disney.'

'You're right. Being happy without drugs or alcohol is quite an achievement.'

Anna looked out the window. 'Even the gardens are perfect. It's like magic – I haven't seen a single gardener working on them.'

'I must say I haven't seen a sweet wrapper, an empty cola can or a lolly stick on the paths. It's impressive; I'm glad we came.' Max gently squeezed Anna's hand; it was such a relief to see her relax.

'The children are happy too,' Anna said, reminding herself that Barney could have moments without anxiety or fear.

As they alighted, Mickey Mouse greeted them with a large placard advertising The Lion King Show at eleven o'clock. Anna looked at her watch.

'We have a half-hour, let's walk around.'

They didn't notice that Barney was disappointed Mickey Mouse didn't greet him with a balloon. Anna then saw another Mickey Mouse standing behind a tree about seventy yards away. Within seconds, Barney was running towards that Mickey Mouse.

'Oska, run after Barney – we're coming,' Anna instructed.

By the time she and Max reached the tree, Oska was standing alone, looking around for his brother.

'Where's Barney?' Anna asked with rising anxiety.

'I don't know – when I got here, he was gone,' Oska exclaimed.

'Well he can't be far; he probably asked for a balloon and Mickey Mouse went to get one for him. He can't have disappeared,' Max said unconvincingly.

'It's not my fault,' Oska protested.

'Of course not.' Anna began to feel it was her fault; she should have held Barney's hand.

They all rushed around in different directions only to return. 'It doesn't make sense! He was here a minute ago, he can't have disappeared.' Max tried but failed to hide his fear.

Anna caught sight of a bright green T-shirt.

'There's one of the staff, let's ask him,' she cried, rushing towards the uniformed young man.

'Where did you say you saw Mickey Mouse?' he asked.

'Standing by this tree. I also saw him yesterday in exactly the same place,' Anna explained.

'That seems a bit irregular.' The man got out a walkie-talkie and Anna heard him ask 'How many Mickey Mouses do we have on duty in The Lion King section this morning? We have a problem, a child is missing. I have the parents with me. Thanks, I'll stand by for instructions.'

Anna's heart was pounding in her chest, a lump in her throat; now beyond panic, immobilised, she hung onto Max.

'It'll be all right, they know what they're doing here, the whole place is so well-run. Really, you're worrying for nothing.' Max struggled to sound convincing.

A jeep pulled up and two men in khaki uniform with security tags on their epaulettes got out. Anna gave a detailed description of Barney and said she had a photo back at the hotel. She listened as they called up another two jeeps with more security men.

'We are sending out a search party,' they told the family. 'He can't have disappeared and we will find him. For now, I think it best if we drive you back to the hotel.'

Max didn't know whether to stay in case they found Barney and he was needed, or to support Anna who was showing every sign of collapse. Sobbing, she explained that Barney was autistic and easily frightened. She gave them Hurrah Hippo, telling them that it was Barney's security toy and he couldn't live without it. The security man ran to give it to his colleagues.

'Will they find Barney?' asked Oska.

'I'm sure they will.' Max struggled to get the words out as the three of them got into the jeep to be driven back to the hotel. It only took ten minutes but felt like a hundred with them all har-bouring the hope that Barney had been found and had been taken directly back to the hotel. This hope was all that kept Anna from a total collapse.

In the hotel foyer the manager, a doctor and a lady dressed in khaki with a badge depicting a Disney World nurse, were there to greet them. The manager told them that their suite was ready and the nurse and doctor would accompany them. Security would be up in a few minutes to get more information but in the meantime they must be assured the entire security staff were working together to find Barney.

51

When they got to their suite there was a tray of coffee, croissants, cakes and orange juice on the table in the lounge. Max found a coke in the fridge for Oska. The doctor gave Anna two Valium tablets and Max poured a glass of water for her, but they didn't dampen her anxiety; if anything, she seemed more alert.

There was a knock at the door and the head of security came in accompanied by another lady. 'This is Amanda and she will be looking after you. I know how difficult this is but I need to ask you a few questions.'

'Of course,' Anna sobbed, tears running down her cheeks. Max passed her his handkerchief.

'Can you tell me when you first noticed the Mickey Mouse?'

'It was yesterday, standing by the tree. I remember thinking, why is he standing there?'

'I also saw him,' Oska butted in.

'Could you tell us what you saw?' Security spoke gently to Oska.

'I saw Mickey Mouse standing by the large tree and I looked through my binoculars and saw that he didn't have any balloons. I thought my brother would be upset because he really wanted a white balloon, but I don't think Barney saw him so I didn't tell him that Mickey Mouse was there. But today Mickey Mouse was standing in the same place and Barney saw him. I knew he would run after him because Barney wanted a white balloon and thought Mickey Mouse would give him one. You see, when Barney wants something, even though he's autistic, he's very clever and will find a way to get what he wants. Barney ran to the tree to see Mickey Mouse, and mom told me to go and get him, but when I got there, he was gone and so was Mickey Mouse.'

Moved by Oska's account, Anna put her arm round Oska, held him close and kissed his head. 'I'm very proud of you,' she said.

'Can I go on the balcony and look at the animals now?' Oska ran out with his binoculars around his neck.

'We have a full description of Barney but we'd like to know more about his behaviour. Is there anything he's afraid of?'

'Almost everything, especially anything new,' said Anna, tearfully. 'He could be hungry now or screaming for Hurrah Hippo.'

'May I call you Anna? Anna, we have thirty security staff out there, they all have a full description of Barney and know where to look.' His bleep went.

'Got it, got it,' he repeated.

'Security have found a van parked in a road at the back of The Lion King section at the edge of our grounds. They got into it and found some Donald Duck and Mickey Mouse costumes. The marshal is sending a search team to fingerprint and remove everything from the van for forensic examination. They also report that this Mickey Mouse cannot be one of our staff and it seems a man has got in illegally disguised as Mickey Mouse. They have now sent out tracker dogs and are combing the grounds. He couldn't have gone far; we'll find him.'

'Oh my God, Barney is petrified of dogs,' Anna exclaimed.

Max went to the drinks cabinet and poured himself a whisky. 'I can't remember, did I give you the photograph of Barney?' Max asked, and went to sit next to Anna on the settee.

'Yes,' Security replied.

'See if Oska's all right, he could fall off the balcony,' Anna suddenly remarked.

Max went out onto the balcony and came back to report that Oska was fine.

'All we can do is wait; we'll find him,' said the Security man. 'I've sent out a message about Barney's fear of dogs, but I wouldn't want to call them off. They are trained to follow a scent and because you gave us Barney's toy hippo, the dogs will be sniffing for Barney. This man will know that security is around and will probably shed his Mickey Mouse costume to mingle among the crowds.'

Another bleep came through. Security replied. 'OK, let the dogs close in.'

Anna looked up pleadingly.

'They've found a Mickey Mouse suit under a bush and the dogs have got the scent. That's good news,' Security told them.

It was one o'clock, almost two hours since the nightmare began.

Anna thought of Barney being hungry, and of what this predatory man might be doing to Barney. 'Oh Max, I don't think I can bear this.' Max put his arm around her shaking body and held her damp, limp hand.

'I know it will be all right,' he said.

'How do you know?' she screamed.

'I just do.' Max controlled his anxiety. He felt terribly guilty. So many times he had thought of Barney as intruding on their happiness. He had even thought of putting him into an institution if his behaviour got any worse. Perhaps Anna had suspected his thoughts and as a result had become even more protective towards Barney. Now he fervently prayed that Barney might be returned to them, whole and unhurt.

Security, aware of their distress, was careful to give them facts, not false hopes.

'Our staff are all highly trained. They will be combing the outer perimeter of the park. The fences are checked regularly for any breaks. It was good that you reported the incident so quickly – no time was lost. Now that the man has shed his Mickey Mouse costume, he may well have left Barney to blend in with the crowds on his own. That would be his best chance of escape but he was stupid enough to not entirely dispose of his Mickey Mouse costume so the dogs have got his scent and, more importantly, Barney's.'

'Where would he leave Barney?' Anna wondered.

'We know he didn't get back to his van where he probably wanted to take Barney. Our staff got to it first and they are surrounding the area. Barney could have been left somewhere on his own.'

Anna recalled all the times she had resented Barney, how she had wondered what her life would be like without him. How he had taken away her chance of being a top designer and she had had to settle for something less. It was almost as if she had now been forced to lose him so that she could value and need him more than any of the sacrifices she had made. Her stomach felt as though it had tightened into a ball. She forced herself to breathe as, paralysed with fear, her lungs no longer seemed to work on their own accord. She would never forgive herself if anything happened to Barney, he was the most precious part of her life.

They heard a buzz on Security's intercom. 'Good.' She looked at him. 'The dogs have picked up the scent.'

The intercom buzzer went again. 'Good, yes, the King of the Jungle suite. They've got Barney, he'll be here soon.'

'Oh Max, you were right, go and tell Oska.' Anna's body started shaking uncontrollably. Max held her and the nurse gave her a glass of water and another Valium, which she could hardly get down her tight throat.

Oska came running in. 'They've found Barney! Can I go and see The Lion King show now?'

'Let's see how Barney feels. Perhaps we ought to have a quiet day at the pool.'

'Yes, that'll be great. I want to go on the water slide,' Oska enthused.

Management accompanied by a young girl dressed in pink shorts and a bright yellow shirt came into the suite. 'Marylou is here to help with Oska. She is part of our children's entertainment team and will help look after him.'

'I want to go swimming,' Oska piped up.

'Oska, you haven't had lunch and we must first see Barney. He needs to see you.'

'I'll call room service,' said the manager. 'What would you like?'

Max replied that neither he nor Anna could eat a thing but he asked for hamburgers without cheese, chips, a salad, and loads of vanilla ice cream for Barney.

The doctor told them that he would want to monitor Barney's condition but felt it best if the family made the first contact with Barney, who would probably not want yet another stranger talking to him.

9

Barney's Back – 1986

Barney, clutching Hoorah Hippo came in flanked by two security men. Sobbing, he ran to Anna. 'Mickey Mouse never came back, Barney wants his white balloon,' Barney sobbed. Max saw the manager make a phone call.

'Where have you been Barney?' Anna asked, trying to conceal her distress.

'Waiting for my white balloon, waiting for Mickey Mouse. He went away to get my balloon but never came back.'

Max saw the manager make another phone call.

There was a knock at the door and two waiters wheeled in a trolley of food. Smoked salmon, bagels, salads, hamburgers, chips, strawberries and a bowl of vanilla ice cream in a bucket of ice. The waiters laid everything out on the large coffee table and wanted to serve the food but the manager told them to leave. Barney rushed to the chips and Anna gave him a plate.

'This is great!' Oska took a hamburger and chips, sat down and said, 'There's vanilla ice cream, Barney.'

Another knock at the door; the girl from entertainment opened it. In walked Mickey Mouse holding a bunch of white balloons. Barney rushed forward. 'It's Mickey Mouse, he's brought Barney balloons. Mickey Mouse got found,' Barney shouted with delight.

'Is there anything else you want, Barney?' Mickey Mouse asked.

'More balloons!' Barney said, now sitting by the table delicately eating his chips one at a time.

The Security Supervisor told Anna and Max that he was still waiting for a full report. However, he felt it unlikely that anything had happened to Barney as the man hadn't had time. He must have been alerted or become alarmed, for he had left Barney sitting on the grass behind a large bougainvillea bush to make his escape. Security were still looking for him and were sure to find him as the dogs were now all converging towards one area.

'I can't thank you enough. I'm so grateful for the way everybody here has been so kind and effective,' Anna said, sitting close to Barney.

The manager looked a bit sheepish. 'Children do get separated from their parents – we have our tried and tested system and we do get them speedily together again – but nothing like this has happened before. This is a wake-up call. In the meantime I hope you can find a way to enjoy the rest of your time here. Amanda from children's entertainment will stay with you and help with the children, and Marylou from security will accompany you wherever you go. We would not want you to suffer a moment of anxiety. Your stay here will be complimentary. We would also like to offer you a complimentary family holiday in the future whenever it suits you. After the doctor's examination there is no need to question Barney, but if anything emerges, please let us know.'

The bleep went again. 'Excellent, thanks.' The manager looked up.

'They've got him. I must go. Goodbye, and call if you need anything – I mean anything,' he added.

'He seems all right,' said Max, watching Barney munching away.

'Can I go swimming now?' Oska asked.

'If you like, I can take Oska,' offered Amanda.

'Barney wants to go,' Barney piped up.

'Barney doesn't like the water,' Anna reminded him.

'Barney wants to go with Oska.' He seemed oblivious of the crisis.

'I'll be with them,' the lady from security offered. 'I expect you could do with a rest. We'll be downstairs and if Barney wants to come back, I can bring him and Amanda can stay with Oska.'

'What do you think?' Anna looked at Max.

'I think it's a very good idea and I know they will both be safe.' Max looked at the security guard.

'You bet, so let's get some gear and off we go,' Marylou said enthusiastically.

When they left, Anna turned to Max. 'Should we go home tomorrow?'

'No! Why? Barney seems all right and Oska is enjoying himself. Not to mention the fact that the weather in London is below freezing. What's more, we suddenly have two full-time babysitters and a completely free holiday. Are you crazy?' Max had a huge grin on his face.

Anna, whilst wanting to be alert could no longer resist the effects of the Valium. 'Max do you mind if I lie down, I can't keep my eyes open.'

They must have been in a deep sleep when they heard knocking at the door. Max went to open the door. Anna heard the children laughing. She couldn't believe that she had slept for two hours.

Oska ran towards her. 'You'll never guess what! Barney went into the water with Amanda and he loves it. We came back because we want to go to the children's show downstairs and Amanda says we need your permission.'

Max, Amanda and Marylou stayed in the lounge and Anna joined them.

'Where is the show?'

'It's downstairs in the Children's Clubroom. It only lasts an hour, and if it's too much for Barney, I can bring him back,' Linda reassured Anna.

Anna was ecstatic. She would never have believed that Barney would survive the ordeal and then be ready to follow Oska to the pool and want to go to the children's entertainment without her.

'What do you think, Max?'

'I think we should take Marylou and Mandy back to London with us.'

When the children left, Max poured himself a whisky. He was surprised when Anna said she felt like a glass of white wine. They sat on the balcony, now relaxed, and mesmerised by the passing scene of the two giraffes still strolling slowly across the 'African savannah'.

'You know what I was thinking, Max? You remember when we first met, you said you had thought of manufacturing a more bread-and-butter line? Well, I know it's years later and we've done well but I think you're right. I suppose being here and seeing everybody dressed in casuals has inspired me, and it would be far easier for me to design trousers and tops in light cottons or silks than those very complicated designs using luxury materials.'

'That's an interesting idea. You could probably knock out a basic pattern in a couple of hours and go straight into cutting without having to make a *toile*.'

'Yes, I feel ready for a new collection. Do you think you can find the fabrics?'

Max was astounded by Anna's inspirational leap. They had not only got Barney back but their intimacy had returned. Max wondered whether the resumption of love-making in their marriage also heralded a return of Anna's creativity. He looked at her and saw her face beginning to resemble its former beauty. The lines and dark rings around her eyes were beginning to disappear, her body that he'd hardly touched for two years was warm and welcoming again. There were so many small differences, each one enhancing the other. Yet was it only the near loss of Barney that had been the trigger for change?

The next five days melted away with Max and Anna relishing the luxury of having Barney and Oska fully occupied and supported by the two Disneyworld helpers. They spent the time talking, just being together, and reminding themselves of their times in Pondicherry, of the earlier years of their marriage and of the peaks and troughs as they built up their business together.

On the morning of their last full day, the phone rang. Max listened, smiled and said, 'Thank you very much.'

Turning to Anna, he said, 'The manager's secretary has booked a table at the Flamingo Restaurant for seven; we just have to confirm or change the time.'

'What about the boys? It's our last night, I suppose we should eat as a family,' Anna replied, unenthusiastically.

The door opened and Oska rushed in ahead of Barney. 'Mom, can we go to the children's magic party and barbeque tonight? It's at seven o'clock?'

'We can take them and bring them back by eight,' Amanda offered.

Barney came in. 'Magic party,' he said.

Anna looked doubtful but relented. 'OK. We are going to have dinner in the Flamingo Restaurant, so any problems, bring them to us. But you can't go to the magic party until you both have a bath.'

'I'll phone down and confirm the Flamingo.' Max seemed elated. 'Oska, you can use our bathroom, and it's my turn to bath Barney.' Max surprised Anna as well as himself.

'Then I'll get on with the packing for tomorrow,' Anna suggested.

The Flamingo Restaurant was dark enough to shade the décor, their table in the corner set well away from the next table. Reclining on the circular velvet cushioned couch, the candlelight reflected Anna's thoughtful expression. Silently they sat contemplating their extraordinary fortune, Anna thinking she would have died if innocent Barney had been sexually abused; Max of how wrong he was in never having really accepted Barney. The more he had tried, the more alienated he had felt from this small, omnipotent being who had blighted his life – and the more guilty he now felt.

The waiter came to take their order. Anna asked for asparagus and grilled fish. Max ordered the *pâté de foie gras, filet mignon* and a bottle of Cabernet Sauvignon.

They talked more openly and fully than they had for years, recapturing those heady moments of falling in love. Both, suddenly hungry, ate voraciously and finished the wine. Later, Max noticed that Anna was becoming a little restless, so he looked at his watch and said that they should get going. She readily agreed and stood up to hurry back to the children.

They got back to the suite just after nine Marylou and Amanda told them that Barney had been enthralled by the magic show and Oska had been called up to take part in a trick and had relished being the centre of attention. They said goodnight and reminded Anna that they would both be back at eight o'clock in the morning.

Anna got up early and completed the packing. Management phoned to tell them that they had arranged for a car for three o'clock to drive them to the airport. Marylou and Amanda arrived at eight with a twenty dollar gift voucher each for Oska and Barney at the gift shop.

Anna hesitated. 'I don't think it's good for Oska to be so spoilt, do you?'

'What about Barney?' Max asserted.

'I don't think he knows the difference between being spoilt or just needing his own way.'

'I agree,' Max said, understanding the point Anna had made.

'It is our last day and I do think Oska is benefitting from all this attention.' Anna sounded as if she was willing to be persuaded.

'OK, the gift shop after breakfast,' Max said.

They had a full American breakfast, waffles and all, then went down to the gift shop, where Barney searched and found a hippo key ring identical to the one he'd chosen before. Oska chose two books, *Birds of Florida*, and *Fauna and Flora of Florida*.

'Good choices,' Anna said.

A porter took their luggage and Amanda and Marylou accompanied them to the entrance, where a sparkling white stretch limousine and a uniformed chauffeur stood waiting. They were further surprised when Amanda and Marylou also climbed into the back, telling them that they had been instructed to take them right to the flight. The limousine waited a moment or two for the manager to come by to give them their complimentary voucher for their future stay at Disneyworld and to wish them a good flight home.

He said that because the whole event had had such a speedy and happy outcome, the media weren't interested in making up any story that might worry other parents and he would be most grateful if the same discretion might be applied in England. Max agreed and they shook hands. The manager said he would be letting them know the outcome of the investigation. Then Mickey Mouse, bearing a bouquet of white balloons, came to the car to give them to Barney and to say goodbye. They couldn't get over this last touch of caring and kindness. Max wished he had a camera to record Barney's smile. It was as if pure joy was bubbling out of him.

At the airport they were given priority. Amanda and Marylou kissed the boys goodbye and handed them over to an air hostess from Virgin who accompanied them right into the plane where, instead of turning right, they turned left into first class. Puzzled and then delighted, they discovered that Disneyworld had upgraded their seats.

Settling down into first class luxury, Anna whispered to Max, 'Isn't this a bit over the top?'

'I think they have behaved impeccably, both generously and wisely. No good would come of it if what happened to Barney got into any newspaper. I am just so grateful. We have had a holiday of a lifetime,' Max said.

10

Reality Returns – 1986

Seven o'clock in the morning they returned to a grey, cold, damp London and to the stark reality of their lives. In Max's study letters and bills were piled onto the desk, yards of printed-out fax paper littered the floor. Oska ran up to his room, and Barney ran into the kitchen demanding toast and butter. Anna followed him and suddenly decided not to go back to the old routine. Finding a sliced loaf in the fridge, Barney sat perfectly still while she made and buttered the toast, cut it in half and put it on a plate in front of him. She was amazed when he started eating it. Only a few days ago he had demanded that everything be cut into small pieces. She also recognised his speech had improved, his vocabulary had increased and he was beginning to use the pronoun 'I' instead of saying 'Barney'. She was amazed and heartened that he had improved so much in one week.

Max came into the kitchen and gave Anna a letter to read.

'Oh Max, I can't believe it. The local authority have approved Barney's placement at Peeling Onions, he can start in the summer term. I don't think I'll send him back to the nursery for six weeks, he can stay at home with me. He has done so well that I'm beginning to wonder whether the nursery experience even for two hours a day is doing him much good. I'm going to be here in the studio starting on the casual collection. And taking him and fetching him hardly gives me any time to do anything.'

'I agree. Why don't we look for a young student or someone to help look after Barney? He seemed to get on so well with those two marvellous Disneyworld girls.'

'Isn't it extraordinary how sometimes the answer is in front of me and I just can't see it?' said Anna. 'This last week with all its ups and downs has released something in me. I feel quite renewed. I hope Bridget comes in soon, I need her to help me unpack.' Anna glanced at the luggage piled up in the hall.

'I'm sure she'll be here – she did fill the fridge yesterday. Perhaps she knows someone who can help with Barney. In the meantime let's have a cup of coffee; the boys seem fine.'

It had been a long time since they had sat down together in their home. The usual morning scramble of Max getting off to work and Anna getting the boys ready or meeting one of Barney's peculiar demands had taken away their time together.

'We must do more of this. Our life is ridiculous the way we both rush around and we hardly ever talk, or when we do, all we do is argue about Barney. I know Barney is very intelligent and I also know he has problems, but what I'm not sure of is how much we are part of the problem,' reflected Max.

'I agree,' Anna replied. 'I can't wait for him to start at Peeling Onions. They have a special programme for mothers and I am going to learn a lot.'

Barney came running into the kitchen. 'Toilet', he demanded.

Anna leapt up from the table and rushed with him to the downstairs loo. 'I'll be back.'

Max left for work, taking Oska to drop him off at school. Since coming home, Anna had been envisioning the designs for her new collection, planning to use medium quality silks in earth colours, adding different trimmings and then blending mauves and other neutral silks for the dresses and the patterned scarves.

'Barney, will you come up to the studio with Mummy? We're going to do some nice drawing.'

Anna was surprised when Barney rushed ahead. 'Barney draw,' he declared. Anna couldn't understand why Barney wouldn't call her mummy.

'Say, "I want to draw",' Anna asked, unsure of his response.

'I want to draw,' Barney repeated.

Anna rewarded him with her best quality drawing paper and three pencils of light, medium and dark tones. She sat on the high stool in front of her drawing board, Barney beside her on the floor. It was so good to be back; her hand swept across the page drawing long baggy trousers with asymmetrical loose tops and one attached pocket hanging over the trouser. She drew narrow trousers with square necked 'A' line tops, and was so engrossed she almost forgot about Barney. Turning to check on what he was doing, she saw he had drawn three Mickey Mouses, two holding balloons, each one expressive, detailed and accurate.

'Barney, that's amazing.' Anna didn't want to alarm him with her surprise. This was the moment she recognised Barney's talent. He was a natural draftsman. He had instinctively understood the relationship between size and proportion and had no need for ruler or rubber to achieve his pure, poetic lines. It was as if the skills she had worked hard to gain at art school had somehow effortlessly been acquired by Barney.

'More paper,' he demanded. Finding a cheaper drawing book she gave it to him. Keeping him busy would enable her to go on working; she felt she was on a roll. The phone rang.

'Hi Max, Barney's a genius.'

'You've said that before. What's he done now, besides getting the entire Disney World Empire from Mickey Mouse to their top management to bow down and give us a free holiday?'

Anna explained, enthused and said, 'Wait till you get home. Also, I've completed four variations of tops and trousers, mix and match ideas. I think we now need quite a few sample materials; as usual it's colour and quality that tell the story.'

'I thought it was going to be a bread-and-butter collection, but knowing you, you can't do cheap. I can't wait to see your ideas. I'll come home early and pick up Oska. I'm beginning to feel quite jetlagged.'

Anna had been absorbed in her work for a couple of hours. Suddenly realising it was rather quiet, she turned round to find Barney fast asleep on his back with a pencil still in his hand. She didn't want to wake him and went across the hall to get his favourite blanket to cover him in the studio. She too was beginning to flag and went to her bedroom to lie down. And fell asleep. She woke up to find Barney standing at the end of her bed holding Hurrah Hippo.

'Barney wants food.'

Anna was touched by his unusually calm approach and wondered too whether she now was less anxious than usual when he was near her. Barney followed her to the kitchen and sat on his chair at the table while Anna hurriedly put some fish fingers and chips in the microwave. She poured apple juice into his special blue mug, and he drank, his eyes glued to the microwave, waiting for it to stop.

It had been a day without Barney's usual routine. No nursery school, a sleep in the late morning and lunch at three o'clock and yet Barney seemed able to adapt. She wondered if it was she who had become dependent on the routine, rigidly adhering to it long after Barney had moved on. She recalled how he dreaded any change, whether it was food, clothing, books, journeys or shops. She had read too many articles on autism. Most of them gave vivid descriptions of symptoms but she couldn't recall any specific and consistent advice on how to change behaviour. The holiday had forced them into a myriad of new experiences and Barney had not only survived – he had thrived.

Anna heard the doorbell and went to answer it. 'Hello, Rob'.

'How was Disney?' Rob asked.

'Wonderful,' Anna replied.

'Can I see Barney?'

'He's in the kitchen.' Anna thought it odd how Rob found the time to visit. She considered formalising the relationship by paying Rob but thought it best to discuss it first with Max. Barney was going to be at home for six weeks before starting at Peeling Onions. It was a long time to keep him busy. She followed Rob into the kitchen and looked at Barney flapping his hands with excitement; he liked Rob.

'How are things, Rob?' Anna asked.

'Terrible! Mum and Dad fight all the time. Dad goes out all the time with Barbara and leaves Mum and me alone.'

'Who's Barbara?' Anna asked, before she realised she shouldn't.

'She was Mum's best friend and Mum says she is a liar and a bitch.'

Anna didn't think Barney should be hearing all this and rapidly changed the subject. 'Oska should be back in a minute, he can tell you all about our holiday. I must get on.' Anna ran up to the studio to gather all Barney's drawings to show Max when he returned.

Soon Max and Oska were home, and Oska came running into the kitchen, calling for Anna. Anna came downstairs to join Oska and Max in the kitchen. Oska excitedly recounted how he was asked to tell the whole class about his holiday in Disneyworld. Max and Anna's eyes met. 'We'll talk about it later.'

She was mortified that their agreement not to disclose their experience in Disneyworld had been broken. She hadn't thought to warn Oska not to speak about Barney's kidnapping, and followed Max into the playroom.

'I'm afraid it's too late, darling. Oska not only told them how and when Barney was kidnapped but also boasted about our freebie holiday, the limo, and every bit of the special treatment. I suspect half the class will be begging their parents to take them to Disneyworld.'

'Yes, but that contravenes our agreement with the manager.'

'We will have to see where it goes. I'm sending a full letter of thanks and praise to the manager emphasising not just how grateful we are, but how efficient and how safe Disneyworld is and what a wonderful place it is for parents and children. I'll send it by courier before anything gets out, but I doubt if it will. We'll speak to Oska, too.' Max paused. 'What's Rob doing here?' he asked suspiciously.

'I've told you, he often comes over. He seems to like Barney and entertains him. It suits me. I think he is so unhappy at home and comes here to get away. Madellaine's marriage is breaking up and apparently Doug has gone off with Madellaine's best friend. I don't know the whole story and I'm sure Madellaine will be in to tell me. It all sounds quite shocking and poor Rob needs a refuge.'

'I'm jetlagged, I must go to bed soon,' Max responded, not wanting to hear the story.

'Before you go to bed, please come up to the studio, I want to show you my working designs and Barney's drawings.' Anna led the way.

Max first looked at Anna's drawings. 'I like them. You haven't lost your touch. I'll bring home some silk samples tomorrow.' Max turned to see Anna holding up Barney's drawings of Mickey Mouse.

'Wow! Did he do those by himself?'

'Totally, I swear.' Anna couldn't hide her delight.

'OK, I agree we have a budding Rembrandt. What can we do with him? Why don't I send them to Disney World as a way of saying thank you,' Max suggested.

'Not until I've made copies, but I do think it's a good idea.' Max's pride in Barney's artwork gave her more pleasure than his approval of her new designs. She so much wanted Max to accept Barney, to value him the way she valued him; she knew that Max was trying and he knew that she was pushing him. He couldn't tell Anna that as much as he tried to love Barney – and in his own way did love him – his love wasn't natural but was more the contrived love of a father's sense of duty towards his vulnerable child. Maybe his expectations were wrong, but he hadn't any specific expectations before Barney came into his life. Oska was such a loving child. He had Anna's nature, and infinite capacity to find the good in everything, delighting in Barney's smallest achievements. He seemed unaffected by or even unaware of Barney's bizarre responses and demands. As for himself, Max wondered if he lacked imagination; he saw life in straight lines whereas Anna seemed to bend reality to suit Barney's behaviour. Anna found a sort of logic in almost everything Barney did. She seemed to have entered into his world of magical meanings and in her own way derived pleasure, whereas he just felt alienated and worried and wondered whether Barney would ever be normal.

11

The Integration Programme – 1986

Although Barney wasn't due to start at Peeling Onions until the summer term, Molly Mandel phoned Anna to remind her to bring Barney to visit a few times. Anna arranged to take Barney to Peeling Onions the next day

It was a sunny spring day. Anna looked at the buds beginning to appear on the skeletal branches of the leafless trees. She felt hopeful, seeing the visit as a new beginning for Barney. He looked particularly cute in brick-coloured corduroy trousers tucked into brown boots, a dark navy polo neck sweater under his camel duffle coat and a light yellow scarf tied round his neck. Anna had hardly pulled out the drive when Barney started to instruct her from his booster seat.

'No. Go straight! Now turn. No! No! Not that way,' Barney screamed. It took Anna a few minutes to realise that Barney had remembered the entire journey from their first visit.

'What next, Barney?' she asked, giving him an opportunity to prove his photographic memory. He recalled the picture of a Peeling Onion on the wooden door and when they arrived blurted out, 'Look! Peeling Onion.'

Anna explained to Barney that they were going to stay for a while and he would see Molly and play with the toys. Barney got out of the car readily and was eager to go through the street gate as Anna opened it. He ran towards the entrance to Peeling Onions and was greeted by Molly Mandel.

'We've been waiting for you, Barney. Take off your coat; this is your special peg. It has a picture of Hoorah Hippo on top, and you can hang your coat here.'

They stepped into the first room that led off to a kitchen ahead. On the right was a large room leading to a garden and from the hall another small room. A staircase led to a lounge and another two rooms and bathroom.

'Would you like to go with Carol and do something nice in the art room, or do you want to stay with Molly and Anna?' Molly asked Barney.

Barney took Carol's hand and led her into the art room.

'Carol is our art therapist. I believe that we should introduce Barney slowly to the other children, and we'll see how he responds. Obviously each child is different and we all have to get to know each other before we can design an optimum programme for Barney. Would you like to come into the kitchen and have a cup of coffee? Carol will call if Barney wants you.'

Anna followed Molly into a basic kitchen with a table and chairs where the children had their meals.

'Something smells good,' Anna remarked.

Molly smiled. 'Wednesday is baking day – you might be lucky and get a slice of our home-made bread when it comes out of the oven.' Molly noted the intensity with which Anna was scrutinising everything. 'Peeling Onions is meant to look and feel more like a home than an institution. We find that everybody relates differently in a homely environment. Staff, mothers and children are on first-name terms. We never have more than six children here and about eight staff.'

Molly got up to put the kettle on while Anna looked out at the garden with its climbing frame, slide, cycles and other toys. A boy of about four ran into the kitchen holding a rubber doll, followed by a teacher. The teacher looked at Molly as if to say, 'This is important'.

'It's fine,' Molly said. The boy pulled a chair towards the sink and turned on the taps. 'I think we should go upstairs and let David do what he needs to do, don't you?' Molly told the teacher.

Anna was heartened that Molly had put the child's needs before attending to her. She got up and followed Molly upstairs; so far she hadn't heard a peep out of Barney who was nearby in the art room.

'I think it's marvellous that each child has so much attention. I never thought it possible but all the children seem so involved and yet they are all so different,' Anna observed.

Molly smiled. 'Of course they are. All children, whether they are autistic or whatever you'd like to call it, are different and need to be treated differently.'

'It seems so obvious when you say it like that. I am probably so anxious I couldn't even think like that.' Anna felt more relaxed.

'Each child responds differently to their family, their surroundings, and most importantly the way they are understood. Our aim is to provide the optimum opportunity for a child to express and develop his talents.'

'How do you do that?' Anna thought of Barney's talent in art.

'We observe each child's responses to specific tasks and together with the child interpret the meaning of their behaviour. If we are right we see a dramatic improvement. We also believe in teaching the basics: maths, reading, writing, plus music, art, swimming, horse riding, and we also have an Alexander teacher who comes once a week. We've noticed that after a session the children seem more relaxed; they stand up straight and generally are more co-ordinated in their movements. The Alexander method releases muscles, opens up the vertebra and allows the body to move in the optimum position for each task. Many autistic children have a stiff gait as if all their anxiety is locked in. I don't know a great deal about it but I have seen changes in the children. Our policy here is whatever works. We find the same with music therapy which helps with their speech as the music therapist makes up songs with specific words that are suited to each child. It is quite marvellous to see and hear the children singing their special song.'

'It all sounds too good to be true.' Anna felt so comfortable in the homely lounge, drinking a mug of coffee.

'I think you will enjoy our mothers' group every Wednesday

morning. It lasts two hours and the mothers discuss anything they like but the main conversation centres on their problems with their child, the siblings and almost anything that crops up. It's surprising how many very small problems can turn into vast upsets because there is no one to listen to what it's actually like living with an autistic child.'

'I've taken up a lot of your time. Perhaps I ought see what Barney's doing.' Anna hoped he hadn't disgraced himself in any way that might have affected his place at Peeling Onions.

There was a noise of chattering and laughter downstairs and a marvellous aroma of freshly-baked bread as they entered the kitchen. Anna couldn't believe her eyes. Barney was sitting around the kitchen table with the other children and teachers, holding a thick slice of bread and butter. Anna, not wanting to break the spell, didn't say a word.

'He's doing well,' Molly said.

The art therapist approached them. 'I'd like you to see what Barney has done.'

The art room floor was covered in sheet after sheet of Mickey Mouse drawings. Barney had arranged them in a pattern around the room, five holding a balloon, then every sixth Mickey Mouse without a balloon.

'Fascinating. We've been to Disneyworld in Florida,' Anna explained.

'Well, something very interesting must have happened there,' the art therapist remarked.

'You can tell from these drawings?' Anna asked emphatically, deciding not to tell them about the incident.

'All I can tell is that Barney is obsessed with Mickey Mouse and is working through some situation but it's early days and the last thing I would want to do is probe. He'll tell me when he is ready. He really is very talented and a pleasure to work with.'

'On your next visit would you like to come to the mothers' group? I think Barney will settle doing art and it will give you an opportunity to meet the other mothers,' Molly suggested.

Going home in the car, Barney again dictated the route and Anna complied. She was wholly gratified by the experience. She could never have dreamed of a place like Peeling Onions. She was moved by Molly's simple yet totally understandable account of their work. She thought Molly was absolutely genuine in the way she responded to each child and certain that she had come into contact with a woman of passion and purpose.

12

Madellaine – 1986

Barney was tired when they got home from Peeling Onions and Anna was sure he didn't need lunch after two large slices of bread and butter. She gave him a drink of apple juice and took him up to his room where he climbed onto his bed with Hurrah Hippo.

Anna was pleased to have the time to reflect on her experience at Peeling Onions. She found some leftovers from last night's dinner and was cutting a slice of roast beef when the front door bell rang.

'May I come in?' Madellaine was standing there with tear-filled eyes, her voice pleading.

'Of course, I'm just making some coffee.' Anna wasn't in the mood for yet another rant about Doug but couldn't reject her. As they sat down at the kitchen table, Madellaine poured out her problems.

'I don't know whether to divorce Doug or wait and see if he comes back. I can't believe that he is so damn stupid to do this to Rob and me.'

'Who is Barbara, do you know her?'

'Of course I know her! Well at least I thought I did. Barbara was my best friend. I don't know how long it's been going on. I should have noticed something when all four of us went to Italy. I actually thought, isn't it wonderful that we're all getting on so well, and I was so pleased Doug liked Barbara as much as I did. I must be some kind of trusting idiot. Poor Rob is really suffering, he won't speak to Doug and says he'll go round and tell him what he thinks of him in front of Barbara. I suppose I shouldn't have run Doug down in front of Rob but I couldn't help it, and anyway, I think children know a lot more than we realise. We just don't know how they interpret it. Well, after all I've said, Rob certainly hates his father. It's not that Doug has been such a wonderful husband but you see I was brought up to trust and I can't get over being treated like this. I suppose I'm rather old-fashioned, and I just can't cope with lies. Doug probably married me for my money, but what hurts is the breaking of trust by both my supposedly best friend and my husband.'

Anna was somewhat embarrassed by Madellaine's further disclosure of her private life. This was the first time she'd seen her without make-up, her hair was barely combed and she seemed to have lost all interest in her appearance.

'I entirely agree with you; loyalty and trust are paramount. Madellaine, you look terrible and I'm truly sorry, but don't let yourself go. You have nothing to be ashamed of. You must make every effort to look good so that Doug can see he hasn't broken you and Rob can see that you're not the guilty one.' It was so unlike Anna to give advice but she too felt contaminated by Doug's behaviour. 'You know you hear these things, you read about them every day in the newspaper and they mean nothing until it happens to you. Really Madellaine, I don't know what to say but at least get a good lawyer and give Doug as little as possible.'

'It's a bit too late for that. My father will be furious with me: I insisted in putting the house in both our names,' Madellaine told her.

'Oh dear, I don't seem to be doing you much good. I really don't know much about these things. I leave everything to Max, so don't listen to me. All I know is I feel so angry; I would be devastated if Max did anything like that.'

'Believe me, I also couldn't have imagined Doug doing anything like that. We had a good marriage,' Madellaine said angrily.

Anna hoped she hadn't sounded smug and tried to retract. 'I suppose in life we can never be sure of anything and when the unexpected happens, we have to think very carefully before we do anything on impulse.'

'I agree with you. That's why I won't divorce Doug. I blame Barbara. I think if a woman is out to find a man and makes herself available, few men can see through it, but what I can't understand is why she decided on Doug. I'll never forgive her and nor will Rob. I suppose I shouldn't set Rob up against his father, but Rob is no idiot and has his own reasons for being furious with Doug. I really admire the way you take care of Barney. I'm finding that Rob is getting so difficult: he doesn't tell me anything and sometimes I wonder what he's up to.'

'I find Rob quite mature for a ten-year-old. He often comes in to entertain Barney; I don't know how he has the patience.' Anna wished that Madellaine would leave. She felt uncomfortable hearing about her marriage and she wanted to go up to her studio.

'Madellaine, I hope you'll excuse me but I have to do a quick sketch before Barney wakes up.'

'I'm sorry, how thoughtless of me,' Madellaine replied, getting up to go.

Anna felt depleted. She had lost both her idea and enthusiasm for the new design. It was as if Madellaine's discontent had seeped into her, suddenly making her feel insecure. She had been so happy after her visit to Peeling Onions, and now, suddenly dispirited, went to lie down on the large couch in the lounge. Her earlier anxiety about the visit to Peeling Onions, followed by the unexpected relief and intensity of her time there, had left her exhausted. It was as if, just when she achieved everything she'd hoped for Barney, she was beset by the fear of losing it all. She couldn't account for these feelings that in a more rational moment she would realise were ridiculous, but somehow Madellaine's unhappiness had stirred an inexplicable fear in her.

She woke up to see Barney standing next to the couch.

'Hi, I know who's a very hungry boy.' Anna sat up, moved by an overwhelming desire to hug Barney, but as she encircled her arms around him he drew away and she felt his body tense as if he was unable or unwilling to mould into her arms. A crushing sadness flooded through her.

13

The New Collection – 1986

Anna was in the kitchen standing by a pot of boiling water when Max walked in. 'What's for dinner?' he asked.

'Spaghetti Bolognese.'

'What's in that big box?' Anna asked, seeing it on the table.

'I brought home a lot of coloured silk samples for you to choose for the new collection.'

'I didn't know we had any, where did you get them?'

'I didn't know either, but Dinah found them. She's proving to be full of initiative. I was telling her about the new collection and she immediately jumped up and brought these in from the work-shop.'

'She's come a long way since I took her on six years ago. She even looks different. I think you should give her more responsi-bility. Perhaps she could help find trimmings and buttons. Dinah's one of those with hidden talents. Would you put the box in my studio? I can't wait to see the silks.' Anna was thrilled that she could take the collection forward.

After Oska and Barney went to bed, Anna and Max went up to the studio where she delighted in spreading the array of colours according to their tone.

'This is quite a find,' Anna said, picking up a range of brown shades going toward fawn, fingering the silk to determine the quality. Arranging the squares across her cutting table she selected an orange and a mauve sample that both blended and contrasted. 'What do you think?' she asked Max.

'There's quite a choice to play with. I'll ask Dinah to check the suppliers so we can get an idea of availability and price. It's supposed to be the bread-and-butter collection, remember.'

In bed, Max gently pulled Anna towards him. Her mind was full of ideas about using the different coloured silk, then her thoughts shifted to Molly Mandel. While her body succumbed, her mind was elsewhere.

14

The Mothers' Group – 1986

The week had flown by. Barney was more settled at home. Bridget, their daily help, managed to entertain Barney while doing the housework. She had found it amusing that Barney would scream each time she switched on the vacuum cleaner and Anna was surprised when after a morning of screams, Bridget had got Barney to hold the handle of the cleaner without screaming.

'Thank you for looking after Barney.' Anna was grateful to anybody who entertained Barney, and even though Bridget didn't seem to have a sensitive cell in her body, Barney followed her around like a puppy. She could only think that Barney could somehow sniff out that Bridget was a good sort. Tomorrow they were going on their second visit to Peeling Onions. There were only two more weeks to go before Barney would start full-time and Anna would be able to take the new fashion collection to the next stage.

It was another beautiful spring morning; the daffodils were in full bloom and at last the buds and leaves on the trees had opened into a flood of green. Barney dictated the journey, Anna taking pride that he had remembered the entire route.

Anna was anxious about meeting the other mothers for the first time. As she stepped into the courtyard, Molly came out to greet her and Barney. Molly explained that each mother sat with their child and his or her teacher for a half-hour before going into the mothers' group and asked Anna if she would prefer to sit in the classroom with the others or be alone with Barney in the art room. Before she could answer, Barney ran ahead into the art room, followed by Carol, the art therapist.

Anna sat on a small chair next to Barney and Carol, who gave Barney a box of coloured felt tip pens and a sheet of paper. They sat quietly while Barney selected brown, yellow and white pens. They watched as his hand moved across the page and slowly and meticulously drew an onion. It was almost a replica of the onion on the front door, only more expressive as he coloured in the brown and gold outer leaves with white tips and a long dark straggly root. He then drew the half-open wooden door around the onion in perspective. Anna was amazed and Carol, who must also have been impressed, didn't praise Barney but acknowledged his effort.

'Barney I'm so pleased that you like Peeling Onions because we all like you and want you to stay. Anna is going with the other mothers, and we are going into the garden with the other children.' Carol spoke in a quiet, unthreatening manner.

Anna noticed how Carol used personal pronouns when talking to Barney.

Anna saw the mothers walking across the courtyard and going through a door. Molly came in to fetch Anna who looked back to make sure Barney was all right.

'Don't worry, you'll soon get the hang of it,' Molly told Anna as they entered the lounge that Anna learned was part of Molly's Victorian home. Molly introduced Anna to the five other women and went to sit on one of a pair of cream and pink, chintz-covered Chesterfield couches. Molly sat on one of the rose velvet-covered Victorian chairs. The green patterned William Morris wallpaper and the Persian carpet in soft colours completed the homely room.

Molly asked if anybody would explain to Anna what the group was about, reminding them that they had all experienced how daunting it could be on the first morning. One mother, Linda, volunteered.

'It's all about us really,' she said, laughing nervously. 'Our problems, how we feel about them, our children, our family and whatever presents itself on the day. Don't worry it takes some getting used to. When I first came, and I think most of us feel this way, I was horrified. I thought I wouldn't dare discuss my personal life with complete strangers. Then as I listened to the other mums, I realised that, yes, I feel like that as well, I've been there. We all support each other because we know that without monitoring our own feelings, little problems become immense. I really can't explain more; just sit back and relax and be assured Molly will always jump in to help us.'

Anna felt comfortable amongst this group of strangers, but was certain she would never discuss her problems with anybody. Her private life was sacrosanct and she deplored this new society that insisted on sharing everything with everybody. She didn't think exposing one's intimate world to others was at all helpful and decided it was best to keep quiet and not say anything that might affect Barney's chances at Peeling Onions.

Anna listened as Angela spoke. 'Yesterday I felt an overwhelming desire to escape, even if it was just to walk to the top of the road. Tony went on and on repeating the same phrase, 'The lights are on, the lights are off', running around the house, operating all the switches. It got to a point where I couldn't take it and screamed at him. 'Leave the lights alone. I've had enough!' Tony threw himself on the floor and I heard him in a low and desperate voice saying: 'The lights are on, the lights are off.' He looked so frightened and I feel so guilty. My husband has no idea how exhausted I am. He thinks going to the office is work – well I'd swop with him any time.' Angela was near to tears.

Jeanette responded, 'I also feel trapped. On Tuesday, Paul asked for an ice-cream. When we went into the shop he shouted, "No ice cream! CHOCOLATE! CHOCOLATE!" The shop was full of people and they all looked at me to control my child. The woman behind the counter said, "Any boy who shouts in my shop will have to go out and come in again and be good." Well, damn me if Paul didn't run out the shop and go back and calmly ask for chocolate. So you see, I don't know how to handle him – one minute he wants something and the next minute he doesn't.'

Molly talked to the group. 'I think this behaviour is all part of the bigger picture. The child isn't sure of what he wants, just as the mother isn't sure. One minute you want to escape, the next minute you feel guilty at the thought of abandoning your child. There is nothing to be ashamed of. Your feelings are quite understandable. Autistic children are living in a world of apprehension and in constantly projecting their anxiety into you, they make you indecisive. There is a repeated spiral of anxiety being transmitted between you.

'Angela, something must have happened to make Tony suddenly become obsessed with the lights. Is he afraid of the dark and if so, it's easy to get a night light. Carol can have a session with him in the art room, she often finds out what's going on. Only by understanding the smallest detail can we intervene. Look how successfully the shopkeeper intervened with Paul – because she wasn't anxious while Jeanette lost her confidence.' Sometimes we're surprised how the children behave differently with a stranger, they seem to sniff out anxiety which makes them feel conflicted. At the end neither Tony nor Angela knew whether the lights should be on or off.'

Anna was riveted to every word. It all made sense to her. She recalled how Max had effortlessly toilet trained Barney. After an hour, a tray of tea and cake was brought into the room, giving everybody a chance to relax from both their expressed and suppressed emotions. At the end of the group, the mothers returned to the unit to fetch their children. Anna was relieved to know that Barney had been fine. One of the mothers, Linda, came up to her.

'How do you feel about the group?' she asked.

'It's early days but I think I learned a lot. Thank you for asking,' Anna responded.

'If you want to know anything more you can phone me, I'll be pleased to help. Here's my phone number,' she said, handing Anna her card.

On the way home, feeling the tension in her body, she forced herself to relinquish her tight grip on the steering wheel and to relax her aching shoulders. Barney was unusually quiet, watching the passing views and monitoring the route. Whilst it had been reassuring listening to the mothers in the group and to know that she was not alone, she couldn't imagine herself expressing her problems. She saw it as a sign of weakness, as giving in rather than confronting life, and believed if once she allowed her feelings to be exposed her entire edifice would crumble. Knowing that Max would see Molly's explanations as sentimental mumbo jumbo, she was not going to discuss them with him. For Max, life was not about talking – it was about doing.

15

The Necessary Collection – 1986

Anna was in the studio putting the final touches to her latest design. She was particularly pleased with the inserts that she'd put into the bottom of the inner trouser leg, giving the leg a longer look without losing its classic appeal.

'That's super,' Max said, watching her trying out different colour combinations with the sample silk squares. 'I like it; I think it makes it morning casual onto lunch time elegance and evening dinner – all in one garment with the addition of scarves, jewellery etc.'

Anna couldn't remember Max taking such an interest in every stage of the design. She felt under pressure to complete her collection, leaving her with insufficient time to mull over and review her work.

'What's the hurry, Max?' Anna sensed his unease and also noticed the tension around his mouth.

'I didn't want to tell you with all the worries you have starting Barney at his new school.'

'Tell me what?'

'Anna, we have a problem. The luxury end of our business is slow. No, it's drying up. Our sales have been steadily falling over the past twelve months and we are now nearing break-even point. Without you focused at the helm, let's face it, the designs have become repetitive and lack your creative flair and finish. Maybe the market for special occasion fashion is changing. I don't know. Another worry is that our designs are being copied but with cheaper fabrics and shoddier finishes, and are selling in the high street. I think some of your original patterns may have been stolen, for just when our collection comes out we see copies in the fashion departments of some stores. It's not surprising that our celebrity customers are turning away. I keep on thinking we should explore manufacturing in India, where the costs are considerably less than here.'

Anna was stunned. Just when she had some hope that Barney would be secure and would flourish at Peeling Onions, her world was collapsing.

'Couldn't you have seen this coming?' Anna asked, unable to hide her disappointment in Max.

'I don't think so. Fashion has always been a feast or famine business and you are only ever as good as your last collection. Then, with you not being around in the factory, the staff culture changed, they were taking short cuts and too many poorly-made garments were getting through the final checks. You know I've always thought we should spread our risks by having a bread-and-butter range, but now it's our only hope. And there's another problem. Dinah found the supplier of the silks you selected for the new collection but they are too expensive. Anna, we have to find cheaper materials, cheaper labour and rethink our market.'

Anna threw the tape measure to the floor. 'I wonder whether I should bother finishing this lot. No sooner does one thing go right in the family then a bolt from the blue destroys us. I can't take this roller coaster life much longer. Today I felt so happy. I should have known it was a warning sign. We have found the perfect place for Barney where he can make progress, and they also help the family and so much more. I was basking in contentment, for the first time feeling really supported and even thought of spending more time in the business, but now there'll be no business to go back to. I don't understand. You must have seen the downward trend in sales. I'm working day and night, I can't do any more! So don't blame me for not being there to hold everybody's hand. That's your job!'

'Don't you think I realise that?' replied Max. 'I've become too dependent on Dinah, who exudes such a sense of confidence that I didn't recognise the gaps in her experience.'

'Now it's Dinah's fault, is that what you're saying?'

'No! It's absolutely my responsibility, I promise you I will do all I can to put it right.'

Anna couldn't bear to see Max looking so defeated. Angry and frightened, she recalled that it was she, against Max's inclination, who had insisted on designing for the luxury end of the market.

'Don't give up on me, Anna. We've caught the problem in time. I'm certainly not throwing the towel in yet.'

'What about our creditors? Don't they have a say in all this?' Anna demanded.

'Between our debtors and creditors, the stock, the tax and the bank, paying off the staff, getting rid of equipment and the lease on the factory, we could just about end up with enough capital to keep us going for a year or two. Look, we still have the house, which must be worth a lot more than we paid for it. I'll keep the office and get Dinah to do more. I'll go to India to look for material and a reliable factory. You just have to complete the collection.'

'What guarantee is there we'll succeed?' Anna asked.

'I don't know, but I'm not going to give up. We can't . . . there's no choice but to go ahead.' Max spoke with more confidence than he really felt.

Those words 'I'm not going to give up' resonated and equated with her feelings about Barney.

'Max, I'll finish the patterns by the weekend and you plan your trip. We started with a lot less money and a lot less experience so we'll just have to re-invent ourselves.'

'Anna, you are by far the most inspiring woman I could ever hope to find. I love you.' Max got up and hugged her. 'Does this mean Oska will have to leave his private school?' Anna asked anxiously.

'Not at the moment. It's no good thinking gloom and doom before we've even started. After all, your name still means something in the fashion industry. I'm sure there will be a lot of interest in the collection but let's keep it under wraps. I think what is happening to us may be a blessing in disguise. Manufacturing in England today is far too expensive and risky. By moving our manufacturing base to India, provided we can find the right people, we could cut our costs by half.'

'Wouldn't it be better to find a buyer for the whole factory rather than sell it off piecemeal? If it can be sold as a going concern there won't be any redundancy payments to make.' Anna couldn't bear to think of all their work being dismantled, but the thought of losing their home was even more frightening.

'There's been a global change in the top end of the market and we can't wait around for the next celebrity to invent herself. The evidence is clear: our order book totals are falling every month. Of course, I should have foreseen this six months ago. I don't want to sink so low as to use Barney as an excuse, but even though I don't often express it, I am consumed with worry about him. And as you know, our business is always volatile. You never know. Last month's poor sales may be next month's bonanza.'

'Oh Max, I've also been so absorbed with Barney's every move that I've neglected you and Oska. I've relied on both of you to be my assistants, as I felt I was the only one that knows how to handle him.'

'I've realised that, but how could I say anything to you when you are doing everything possible to help the family. Is there anything I can do to help you?' Max looked around the studio: every surface was covered in papers, silks and drawings.

'You can make me a strong cup of coffee because I'll probably be working through the night, and you can take Oska to school tomorrow and help a little more with Barney. I must sort out the patterns and match them to the colours.'

'How many designs do we have?' Max asked.

'Six, which I suppose is the minimum for a collection but as they are mix and match, probably a lot more. I would like to make them up here, so that you've got the best samples of quality, design and finish which is our trademark. Then I think you should take them to our best customers and get their orders before we go into production. I also need our top pattern cutter and seamstress to be available tomorrow. I'll pop down and supervise.'

'I think you will have to come with me to India to sort out the production.' Max knew he was stepping into a minefield.

'What about Barney? He will have just started at Peeling Onions. We've never left him before, who would look after him?'

'This isn't a joyride Anna. Our whole future is at stake, Oska's education, our home and God knows what else. Can't we get Bridget to stay here for five days and pay Rob to come in the late afternoon to entertain Barney? If we do it in the middle of the week, Barney will be at school most of the day.'

'I thought you disliked Rob,' Anna retorted. It was unthinkable to leave Barney. 'And how will Barney get to school?'

'Perhaps Madellaine would drive him? It would just be for five days,' Max pleaded.

'I think it's all too complicated. We can take him with us.' Anna was emphatic. 'Bridget can move in and look after Oska.'

'How do you think we will be able to negotiate anything with Barney running around screaming for hamburgers in Hindu India?' Max sounded more worried than flippant.

'Come on Max, don't be so negative, you know Barney behaves better when you're around.'

'We'd only be in India for such a short time. I'd better go and work more on the figures. We still have quite a lot of stock to get rid of and I am not accepting bargain basement prices.'

'Max, leave me to finish these designs. Get Dinah to send over the silks and I'll tie up the colour combinations and come into the factory when I've sorted it all out. I'm not going out all day and I'll ask Bridget to stay late and help with Barney.' Anna felt energised by the challenge. She thought how much energy she had for everything else but how quickly Barney exhausted her. Anna had fought exhaustion all her life, from the moment she could remember coming home from school at the age of five to help her invalid mother. This is what had shaped her expectations – she could never believe in magic or life being too easy. Anna had been up most of the night and Max thought she had probably finished the patterns as he watched her finally come to bed and fall into a deep sleep. He sneaked out of the room to get Barney up and make breakfast for the children.

At breakfast Barney watched Max like a hawk. 'He won't eat that,' Oska told him as Barney left the second piece of bread. 'You first have to put the butter on, then the Marmite, and then cut it up into small squares and put it on his blue plate.'

'I thought he was over that,' Max said.

'He is, but today he is anxious because mum isn't here, so just do it and he'll settle down,' Oska instructed.

Max heard Anna coming down the stairs. 'Are you being a good boy, Barney?' she asked, watching him neatly picking up one square at a time. 'I see he's gone back to bits and pieces again,' Anna remarked.

'I told dad to give it to him like that,' Oska said.

'Thanks.' Anna thought it was a small regression considering the immense task ahead of them. She was having second thoughts about taking Barney to India and called Max into the lounge to talk in private.

'I don't think it's such a good idea to take Barney with us. He'll struggle with the change and it must be better for him to be in his own environment.'

'I thought it was a daft idea last night, so I'm pleased you've come to your senses. He would be terrified by the hordes of people, the smells, the strange sights. I remember my first reaction to India, I felt as though I might disappear and never be found again. Surely being here amongst the things he knows is the better option. Why don't you speak to Molly and get her advice?' Max suggested.

'I'm going to Peeling Onions next week so I'll ask her then, and I'll also speak to Bridget and Madellaine.'

Max left to take Oska to school and Barney seemed content watching television in the playroom. Anna sat at the kitchen table, her hands wrapped round a mug of coffee. She thought of her isolation. It was extraordinary that when it came down to it neither Max nor she had any family who could help. Her older married sister with three children lived in Manchester and helped with their disabled mother. Her father, head of the art department at the local grammar school, could hardly come down to London to look after Barney. Max's elder brother Harold, was mildly eccentric and lived with their mother in Rottingdean. He never married, had remained the bookkeeper in the same firm and although intelligent seemed dependent on their mother. After their father died, their mother had bought a local tea shop and she and Harold lived in the flat above.

Anna sipped her coffee, realising that there was nobody they could turn to. She was deeply disappointed in Max and couldn't understand how he could have let what had been a successful business run down. Perhaps it wasn't entirely his fault. Society had changed, become less formal, and it was she who had insisted on special event gowns. Now it was all jeans, the tighter the better, and her new collection wasn't so far off the current trends. She had to save the business – there was no time for self-pity and there was no other way but for her to go with Max to India. It was the place where ideas bounced off the materials and she had to immerse herself in the exotic pickings.

Bridget walked into the kitchen. She had been with them for six years with hardly a day off. 'Here comes trouble,' she joked, as Barney ran towards her waving his hands with excitement, only to then immediately run back to watch television.

'Bridget, I want to ask you a big favour. Max and I have to go to India for five days, and I wondered whether you would move in and stay with the children? I wouldn't ask you but it's very important.'

'Now when would that be?' Bridget hadn't said no, but she hadn't said yes either.

'In the next two weeks, ideally. But whenever it suits you, really, everything depends on you.'

'I'd like to help you but you see my niece is coming down from

Dublin next week and I promised my sister I'd look after her. She's coming to look for work, so I don't know how long she'll be staying with me.'

'She could stay here, and if she's good with children, I'll pay her to help with Barney.' Anna felt elated, everything was falling into place and all she had to do now was save the business.

'She's the eldest of seven so I think she knows something about nippers, although Barney is quite a handful, but not with me. Barney and me get on fine.'

Anna wasn't entirely sure whether Bridget had agreed. 'So what do you think?'

'Yes, I'll help you and Brie can stay here with me. I think she'll be pleased with the extra pennies while she's waiting to get a job.'

'Bridget, that's marvellous! I can't tell you what a relief it is to know that I don't have to take Barney with us.'

'What a ridiculous idea! How do you think he'd cope with the smell of all that curried food? He won't come into the kitchen if I'm cooking cauliflower!' Bridget exclaimed, loading the dishwasher.

Anna immediately phoned Max to tell him of the new arrangement.

'Do you really think we can leave Barney? What if he regresses? I've read about how autistic children react to shock.'

'I think you should speak to Molly but I'm struggling between what we owe and what we are owed, trying to pay the wages and sell the stock. It's not easy and the last thing I want to do is take out another mortgage on our home.'

'I didn't realise that there is such time pressure. How bad is it?' Anna felt depleted; she loved the house she'd put so much into refurbishing. She was always pleased to return to it and never felt bored at home. It was her creative space and emotional comfort.

'Anna, I know this is a shock but we can build it up again; no one has taken your talent away. I've started contacting a few top end fashion houses and Frank James is coming over this afternoon to talk.'

'Do the staff know what's going on? Because for heaven's sake they mustn't get a sniff of it.'

'Well,' he paused.

'Well what?' Anna retorted.

'Of course Dinah knows, she's my Girl Friday.'

'OK, but swear her to secrecy.'

Anna went up to the studio. She had two more patterns to sort out and the colour samples for contrast and blending. Suddenly an idea came to her. She looked at the twelve pieces – six tops and six pairs of trousers – and decided she needed four skirts and six scarves to expand and enhance the mix and match concept. She would call the collection '24/7' to describe its intent. In the new world of the executive woman who met over business lunches and meetings, and who travelled, she could dress in the morning and go through to a cocktail party or an evening event in the comfort and elegance of the 24/7 collection. With the right quality, crease-resistant silk, the whole collection would be light to carry, take up little space and could be folded and packed in an attractive silk bag. She now had to design the four skirts from mini to maxi – a wrap-around, an A-line, a mini and an elegant evening skirt with side slits. Simple, compared to the detailed shapes that she'd devised for the luxury end of fashion. Anna started making drawings as her mind spun with excitement.

She'd been in the studio two hours and hadn't heard a peep out of Barney. In the hall she found Bridget emptying the bookshelves in Max's study and dusting them while Barney put each book back in its place, hardly noticing her. It was like a cloud lifting, seeing Barney even for that brief moment manage without her. She could see her way forward; all she had to do was the work and she wasn't afraid of that.

The phone rang and she heard Max half whispering excitedly.

'Frank James Fashion is interested in taking over the whole lot, with one sticking point. They want all your original *toiles*.' Max paused as if expecting her objections.

'Max, if we can sell the whole shebang as one, it couldn't be better. We'll have no liability to redundancy, you'll easily be able to pay off all the creditors and we should have something left over to finance the new collection.'

'Anna you're marvellous! By the way, Frank James also wants our "Anna" label.'

'That's OK. I've already thought of another label.' Anna couldn't wait to tell him of her breakthrough. 'What about calling it 24/7?'

'That's brilliant! I think you've caught the zeitgeist. Well, we still have a long way to go – I think Frank James is looking for a bargain.'

'Don't let him know how desperate you are,' Anna warned.

'I think he's already got whiff of the perspiration running down the inside of my shirt, and wants to take me to the cleaners.'

'Max, don't give up. Please fight for me, for Oska and Barney. I must get back to work. Good luck.'

After putting the phone down Anna felt worried. Max wasn't as strong as she was. He was fine when things were going well but gave up too easily when he came up against a really major problem. She hoped he could sustain the negotiations. She was also worried that Dinah knew too much. Although she had no reason not to, there was something about Dinah she didn't quite trust. It was the way she always appeared to be doing the right thing, as though there was a sign above her head proclaiming 'Trust me, I really do care'. Pushing the thought away Anna went back into the studio to work out the skirt and top combinations.

Anna woke up after an unusually disturbed night. What if they couldn't get the right price? What if they had to sell the house? She needed to talk to Molly about leaving Barney at home. There was so much to think about and to organise, they were leaving in five days. And they were still waiting to hear from Frank James, who bit by bit was stripping Max down to the bare bones of the business, especially after his accountants had examined the books and done due diligence. Last night she and Max had worked out the absolute lowest figure they would accept, below which the deal wouldn't be worth doing. Even at the lowest price they could, if they were careful, end up with enough money to pay for their trip, the new collection and a few months' living expenses.

Anna again came up with a plan. She would do finished drawings of her design concept and Max would take them to buyers who knew Anna's work. He shouldn't lose sight of or leave any of the drawings with them, as they both knew how easily designs could be copied overnight. He would have to insist on the buyers confirming orders so that they could work out their production and delivery schedules to encourage Frank James. Max agreed it was well worth a try, and Anna felt that she had got over another hurdle.

Later that day, just as she was beginning to think that they had a workable plan, Barney collapsed in a major tantrum. She ran into his bedroom and found that he was tearing bits of transparent sticky sealing tape off from the reel he had taken from Max's study.

'It's breaking! Mend the cracks!' Barney shouted, looking at the lines in his hand and covering them up with the tape sobbing, 'Make them better! Mend Barney! It's broken! It's broken!'

Anna felt distraught. 'It's all right, Barney. Look, Anna has lines, Max has lines, Oska has lines. Your hands won't break.'

Barney hardly listened as he tugged at the tape, twisting it trying to find straight bits to stretch across the lines on his hands and so making it difficult to cut. Anna could see that Barney was incapable of escaping from his terror and all she could do was let him complete what he had started. Eventually he would use the whole reel. It was nine o'clock and Barney should have been asleep. Max was still at the office.

Oska came in. 'What's up?' he asked. 'It's OK, Barney, just wait. Oska will fix it.' Oska ran downstairs and returned with a pair of Barney's gloves. 'Here, put these on,' he told Barney.

Barney let Oska unwind and take off all the twisted tape and put on the gloves, then taking Hurrah Hippo he turned over and rocked himself to sleep.

Anna went back to the studio to do some work but the worry of leaving Barney dominated her thoughts. How would Bridget cope with Barney's unpredictable tantrums and bizarre demands; it was one thing to explain Barney's routine, to write out a list of his likes and a bigger list of his dislikes, but she could never explain to herself, let alone to Bridget, how to deal with his anxiety attacks. She would have to rely on Oska, who had experienced enough of them and sometimes knew better than she did what Barney needed.

She realised that she was becoming more dependent on Oska and wondered what effect it might be having on him. She wondered why he never brought any friends home and, as if knowing he might be needed at home, usually checked with her if it was all right to go out to see a friend. Max was right in regularly reminding her about the sacrifice Oska was making and had independently researched boarding schools and communities for Barney, but she wouldn't listen or discuss any such possibility.

'What happens when we die? Do you expect Oska to look after Barney? I don't think you're being rational about Barney's future.'

Then Max, seeing the pain on Anna's face, would feel guilty but would go on as it was clearly important for them to start thinking about Barney's future. These discussions would always end in the same explosive way with Anna going up to her studio while he sat alone in the kitchen. At those times she knew Max had a point but she couldn't explain why she couldn't even think about sending Barney away.

Anna, too upset to complete her drawings, went to bed. She wasn't going to tell Max about the sticky-tape incident. She accepted that they both dealt with life differently but perhaps the judgements she made about Barney were entirely emotional and other thoughts should be used in making decisions. It seemed absurd because when it came to the business, or buying a house, she remained pragmatic and had proved that she was capable of clear thinking.

'Have you eaten?' she asked, as Max came into the bedroom.

'I've had a sandwich but I'm not hungry. Frank James only left about an hour ago. Nothing is resolved.'

'What's the sticking point?' Anna knew it was the money.

'There's no point in throwing the business away.' Max sounded depleted.

'Can't we offer him something extra?' Anna said, sitting up in bed.

'Like what?' Max replied.

'I could contract to do him one design a year for three years. I can practically do our new collection standing on my head, so I'll have more time and less pressure.'

'It's worth a try,' Max agreed, sounding desperate.

'Things will look better in the morning,' Anna said, not knowing whether she was trying to cheer up Max or herself.

Anna's night was filled with disturbing dreams, none of which she could remember when she woke up. She was pleased that Max was in the bathroom getting ready for work; she had to keep him motivated and away from Barney. Getting out of bed, she went into Barney's bedroom. Whilst Barney now managed to go to the toilet on his own during the day, at night he wet the bed and she could never get used to the strong odour of stale urine soaking his nappy and the bed. Barney followed Anna into the bathroom. She filled the bath while pulling off his nappy and smelly pyjamas and put his collection of plastic duck, hippos and sponges into the water, filled it with peach-scented liquid soap and helped him climb into the bath. She let him soak and play while she hurried into the bedroom to talk to Max.

'Have you decided what to do?' Anna asked.

'Yes. I think your idea of doing a design a year is a good one, but I'll offer it for two years so we have some wiggle room,' Max said.

'Good thinking,' she said, and hurried back to Barney.

Sitting at the side of the bath she wondered whether she had transmitted her anxiety to Barney. Anna also suspected that he knew without being told that she and Max would be going away. Why else had he suddenly become so fearful? She pulled out the plug, and Barney dutifully climbed out. She dried him with towels as he cleaned his teeth, and she brushed his long thick hair, and dressed him. Today they were going on their third visit to Peeling Onions.

16
The Visit – 1986

Barney dictated the route as usual and seemed much calmer. Molly was there to greet them and suggested that Carol take Barney into the main workroom to sit with the other children. Barney didn't object so Anna asked Molly if she had the time to see her alone.

'Of course,' Molly agreed, thinking that Anna, like Barney, had also made progress in that she was secure enough to request a meeting. They went into the art room that doubled up as a meeting room for private talks. Molly sat opposite Anna and waited for her to begin talking. Anna burst into tears.

'Has something happened?' Molly asked.

'Just about everything is going wrong,' Anna blurted out.

Molly didn't probe but offered Anna a tissue to wipe her eyes.

'I have to go with my husband on a business trip to India. We've never left Barney before. If I don't go our business could collapse – we'd have to sell the house and God knows how we would manage.'

'I didn't know you worked.' Molly spoke quietly.

'I'm a dress designer and the business depends on my creative input. Since Barney was born I've been working from home so that I could be with him. I haven't put enough time or energy into designing the collections and scrutinising quality control and I'm sure that's been a major reason for the collapse. We have to go to India to save the business. Max can't go on his own and I don't know how Barney will survive without me.'

'What about your older son, how is he managing?'

'I feel very bad about Oska. He hardly gets any attention and he spends most of his free time helping me with Barney. You see, right from the word go, Oska seemed to accept that Barney needed the lion's share of attention. He is so good-natured and doesn't complain; I'm sure that one day he'll protest, and I don't blame him,' Anna sobbed.

'There are times in life when we are faced with difficult choices, yet we have to decide. What plans do you have for Barney's care?' Molly asked.

'My daily help, Bridget, who's been with me for years, has agreed to move in with her niece for five days.'

Somehow sharing the information with Molly helped Anna to believe in the possibility of leaving Barney.

'She must know Barney well and you know her well. It's quite common to think that you are the only person who can meet Barney's needs but perhaps that's part of your anxiety.' It was clear to Molly that Anna needed to make a decision.

'I don't think Bridget could have handled Barney last night.' Anna related the sticky-tape incident to Molly.

'Perhaps it wouldn't have happened if Bridget was there. Mothers have often told me they can't believe how well-behaved their children are here and how they change as soon as they get home. I'm not saying Barney won't miss you but from what you say, you have no choice.'

'I don't. Max needs me and I can't let him down.' Anna looked up at Molly as if needing her permission.

'Perhaps in the long run you won't be letting Barney down if you put your husband and the business first. From what you tell me, you would be letting the whole family down if you don't go to India.'

'I didn't think of it like that.' Anna visibly relaxed.

'It might be a good idea to bring Oska with you to visit Peeling Onions. Oska will feel reassured, knowing that Barney is in a good place. From what you've told me, Oska seems unusually caring and he would be comforted to see how well Barney is settling in, and to know that if something untoward crops up, he can phone me. I know Barney isn't officially starting here for two weeks as his referral hasn't yet come through, but perhaps he could come here from half past nine to three every day? If we are asked we can say it's part of the integration programme,' Molly suggested.

'That would be marvellous. Bridget could take and fetch him by taxi. I really can't thank you enough.' Anna couldn't believe how everything seemed to be working out. Her sense of relief was palpable.

'I hope you will come to me with any problems. Sometimes together we can find solutions that can prevent things getting worse.' Molly got up. 'Let's go and see how Barney is doing in the work-room.'

Barney was sitting with Carol, engrossed in number learning. He didn't even look up when Anna walked towards him.

'I see what you mean,' Anna smiled, 'Thank you so much.'

17

The Last Chance – 1986

Anna was surprised to find Max on the bed when she got home at two o'clock. Asking Bridget to give Barney something to eat and to put on his favourite video she went upstairs again.

'What's happened?' Anna asked Max, afraid to know the answer.

'I think we almost have a deal. I'm going back at five o'clock when the lawyers will join us.'

'But what's the deal?' Anna asked impatiently.

'You're the deal, darling. One "Anna" design a year for three years. It was a good thing I offered him a two-year deal first because, like the bully he is, he only shook hands on the three-year contract.' Max looked exhausted.

Anna told him about her talk with Molly.

'We're very fortunate. It isn't easy to find good people. I really think that Barney will improve at Peeling Onions, although I just can't deal with the name. It's bizarre.' He sounded near to collapse.

'I think the name tells a story,' Anna explained.

'I think "24/7" tells a great story,' Max said before falling asleep.

Anna went up to the studio to finish some drawings.

Later, seeing the time and running down to the bedroom, she shouted:

'Max, it's four o'clock! Aren't you supposed to be meeting the lawyers at five?'

Max leapt off the bed. 'Thanks for waking me. I was dreaming of being with you in Pondicherry. We were walking down that side street leading to the silk shop and Narendra was standing outside with an enormous smile.' Max rushed in and out of the bathroom and grabbed his jacket. 'I'll phone you.'

'Good luck,' Anna shouted from Barney's room. She heard Oska coming up the stairs. 'Dad nearly knocked me over, why is he going to work at four o'clock?'

'Oska, I'll know for sure tonight so I didn't want to say anything until it was certain. Max and I may have to go to India for five days on business. We have to do an urgent buying trip, otherwise the business might have to close.'

'Does that mean I won't be able to stay at school?' Oska asked.

'What makes you say that?' Anna asked.

'Last night I heard you ask Max if it was the best deal he could get and he answered "It's the only deal and we have to make it work".'

'Oh, Oska darling, you mustn't worry, things will work out. We're just going through some problems and we'll sort it out. I know I've haven't been around much but I've been working hard to help Max. We Elliotts don't give up!' Anna sounded upbeat.

'When are you going?'

'Hopefully in ten days.'

'What about Barney? He might go nuts,' Oska said. His sense of responsibility to Barney affected Anna, who told him about all the arrangements and said that she was going to go next door and ask Madellaine to help.

'Well, I don't want Rob coming around,' Oska said.

'OK, I'll tell Madellaine that Bridget doesn't want any more responsibility while I'm away. I don't want to upset Madellaine as she's been very kind to me.'

'It's not our fault that Doug left.' Oska sounded emphatic.

'Oska, please don't talk about things you don't understand.' Anna felt out of her depth with Oska, who seemed very perspicacious for an eleven-year-old.

Anna went to find Barney. 'What do you want to eat?' she shouted after Oska, hoping he wouldn't see through her effort at holding the family together when all she wanted to do was get into her bedroom, shut the door and lie down.

In the kitchen Barney ate his macaroni cheese without making a sound or looking up to make eye contact. Although Anna had got used to the silences, had almost relished them, today she felt saddened by his stark avoidance of contact. It was as if he was leaving her before she could tell him that she was going to India. She didn't know where to start, how to explain he would be going to Peeling Onions every day, and that Bridget and her niece Brie would be staying in their house. Whilst she usually felt that Barney knew a great deal more than he let on, she could never be sure.

Anna heard the phone ring and rushed to pick it up. She heard Max's tired voice.

'We've signed.'

'Did we get the best deal?' she asked.

'There wasn't a queue hammering down the door. Let's say we got the only deal and, according to my figures, we'll live to see another day.'

'That means we'll go to India.' Anna needed to be sure.

'Yes, we have to. I've just drafted a long fax to Narendra in Pondicherry. I'll be home in a couple of hours after I've cleared my desk.' Max sounded exhausted.

Oska walked into the kitchen.

'So you're going to India?'

'In about ten days,' Anna replied, automatically observing Barney's sustained withdrawal.

'There are elephants in India,' Barney suddenly piped up.

'How do you know that?' Oska asked.

'There are elephants in Africa but they are much bigger than the elephants in India,' Barney went on.

'I've seen him read those books on nature and he also likes to watch nature programmes on television,' Oska said proudly.

'We'll have to buy Barney some more books,' Anna said.

'I'd like some more books on military history. You also promised to buy me some more model soldiers for my Battle of the Somme,' Oska asserted.

'You're quite right, Oska. We'll all go shopping at the weekend.' Anna instantly regretted saying this as she realised that she needed every working hour to complete her package for India. She hoped Max might be able to take the boys shopping. She had all the patience in the world when it came to textiles but she was far from enamoured with the never-ending cycle of shopping for food, household goods and children's books and toys.

18

Pondicherry – 1986

The prospect of Bridget and Brie coming to stay in their home created excitement and distraction for Oska and Barney, with Oska looking forward to manipulating bedtime rules, and Barney to the fun when Bridget would play the piano and sing Irish songs.

At first Anna was rather irritated by the way Brie draped herself across the newly-upholstered settee in the playroom, dropped her sandals over the arm of the chair and watched TV for hours with Barney. But when Anna complained to Max, he said:

'I don't get it. Aren't you relieved that Barney is relaxed? Who cares whether he watches *Blue Suede Shoes* ten times a day. Let's just focus on one thing at a time. I'm not a woman, so not being able to multi-task, I'm excused from multi-worrying!'

Ignoring his joke, Anna understood Max's irritation. 'You're right, I suppose I'm just getting anxious about everything.'

'We've had a hell of a week and have been lucky to get out of the business. I don't know why but I keep having a feeling that Dinah has something to do with the way our designs are being copied.'

'Do you have any evidence? It's unlike you to rely on a feeling – that's more my department – although Barney said something odd the other day when Dinah dropped off some more silk samples.'

'What?' Max looked at Anna, surprised that she should think they were so desperate they now had to rely on Barney.

'Dinah and I were sitting in the kitchen having coffee and Barney came in. You know how smarmy she can be with Barney – she even changes her voice when she talks to him: "Aren't you coming to say hello to Dinah, Barney? If you say hello you can have some chocolate". Dinah took out a bar of chocolate from her bag. Barney rushed forward, grabbed the chocolate and shouted, "Barney's afraid of Dinah" and ran out!'

Anna was surprised when Max added, 'So am I.'

'Well why don't we get rid of her?' Anna asked.

'We will, when the time is right. But for now we're starting from scratch again. We will have to set up a whole new structure in Pondicherry and get the new collection going. Dinah has become too powerful. She thinks we can't do without her and while there's never a right time, now is certainly a wrong time to let her go. And, as you say, I haven't got any evidence she's doing anything wrong.'

They had to get up at five o'clock in the morning to get to London Heathrow for the twelve-hour flight to Pondicherry. Anna felt a frisson of excitement and freedom as she sneaked out the house without waking anybody. In the taxi she told Max that she felt as if she was running away for a naughty weekend. Max laughed.

'Are you quite sure that you don't have Barney packed away in that case?'

'It did cross my mind.'

She felt saddened and hurt by Max's veiled criticism of her pre-occupation with Barney. She wanted to scream and tell him that she'd had enough and couldn't do any more and if it wasn't for Oska who was so helpful, she would have given up. Then just as she managed to stop herself from saying anything, Max put his hand over hers.

'Darling, I'm sorry, I know how hard you work to hold everything together and you deserve better. Let's try and make something of our time away from Barney.'

Warm, all-enveloping sunshine greeted them at Pondicherry airport, where Narendra, a tall, thin, well-dressed man, welcomed them warmly. He hadn't seen Anna for ten years and was struck by the way she had aged. She looked twenty years older, thin rather than slim, her faded hair neatly tied up in a chignon emphasising her sad eyes. Narendra felt the overwhelming desire to cheer her up.

'Everything is fixed up. One appointment this afternoon after you've rested. It's a small factory and they do good quality work and the owner, Agrim, is my wife's cousin. Another factory tomorrow morning, much bigger, a little out of town. They are eager to expand but I don't know the quality of their work. Then on Wednesday we have two meetings with silk suppliers. There is a new material, seventy per cent silk, thirty per cent synthetic. You can't beat the price and it doesn't crease, but I'm not sure you will like the colours.'

'You've been working hard, Narendra,' said Max gratefully.

'Max, I want to help you – you are like family. Just ask and I'm here.'

Anna thought of how alone she had felt in London and now after less than thirty minutes here she felt safe and cared for.

The roads were lined with jacaranda, the cascading blue flowers vibrant yet cool against white colonial buildings in colourful gardens. Anna relaxed as the passing scenes took her back to the time she had met Max here. London with all its stresses seemed far away.

The Park Hotel was surrounded by wide lawns with shaped flowerbeds of tropical plants, through which a stone path led up to a covered veranda dotted with rattan tables and chairs. The bowls of marigolds on each table and the floral-patterned cushions on the chairs gave the porch a homely yet exotic feel. The dark inner hall with its comfortable leather couches reminded Max of an Edwardian club. They followed the porter through a glass door in the inner hall leading onto a square courtyard with potted plants, tables and chairs, and then to their spacious room with its high ceiling and rotating fan.

'This is perfect,' Anna said, flopping onto the bed.

'I'll have a shower,' Max said, covering her with the white bedspread.

When he came out of the bathroom, Anna was asleep. Refreshed after his shower, Max lay down next to her in his towelling gown.

107

He woke up to hear the phone ring. Narendra was in the lobby waiting to take them to the factory.

Anna leapt out of bed and told Max that he should go to Narendra while she had a quick shower before joining them.

'You look so much better,' Narendra enthused, seeing Anna dressed in one of her samples as she walked towards them.

'I'm over my jet-lag and eager to see the factory.'

The drive through roads lined with flame-red trees stirred Anna to thoughts of a fresh colour palette for her designs.

They stopped at the factory, a colonial-style, two-storey building on the outskirts of Pondicherry that gave no indication of how large it was inside. Entering through rather grand wooden doors, the art nouveau tiled floor felt cool after the humidity outside and, through the internal glass windows, they could see an enormous room filled with machinists and machines and hear a cacophony of sewing machines, rotating fans and chattering workers.

'We are going upstairs to the office to see Agrim,' Narendra told them. Agrim, a stocky man of about fifty, came out to greet them. Following the somewhat effusively courteous welcome and an ice-cold lassi, Anna explained her overall design concept and laid out her patterns, drawings and colour swatches on the desk. She stressed to Agrim that her main concerns were the quality and price of the material, its durability, its degree of crease resistance, its washing machine response and its colourfast quality, all while retaining the feel and appearance of silk.

'I have just the answer.' Agrim left his office to return with a selection of materials.

'It feels like silk,' Anna said, fingering the material. She liked the muted tones of khaki, green, brown, beige, terracotta, purple and gold ochre.

'It's better than silk, hangs better, doesn't crease and is extremely good value for money,' Agrim told her. After two hours of discussion and a full inspection of the factory, Anna felt she needed to go no further. The problem was solved. She could see that 24/7 was becoming more than an idea.

Narendra put his arm round Max. 'Now I must take you to my home. Amala has made us a wonderful dinner.'

The front garden of Narendra's large rather run-down bungalow was filled with oleander bushes and marigolds. It led onto a sizeable covered veranda strewn with rattan chairs and tables. Amala came out to greet them like long-lost relatives, her face shining with warmth and affection as she offered them cool drinks of lassi or chai. In the bungalow, at the end of the lounge the full sized wooden table was overflowing with dishes of roti, chapatti, dahl and chole kept warm on hot plates. Anna's eyes adjusted to the dark interior with its aroma of curry.

'Narendra, may I make a short phone call home?'

'Of course.' He had their phone number at the ready, spoke rapidly with the operator and Anna spoke briefly with Bridget.

Max breathed a sigh of relief at Anna's enthusiastic exclamations, and when she had put the phone down she told Max that Brie was helping Barney with his reading and how much Barney was enjoying it.

'He's very clever. God knows what goes on in that head of his,' Max replied.

'Do you think he will ever be accepted at a normal school?' Anna asked.

'I think if our collection succeeds, we might be able to find and afford a small private school and bribe them to take him,' Max said.

Narendra returned. Max tucked in, while Anna barely coped with a piece of roti and a glass of chai.

'I was very impressed with those materials we saw today,' Anna told them.

Max added: 'I was thinking if we could have all our designs made here and find someone here to manage the production and delivery, we wouldn't have to travel and would probably save hugely on production costs.'

'The key is quality control,' Anna said emphatically.

'Narendra, would you be interested in some sort of partnership? We need to have someone we can trust.'

The evening meal proved to be a life-changer. Narendra admitted he was also thinking along the same lines and he thought Agrim's factory was ideal for their purpose. He suggested that they still make the trip to the other factory in the morning to compare the technical skills and the costing.

It was midnight before he drove them back to the hotel, the balmy night air filled with the scent of frangipani blossom. Anna was unusually relaxed and, reminding them both of the time they first met in Pondicherry, quite naturally they fell into each other's arms.

Both were in a much lighter mood as they sat on the veranda having breakfast. Anna was pleased to have an English breakfast of toast, homemade marmalade and coffee.

'Max, everything seems to be falling into place.'

'I think I'm falling in love with you all over again.' Max said, and noticed her blush.

They saw Narendra coming up the path smiling. 'Good morning, did you sleep well? Are you ready?'

In the car, Narendra was less deferential and more businesslike.

'Let me do the talking. I know Mr Desai and he runs a very tight ship. Believe me he is one of the wealthiest men in Pondicherry – and one of the meanest.'

'What has he got to offer that Agrim hasn't?'

'His factory is a much bigger outfit, they employ four times the number of workers and supply good-quality garments all over the world. He'll name a price and won't budge by more than four per cent.'

It was past two when they drove back to the hotel to have a late lunch. Anna had already made up her mind. She couldn't work with Mr Desai. She had to admit that everything she saw was impressive but it was too regimented. Their business would be too small a part of his business. She preferred to have more power to control both design and quality. She also saw Narendra's relationship with Agrim as an advantage.

Over lunch, Anna discussed her reservations with Max and Narendra. They agreed that they should focus on producing samples and pricing. Since Narendra was offered a share in the business his enhanced enthusiasm made them realise how jaded and tired both had become. Narendra suggested taking Max to another silk wholesaler to look for trimmings and compare prices and on the way dropping Anna off at Agrim's factory to meet with his pattern cutter.

There she walked round the factory and having inspected the quality of stitching said that she wasn't happy with the quality of the buttonholes and that she wanted more hand finishing. Agrim promised to have samples ready by tomorrow evening. It was a full day of discussions and hard work. Max told Narendra and Agrim that both he and Anna were exhausted and needed an early night. They would make an early start tomorrow morning.

Back at the hotel, Anna phoned home. Bridget told them that everything was fine. Barney no longer demanded his food be cut up into little pieces and hadn't had one tantrum. He liked going to Peeling Onions, and Molly had asked her to tell Anna that it was a joy to have Barney.

'I can't believe it! All those sleepless nights of worry, all that anxiety, and everything is turning out better than we expected,' Anna reflected.

Max noticed that Anna was beginning to lose much of the tension in her face, her mouth was relaxed and the dark rings under her eyes had gone. Whether it was the balmy weather, the new hope for their business or the relief that Barney was fine, Anna felt quite calm. It was as if she had used up all her emotions prior to the trip. And the few days in Pondicherry were proving to be more than just a battle for their economic survival for their revived sensuality had brought her and Max together again.

Packing to go home, Anna remarked: 'I feel as though I've been here for much longer than five days, we've achieved so much.'

'I think the last touches you added in choosing the perfect buttons for the collection took it into a new dimension,' Max added.

'Max, I was thinking . . . if Brie is good for Barney, could we afford to keep her on for a while? It would allow me to give Oska more attention.'

'Very good idea, I hope she wants to stay. All this "work and no play" life will destroy us both. I can't remember being so happy. Now that we've got rid of the factory and Narendra will oversee the production and delivery, I can concentrate on the marketing.'

It was a hot and sticky evening when Narendra took them to the airport.

'Max', he said. 'I remember when you came here twenty-two years ago. Who would have thought then that I would be more than just your landlord?' Narendra hugged Anna and stood there waving as they went through passport control.

In the duty free area, Max stopped by a shop, its window overloaded with sparkling jewellery and glistening gold. 'I want to buy you something special to remember this trip.'

'Max, thank you but it's been special enough. Let's not spend money before we get it, but we must buy something for the boys.'

19

Return from Pondicherry – 1986

London seemed unacceptably cold for the end of April. Anna hoped that they would arrive home after the boys had left for school. She hadn't slept much on the flight and was anxious about how Barney would greet her.

Bridget came out of the kitchen to meet them. 'Welcome home! The boys have just left. They like Brie to go with them in the taxi. I'll put the kettle on.'

Sitting around the kitchen table, Bridget told them Barney was very clever. 'He can read properly now and has a remarkable memory. He knows all the songs that Brie taught him and enjoys music and when she told him that you were coming home today, he said, "See Anna after school".'

'How's Oska been?' Max asked.

'A real bossy boots, that one. He kept on telling us what to do with Barney. Barney doesn't like this, Barney doesn't like that, he needs his favourite programme now . . . He's a good brother, the way he looks out for Barney.'

Max was pleased to hear how responsible Oska was becoming, while Anna thought Oska was taking on too much responsibility.

Anna couldn't believe that Barney had made so much progress in one week. She couldn't wait to see him and hesitated to tell Max, who was wondering whether he should go into the office or give it a miss for a day.

'I thought we should both go to pick up the boys from school today.'

'I was thinking of going into the office, there'll be a mass of stuff piling up,' he replied.

'I think you should take the rest of the day off. Of course, I could go alone but think how they will respond seeing the two of us. We could then take them out for tea.'

'You're right,' he said. Although eager to get back to work, he didn't want to disappoint Anna.

'Let's go upstairs and have a lie down. We need to be fresh for the onslaught.'

They arrived fifteen minutes early at Peeling Onions. Barney was sitting with Carol in the large workroom. The other children also seemed hard at work. Anna looked at him through the window and wondered whether Max also felt a frisson of pride and hope. Molly came out to greet them.

'I'm so pleased to have Barney. He is a very talented little boy. It's a very good prognostic sign when a child settles so quickly.'

'Do you mean his autism will go away?' Max asked.

'I didn't say that – I didn't mean to give that impression. What we like to see is a child realising their potential and Barney clearly is like a sponge; he absorbs everything and it seems so effortless. Peeling Onions is the right place for him. Inappropriate treatment can not only hold a child back but may also be harmful.'

Barney came rushing towards them. 'Anna's home, Max's home,' he shouted. Max picked him up and Anna joined them in a hug.

'That was a very positive welcome. Would you like to show Anna and Max your drawings?' Molly ushered them into the art room.

Barney went to his shelf on the art trolley and pulled out a pile of his drawings. Bowls of apples, a boiled egg in an eggcup, the table set for lunch, all showing excellent form and proportion.

'They really are good,' pronounced Max.

'They're wonderful Barney, I'm so proud of you.' Anna could hardly believe Barney's progress.

'Did I tell you about Oska's visit to Peeling Onions?' asked Molly. 'He came with Bridget on the day after you left. Apparently after you told him that he was welcome, he wanted to make sure that Barney settled and see that Bridget was OK on her first visit. They both stayed a while. Oska is very impressive, so mature for an eleven-year-old. Of course all the staff welcomed him and we had a chat. He was interested in everything and asked if he could visit again.'

Once in the car, Max was delighted with Barney's meticulous instructions as he guided them to Oska's school.

'Mummy! Daddy!' they heard Oska shouting as he ran up to their car.

Max got out of the car to give Oska a bear hug while Anna waited her turn.

'Would you like to go out for tea?' Anna asked.

'Hamburger and chips, vanilla ice cream,' Barney replied.

'Some things don't change,' Max said smiling and they all laughed.

Anna had been worried that Oska and Barney might not forgive her for going away and so far she was surprised by their welcome. Her few days in Pondicherry had also made her realise how much Max needed her. She determined to get extra help in the house and hoped that Brie would agree to stay and work for her. More than ever she believed that with the right approach Barney would realise his potential and his progress made at Peeling Onions proved her point. It was only a matter of creating the structured environment for him that would also liberate her.

20

Six Years Later – 1992

Anna had long dreaded the day when Molly would tell her that Barney had to leave Peeling Onions. Now twelve years old, he was a replica of Max with his big-boned physique, square jaw, thin mouth, prominent straight nose and hefty physique. She too could see that he no longer belonged amongst the delicate pre-school children and that Molly was doing her best to accommodate him. Barney spent much of his time with Carol in the art room, painting, and reading the books Anna brought in to keep him occupied. He seemed to benefit from self-learning and from the one-to-one attention and showed extraordinary arithmetic agility. He could add, subtract, multiply and divide complex numbers in seconds and he could calculate what was and will be the day of any given year in the past and future. He had also become quite articulate but tending to go off on a monologue of his own interest, found it difficult to engage in a conversation.

Molly thought it more important for him to be content than to force him into any system that increased his anxiety. Anna, however, worried that by not providing a more varied programme, Barney was becoming resistant to change. When she discussed this with Molly, Anna understood that Barney's resistance to change had to be balanced against his motivation to develop in areas where he was capable of growth. Anna recalled how she too was resistant to the wider curriculum at school and, preferring art, where she could succeed, had failed miserably in the other subjects, so adding to her lack of confidence.

Anna realised that she wasn't making much effort to find another school for Barney as she didn't want to give up the support and anxiety-free environment of Peeling Onions. Three years ago when the local education authority had wanted to place Barney in a special school, she'd rejected this suggestion as unsuitable. Molly had supported her and proving to the Educational Psychologist how much Barney had developed at Peeling Onions it had been agreed that it was better for him to stay with them than go to an inappropriate placement.

Anna also realised that she needed the mothers' group, where she was amongst women who shared her pre-occupations. Anna valued the group where, even though she was limited in volunteering her thoughts and feelings, she shared a lot in common with the other mothers who also found difficulty in separating from their autistic child. All agreed that at times their child could be so in tune with their feelings they felt that their child was telepathic. She recalled Susan announcing:

'You know, if this group was tape recorded, I'm sure we would all be considered mad, but then we are living in a mad system and our weekly group helps to contain my madness from the outside world.'

Molly smiled reassuringly. 'We shouldn't be so hard on ourselves. I challenge anybody to live with a child who is perpetually anxious when no-one can explain the cause or optimal treatment. Professor Kanner first described the condition in 1944, but it's now 1992 and whilst we seem to be recognising more and more children suffering from different degrees of autism there are so many different opinions as to the cause.'

Anna felt devastated when a mother suddenly broke down. 'It's not just my child – it's my marriage. I've been so involved with my child I didn't know that for the past five years my husband has been having an affair. I thought my fifteen-year marriage was OK, so you can imagine what I felt when my husband announced he was leaving.'

All the mothers were visibly shocked. There was a palpable silence. Then another mother said she didn't know what to expect

117

of her marriage; her measure of success depended on the degree of help her husband gave her with her daughter, adding: 'I can assure you that after a day of looking after my daughter, sex is the last thing on my mind!'

The group was very quiet as each mother was moved by the honesty and courage of those who spoke of their experiences. Molly, always in touch with the group feeling, told the mothers that whilst she understood it was difficult for some to talk about their problems, the group as a whole could feel let down, as everyone had an obligation to help each other. Although she appreciated how difficult it was to express one's feelings in a group, there was nothing to be ashamed of, as she was sure that listening led to a deeper understanding.

Anna didn't quite understand what Molly was getting at and felt she may be directing this at her. She resented any intrusion into her private life and felt an overwhelming desire to be free of Molly's scrutiny; her need for privacy was paramount. Despite that, she admitted to herself that over the past six years she had noticed how each mother had become stronger and more confident in dealing with their family, some even going on to pursue careers. Most of all, she learned that there would always be good and bad days living with Barney.

It was so different with Oska. He hardly complained and was now doing reasonably well at school. Sometimes Anna worried that he never had more than one or two school friends and didn't invite them home. She assumed it was because he thought Barney would embarrass him and he would find it difficult to explain or apologise for some of Barney's peculiar and intrusive remarks, especially when he played with words and would suddenly laugh, as if engaged in a private joke. But Oska's love and care for Barney was extraordinary and exemplary. His interest in military history had also advanced from setting up his toy soldier battles to reading voraciously and to visiting military sites and museums. He had also joined the cadet's section of a local shooting club and learned about different guns.

With both the boys gainfully occupied and the family more settled, she and Max were able to focus on their business. Narendra was proving to be a reliable partner and Anna was able to bring out a new collection each year, expanding her 24/7 label, to 'Cruise Wear', 'Special Occasions' and 'Executive Girl'. Each collection was sold in the ready-to-wear department of a number of high quality stores. There was a steady flow of orders in London, Paris and New York, they could rely on Narendra not to miss a delivery date and step by step their financial position had improved. In addition to her collection, Frank James had commissioned her to design specials for his collection, as the celebrity culture was on the increase and her designs were again in demand. She felt happiest when she could escape to her studio and fill her mind with creative ideas.

21

Anna and Madellaine – 1992

Anna hadn't seen Madellaine for a couple of weeks and decided to knock on her door.

'Anna, what a lovely surprise! Come in. Coffee? Let's sit in the lounge, it's more comfortable.'

Anna sank back in one of the armchairs. Looking round the pleasant room, she became aware of the emptiness of the house.

'You look a little down Anna, is anything wrong?' Madellaine asked, for it was unusual for Anna just to drop in like that. Anna told her about the mothers' group and one of the mother's poignant account of the breakdown of her marriage.

'I still haven't got over Doug leaving me the way he did,' I think a lot depends on how it's done. It's much more difficult to move on when you've been betrayed by the person you most trusted. It's more difficult to resolve because there is no closure. It's not that I want Doug back – in fact I wouldn't take him back – but what I resent most of all is what it's done to Rob. I'm now very worried about Rob. He doesn't tell me what he's doing or where he's going. He doesn't bring friends home, so I don't know what to think.'

'How's he doing at school?' Anna asked.

'He's supposed to be doing his GCSEs any moment and, quite honestly, I never see him working and when I try to talk to him, he just runs out the room.'

'Does he talk to Doug?' Anna knew that he didn't because she had once asked him and Rob vowed that as long as he lived he would never talk to his father.

'As much as I resent Doug I do think that I shouldn't have

involved Rob. Doug is his father and it's vital for him to have a relationship with his father. Unfortunately it's only now that I realise this and I know he is suffering. You see, I think Rob is rejecting Doug because he has witnessed my unhappiness but he really does want to see his father. I suppose his anger towards me is part of it. I feel more than ever I must try and get Doug and Rob together again. Does Rob still come over to see Barney?' Madellaine asked.

'About twice a week. He's very kind to Barney and I'm pleased he feels comfortable with us. Is Doug happy with Barbara?'

'How would I know? I hope not. I don't know what he sees in her; at least I had some money.' Madellaine sounded bitter.

'Madellaine you're only forty-five. You have every chance of meeting someone new.'

'You're right. I could do with losing some weight, though. Will you promise to design me an outfit if I slim down a bit?'

'It would be a real pleasure. I know I've also let myself go, but it seems so hard not to give up – or maybe it takes up too much of my time to take care of myself when there are so many other people I have to take care of. I put myself at the bottom of the list, not consciously, and I suppose as a designer I should at least try and look the part,' Anna reflected.

'I'm afraid I don't even have that excuse, just a touch of low self-esteem, laziness and nowhere to go. I think you're the only person I see these days,' Madellaine admitted.

'What do you do all day?' Anna asked.

'I read, I worry about Rob, the garden, a bit of embroidery, that sort of thing. I'm thinking about doing some voluntary work – after all I do have an 'ology of sorts.'

Anna's expression of surprise helped Madellaine admit to her past achievement. 'I got a 2-1 in biology at Birmingham, so you see I should know something about metabolism and weight gain.'

'I had no idea! Why are you so modest? Did you work after you left college?' Anna regretted underestimating Madellaine all those years.

'I worked in the IVF laboratory at The London Hospital. That's where I met Doug. He worked as a computer hardware engineer. Don't laugh! I fell pregnant the first time.'

'What do you think went wrong in your marriage?' Anna asked.

'I think I tried to hold myself back. You see instinctively I knew I was smarter than Doug and I didn't want to undermine him. I think that some men feel a woman's intelligence as a threat and eventually run away. Doug certainly doesn't have that problem with Barbara! I don't know how I tolerated her as a friend for so long.'

'Why haven't you followed a career?' Anna asked.

'It's quite simple: I had to be a mother and a father to Rob and I didn't want him to feel that I'd abandoned him. That's why I admire you so much, managing two jobs.'

Anna couldn't control her impulsivity. 'Would you like to come and help me in my studio? Nothing too demanding, cataloguing my patterns, sorting out the mess, that sort of thing?'

'Oh Anna, I'd love to. I promise I'll be quiet and let you get on with your work,' Madellaine responded.

'Good, I'll speak to Max and work something out. Now I must rush.' Anna noticed how Madellaine's expression had changed, which made her feel pleased that she'd made the offer. She now saw Madellaine differently.

22

The Dinah Dilemma – 1992

After dropping Barney off at Peeling Onions, Anna decided to go to the office to look through the order books. She walked through Dinah's room, which was empty, and into Max's office, where Max, surrounded by and studying papers, not looking up, said: 'I thought you weren't coming in till midday?'

'What are you talking about?' Anna sounded confused.

He looked up. 'Anna! What are you doing here?' Anna thought she detected a blush, accompanied by a guilty look.

'I decided I'd come in and look at the orders and thought we could go out for lunch. I've got a bit of cabin fever being at home all week.'

'Wonderful idea.' Max's contrived enthusiasm went unnoticed.

'Where's Dinah? I thought she started at nine o'clock.'

'I gave her the morning off to do some shopping. She's been doing quite a bit of overtime lately.'

'Good. It's important to reward loyalty. I'd like to see the comparative figures for each collection.' Anna took out a box file labelled 'Cruise Collection Paris'.

'I thought so,' Anna asserted. 'Cruise wear is not doing all that well and it's quite obvious when you think about it. Two women would be horrified to find each other wearing the same outfit and that is bound to happen in a targeted venue. I'll have to think about it.' Anna made a few notes on the page.

'All the other collections are exceeding expectations,' Max pointed out.

'It's about time we ran another colour range, maybe even a

mixture of prints and plains. I'll get Dinah to ask Narendra for some samples.' Anna looked at her watch. 'Let's go to lunch.'

'We should wait for Dinah to return to hold the fort.' Max seemed unsettled.

'Max, you know I have to pick up Barney by three. It's twelve now, I thought you said she'd be back by twelve.'

Dinah walked in surrounded by designer label bags filled with clothes, shoes and handbags. Anna hardly recognised her. Her highlighted reddish hair, heavy make-up, gold earrings, glamorous, wrap-around fuchsia dress and high-heeled shoes seemed unsuited for the office. 'Hello, Anna, what a lovely surprise,' Dinah gushed.

'Same here, I hardly recognised you. Are you going somewhere special?' Anna thought Dinah's sense of fashion was clearly over the top.

'It's my birthday and I am going out for dinner after work.' Dinah blushed.

'I hope he appreciates you.' Anna instantly regretted her remark. Why did Dinah make her feel uncomfortable, making her say the first thing that came into her head?

'Of course he does, otherwise I wouldn't make the effort.'

'Happy birthday, I hope you have a lovely evening.' Anna didn't notice Max walk past her and wait impatiently outside the office.

'Thank you. I must say you look stunning, considering the amount you get through in the day.'

Anna knew Dinah was disingenuous. Dressed in her working jeans she had impulsively decided to come into the office after dropping off Barney and was a very long way from looking stunning. Anna caught up with Max.

'We haven't upped Dinah's salary, have we?' Anna asked Max.

'Certainly not. She's doing less work now the factory is sold.'

'Well, how can she afford all those designer labels? She looks like she's rolling in it.'

'Now that you say it, I agree. Maybe she's got a sugar daddy.'

'Max, don't you find her a little over-familiar?'

'I do, and what's more I find that she's become rather controlling. I'm a little weary of her.'

'I can't stand the way she tries to compliment me. How could she say I look stunning, I know when I Iook stunning and it certainly isn't today.'

'I suppose you're right but quite frankly I am pleased that she is so accepting of Barney. We don't have many friends who feel comfortable with us,' Max remarked.

'We have Madellaine and during lunch I must tell you about her – she isn't what she seems.'

'I admit I hardly know her, but she seems a decent enough person.'

'She is, Max – she could have had an interesting career as a biologist but after Doug left her, she decided to give all her attention to Rob.'

'I owe her an apology. I have no idea how to assess women. I thought Dinah was marvellous and now I doubt my judgement. People just are never what they seem, are they? I suppose I'm very lucky I found you.'

23

Barney's Assessment – 1992

Anna arrived in time to fetch Barney who was waiting by the window.

'I'm so sorry I'm late.' Anna disliked being late for anything. She regarded punctuality as the minimum of good manners and to keep anybody waiting was akin to stealing their precious time.

'We've had a good day, with an interesting development,' Molly informed her. She told Anna that she'd had a phone call from the local authority's educational psychologist who was alarmed to discover that Barney hadn't been assessed for three years. It was inappropriate for a twelve-year-old boy to continue at Peeling Onions. Barney had to be properly assessed for secondary education.

'What does that mean?' Anna asked.

'I really don't think we can keep Barney here. Joan Kindle, the educational psychologist, is visiting next Tuesday to give Barney a series of tests, and we'll know more after that. I agree with her. Barney is ready to move on. The only reason the local authority have allowed Barney to stay here is because they can't find another suitable placement. He is high functioning, even brilliant, his main difficulties are his impairment of social interaction. We have to find a school that will accept his idiosyncratic behaviour.' Molly sounded determined.

'There must be a sympathetic headmaster who will acknowledge Barney's ability. I will try, and can only try and won't give up. I'll never forget how much you've done for Barney and also for me. I will also write to the local authority, telling them how Barney has flourished at Peeling Onions.'

'It's not just one-way, you know. We here have also learned a lot from Barney and your family and that knowledge will go a long way to helping other children. Let's wait and see how Barney performs in the tests.'

Anna couldn't believe the day would come when they had to leave Peeling Onions. She had kept putting it to the back of her mind. She couldn't face going into the real world, it was like stepping out of a warm bath into a freezing room. But at the same time she also knew that she was holding Barney back because it suited her. She couldn't wait for Max to come home so that she could tell him of the impending change.

However, Max phoned at six o'clock to say a new buyer had walked in at five o'clock and he was taking him out to dinner, so wouldn't be home until later.

'Two meals in one day, I hope it's worth it.' Anna didn't feel like telling Max over the phone about the impending change in Barney's education. Unnerved by abrupt changes, she was most comfortable when life flowed smoothly from one situation to another and worried how she was going to explain this immense change to Barney. She recalled how when she had first brought Barney to Peeling Onions, she would have her first cup of coffee of the day in the unit and only then would she feel sufficiently settled to go home and work. She had also formed a bond with two other mothers who had helped her through many a crisis. She recalled the caring culture in the unit had made her into a better person. It had opened her mind to think differently about life. She looked for the reasons why people behaved in a certain way and had become quite astute at understanding their motivation, recognising anxiety in others and, most of all, insincerity. She learned too how much she needed honesty in her dealings and had become impatient with small talk and flippancy. She smiled to herself when she thought of Barney. He was never flippant, never engaged in small talk and above all he was without guile. She also enjoyed being with Oska, who, caring and loving from the start, had now become more caring and serious. She thought of Max who could be so loving, yet there were times when his judgment worried her. She could not forget when they had been on the brink of bankruptcy. It was not only that he had failed to keep control of the business but that he had failed to tell her what was happening.

The following Tuesday, Anna told Barney on the way to the unit that he would be having a test this morning.

'I know, Molly told me and I'm very clever so I needn't worry.'

'You are very clever and I'm very proud of you,' Anna said, delighted.

After nearly six years, Barney had stopped directing Anna through the traffic, now confident she would find her way, and instead busied himself identifying every passing car. He knew their engine size, manufacturer and current price. Barney's eyes were glued to the passing traffic; he was on the look out for a Porsche Cayman, BMW M6, Ford Mustang and an Audi 214, which made it difficult for Anna to distract him.

'Have you seen any of your favourite cars?' Anna asked.

'Not on this route. At the weekend we should drive to Surrey where we are more likely to see the more up-market cars.'

'Do you like sports cars, Barney?'

'I like the design, but I wouldn't like to drive one because they are too dangerous. I don't think people should be allowed to drive a Porsche on the roads when children are going to school. A Honda or Volvo is much safer as they're built for domestic use.'

Anna's attempts at having a conversation with Barney usually ended up with Barney giving a monologue on his obsessive interests and once he started it was impossible to direct him away.

'Barney, when the lady comes to give you the test, don't forget to say good morning to her.' Anna wanted Barney to be seen in the best possible light. She was terrified that he might land up in some school for the mentally handicapped.

'She isn't a lady, she's an educational psychologist, and it's her job to see how much I understand. She asks me to do different tests and asks lots of questions and I have to answer them and also write down words. I have to know the meaning of words and how to use them. I have to recognise pictures and talk about them,' Barney said, without a hint of concern.

'Who told you about it?' Anna was amazed.

'I read about it in Oska's encyclopaedia: "How to become an educational psychologist and what an educational psychologist does". I think it's boring and I don't want to become an educational psychologist even when I'm grown up.'

Anna remembered her sister Laura giving Oska a set of second-hand encyclopaedias that Oska had swapped with Barney for his set of toy soldiers.

'So when do you read your encyclopaedia?' Anna asked.

'Every night before I go to sleep or if I want to find out information. Yesterday I heard you tell Madellaine that she did well to get a divorce, so I thought I would like to get one and I didn't know what it meant because it didn't sound like any words I knew, so I looked it up in the encyclopaedia. It says it means to legally dissolve marriage to terminate a marital union. Then I read about no-fault divorce laws, which is a legal action between married people to terminate relationship. No-fault divorce means that the court does not need to know the reasons for the divorce. Well, I think that's wrong. Rob told me that his father Doug is very wrong. He went off without even telling Madellaine that he liked Barbara better. Rob is very cross with Doug and so am I. No wonder Madellaine is called Mad-ellaine. Wouldn't you be mad if Max did that to us? Rob is pretty mad at his father and how can there be a no-fault divorce when Doug is definitely at fault and he can get away with it?'

Anna didn't know whether to laugh or cry. All that information going around in poor Barney's head. His brain seemed to be wired differently. Anna worried how he would do in the tests this morning.

Barney walked confidently into the quiet room. Since he was so much older than the other children he spent most of his time on his own with Carol. He had also been given tasks to help the younger children, like reading with them or maths games. He seemed to enjoy having responsibilities but had little patience if a child didn't instantly conform to his way of doing things. Molly watched for this tendency so as not to upset any of the other children.

'You can collect him at the usual time,' Molly told Anna, who realised that both Barney's and her future were at stake.

'I'll be at home if you need me.' Anna waved goodbye.

She couldn't imagine where Barney would fit in and the thought of a new school seemed like a major intrusion. Barney had been at Peeling Onions for nearly six years and had developed beyond their expectations. But by law he had to attend full-time education and she would have little choice but to accept their recommendations. At home she couldn't settle down, and her mind wandered to what Barney was doing and how he was coping. Willing the morning to pass, she was pleased when the bell rang and Madellaine walked in.

'It's good to see you. I'm in such a state, Barney is being assessed by an educational psychologist this morning.'

'What does that mean?' Madellaine asked.

'It means that depending on the way he performs, they will make a decision as to his future education and we have little choice. He has to leave Peeling Onions.'

Madellaine followed Anna into the kitchen. 'It may be a good thing. Barney's really grown out of that nursery school; he needs to broaden his horizons.'

'But he's done so well there,' Anna protested.

'Well, how do you know he won't continue to do well? He's had a pretty good grounding and you can't hold him back because he's so happy there. You know, Anna, sometimes I think you like everything to be the same, no ruffles to upset your calm. Even a calm sea has waves.'

'I know you're right but I just can't get my head around moving him to an unknown environment.'

'I think Barney is going to be fine. You should try living with

Rob! Honestly, I'd swop Rob for Barney any day,' Madellaine said, sadly.

'What's he done to upset you so much?' Anna asked.

'Try being suspended from school for smoking pot.' The tears welled up in Madellaine's eyes.

'Oh Madellaine, what did you do?'

'After a long wallow in self-pity, I swallowed my pride and phoned Doug.'

'Wow! That took some doing, well done,' Anna said supportively.

'It wasn't that difficult, you know. When a mother fights for her child there isn't such a thing as pride.'

'How did Doug respond?'

'Look, it's eight years now – Rob was seven when Doug left and Rob doesn't have a forgiving nature. He's not a child any more and I think Doug doesn't quite know how to make contact. Rob is out to punish him and to be honest I hope Doug gets his comeuppance.' Madellaine sounded bitter.

'What do you hope Doug can achieve?'

'First of all, he can go to see the headmaster and explain how the break-up of our marriage has affected Rob and find out the extent of Rob's problems. Perhaps we have left it too late but we have to start somewhere.' Madellaine sobbed profusely.

'It's difficult for me to see Rob the way you describe. He's always so perfectly behaved when he comes over, and so kind and patient with Barney.'

'We can never see our children as others see them,' Madellaine sighed.

Anna felt a bit distracted worrying about how Barney was getting on with the tests and she invited Madellaine to stay for lunch, mainly to fill another hour before having to leave to pick up Barney. Madellaine too was at a loose end and admitted that she really couldn't concentrate on helping Anna in the studio.

'What would we do if we didn't have each other to talk to about our problems?'

Anna had never seen Madellaine at such a low point. 'Do you know anybody who doesn't have any problems?' Anna asked.

'Perhaps we aren't asking the right questions. We don't really have problems – we just have the wrong expectations,' Madellaine stated.

'That's a good way of explaining our disappointment, I feel so much better now.' They both laughed.

'Don't you ever get lonely?' Anna asked thinking of Madellaine alone in her big house.

'I can feel lonely in a room full of people. I think if I look back, I even felt lonely with Doug,' Madellaine admitted.

'I suppose there are different kinds of loneliness. I feel lonely when I'm with Barney. He seems so self-contained or detached. I try to make contact with him and it's a struggle. It's as if he's having his own conversation and won't let me in, so I just encourage him to talk about whatever he likes. I suppose I've got used to it and don't notice it so much but then when Oska suddenly comes into the room, I have a different feeling. I suppose we have to think of the times when we didn't ever feel lonely. Perhaps it was at the beginning of our marriage when the love and chemistry fulfilled our needs. But that changes with the children coming along and a new and more dependent intimacy with the children takes over. I don't know, I've never thought about it too deeply. I just got on with life as it was presented to me. But I must admit I am beginning to feel the gaps,' Anna reflected.

'It must be very difficult living with Barney. We find him charming and interesting but I wonder whether other people do?' Madellaine hoped she hadn't offended Anna.

'I think Max finds Barney very difficult. He doesn't see him the way I do and I've noticed how Oska tries to explain Barney's behaviour to Max. Oska finds aspects of Barney interesting and has much more patience with him than Max,' Anna admitted.

'Men see things differently; they seem to have a blind spot when it comes to understanding emotions,' Madellaine commented.

They spent a cosy hour discussing the men in their lives, until Anna looked at her watch.

'It's two thirty! I have to fetch Barney at three. Thanks for coming over, Madellaine, I really valued our conversation today.'

24

Barney's Results – 1992

When Anna arrived, Molly was smiling. 'Barney is finishing off a painting.'

'How did it go this morning?' Anna couldn't wait to be told.

'Barney was remarkable. He seemed to enjoy every part of the test. He scored in the highly gifted range and the educational psychologist was totally surprised with his concentration. At the end of the test, he asked if he could do more tomorrow!'

'We know he's extremely intelligent, but he's also socially inept. How will he fit into a normal school?' asked Anna anxiously.

'I think he will. We've mollycoddled him too much, if you get my meaning.'

'Absolutely,' Anna agreed.

'It's time for him to go out into the real world. Peeling Onions was just meant to be a springboard. Barney will find it difficult but I will always be here to talk things over with you and he can visit if it's appropriate. Anna, Barney has to move on.' Molly put her arm around her shoulders. 'Let's wait to see what the educational psychologist recommends.'

'Can I still come to the mothers' group?' Anna asked.

'Anna, I really think you also have to move on! I told you, I'll always be here and you can phone and come and talk things over with me. When I get the report and recommendation, perhaps Max and you should come together and we can discuss them.'

Anna went into the art room to fetch Barney. Watching him complete a picture of a vibrant sun that filled the page, a feeling of deep loss swept over her. But as she looked at Barney's glowing sun, she felt the cloud had lifted for both of them.

Anna phoned Max to tell him about Barney performing in the highly gifted range in the IQ Test.

'What does that mean?' Max sounded as if he didn't believe her.

'His actual IQ score was 142; I doubt whether you or I would achieve that. Most university graduates score about 120 or more, but Barney, with all his problems, is exceedingly bright.'

'That is wonderful, especially hearing it from an authoritative source. What next?'

'He definitely has to leave Peeling Onions, and the local authority have to find him a school placement,' Anna told him.

'Can't we get him into a good private school? The classes are smaller and maybe they would be interested in taking him.'

Anna was delighted to hear Max talking with such concern about Barney.

'I agree, we'll both have to go along to a meeting with the educational psychologist and discuss all the options. In the meantime, let's just enjoy the good news that our son is a genius. What time will you be home?'

'Oh damn! There is a new buyer coming to the office at six, it shouldn't take too long.'

'Max, this is happening too often, can't you tell them to come during office hours? You remember when we came back from India, you were the one that said we had to change our priorities, and that finding enjoyment in life was more important than work. I'm tired of waiting for you every evening and you should also be here for the boys.' Anna was annoyed.

'You're right! I'm going to phone up and re-schedule the appointment. I'll see you soon. I think we should take out our genius for dinner to a restaurant where amongst other things they serve hamburger and chips.' Max said goodbye and feeling all hot and cold, shivered. He didn't like lying to Anna but Dinah was in his office listening to his side of the conversation.

'This has got to stop.' Max was emphatic as he addressed Dinah.

'Don't give me that "It's not you, it's me" story,' Dinah threatened.

Max was intimidated by Dinah's outrage. Anna was so different – she hardly ever made demands on him and had always fitted in with his plans. Perhaps it was because of Anna's passivity that he enjoyed the challenge of a strong woman like Dinah.

'It has to stop. I mean it.' Max banged on the desk, picked up his keys and left. On the way home he stopped at a flower stand and bought a large bunch of red roses.

Barney heard the front door open. 'It's Max,' Barney shouted. 'Max is coming to take us to a restaurant. Hamburgers and chips, hamburgers and chips.' Barney flapped his hands with excitement.

'I never expected you so soon.'

Max handed Anna the roses.

'Thank you, Max, you make me feel like a pop star. Who said romance is dead? I'll go and change.'

25

Max's Surprise – 1992

The Italian restaurant was practically empty at seven o'clock and there were plenty of staff around. Max ordered osso bucco, Anna felt like veal chops, Oska wanted a fillet steak and chips and the waiter assured them, although it wasn't on the menu, he could persuade the chef to make a hamburger and chips for Barney. For starters, as Barney was hungry, Anna ordered a small portion of fettuccini with tomato sauce and no cheese, while the others had a selection of antipasti.

'Well, tell me about your test, Barney', Max asked.

'I'm very clever and it's a problem because I have to go to another school even though I don't want to leave Peeling Onions. People at the other school won't understand me and I don't like being with a lot of boys because they can harm me. I know I'm different.'

Tears welled in Anna's eyes. She had never envisaged that Barney had any insight into his problems and wondered whether he was just repeating what he'd heard.

'We will find a school for you where the teachers do understand your worries,' Max said.

'I don't want to go to Rob's school because they don't like Rob and everybody is very cruel to him and now he might not be able to take his exams,' Barney told them.

'How do you know all this?' Oska intervened.

'Rob told me,' Barney replied.

Max looked sternly at Anna and Oska said, 'I told you that Rob isn't good for Barney. Why don't you listen to me?'

'I promise to talk to Rob, next time I see him. He shouldn't fill Barney's head with things he doesn't understand,' Anna assured them.

'I do understand!' Barney was emphatic. 'If you smoke pot, you can be kicked out of school. Pot isn't the same as cigarettes or cigars or a pipe. Pot makes you feel good but the government doesn't like people to feel good because it's bad for them. Maybe I can go to Oska's school, they don't hurt people there,' Barney added.

'I don't think so. No way! It's not the right place for you, Barney. Of course I would love having you there, but I think you might be too clever for my school.' Oska didn't sound too convincing.

'You might be saying that because you don't want me to come to your school even though you love me. You might be afraid that the other boys might hurt me,' Barney said, without a hint of resentment. Max and Anna caught each other's quizzical expressions.

'Don't worry Barney, Anna and I will find you a school that will suit you.'

Oska didn't respond but he felt trapped. He just wanted someone to consider his position for once, without making him feel guilty each time Barney was disappointed, which could lead to him having a tantrum. He thought how much he tried, in fact had been trained, to put Barney first and how much he hated Rob for trying to be the big brother to Barney.

Max's hope that this would put an end to that topic was realised by the arrival of Barney's fettuccini and they all relaxed as Barney focused on each mouthful.

Anna turned to Max. 'By the way, did Dinah order the colour samples from Narendra?'

Max wondered if Anna noticed his face flush, and wondered why Anna had chosen just that moment to mention Dinah.

'I'm not sure, but I've got a better idea: why don't we all go to Pondicherry for a short holiday? There are quite a few odds and sods to sort out with Narendra. We could stay at one of those good hotels on the beach and you could refresh your ideas with another look around the factory and the latest fabrics,' Max suggested.

'Could we really do that?' Anna was excited. 'I do need to refresh my ideas and I think we all need a holiday. Oska will love the beach and Barney will be able to show us around so we don't get lost. I never was all that happy with Dinah getting the samples, she really doesn't know much about material, and even less about colour. Have you noticed how she turns herself out lately? There's a word for it but I won't say it in front of the boys.'

'Say what?' Barney demanded.

'It's rude to make remarks about the way other people dress. We all have different taste and we should wear what suits us,' Anna said, reminding herself of Barney's propensity to repeat or misunderstand everything he heard.

'Rob said you used to dress like a hippy and he wished Madellaine would dress like you, but she's too fat,' Barney said, waiting for his hamburger and chips.

'OK, I've decided we'll go to Pondicherry for the Easter hols,' Max said. It sounded as if he had resolved more than a family problem.

26

Good News/Bad News – 1992

The following morning Max walked into his office determined to have it out with Dinah. He couldn't imagine a stronger message than telling her to book four plane tickets and a hotel for him, his wife and children in Pondicherry for the Easter break.

It had started well. Dinah arrived and Max announced, 'I've decided to go to Pondicherry for two weeks over Easter.'

Dinah's instant smile made him realise he had made matters worse. 'When do you want me to book?' she asked.

'I'm waiting for Anna to phone with the exact dates of the school holidays,' Max replied – but Dinah still didn't get it.

'Do you want us to go before or after the school holidays?'

'Dinah! Of course Anna and I want to go during the school holidays. We're taking the children and Anna also wants to research some new materials.' Max was alarmed at her supposition.

'Oh she does, does she! Then tell me, why did you ask me to ask Narendra for samples?' Dinah was annoyed.

'Anna thinks it's best if she selects them herself. After all, she is the designer,' Max reminded Dinah.

'And what am I?'

'Dinah, I'm really sorry, but I've been very stupid. We have to end this. I will quite understand if you want to resign. You have done a lot for the firm and I'll see you right.'

'Are you sacking me?' responded Dinah indignantly.

'Of course not, I just thought . . . '

'You just thought it would be convenient if I left and you

wouldn't have to face me every day. But take it from me, I have no intention of losing my job.'

'I'm pleased to hear it.' Max thought he should keep quiet, he could see he was digging himself in deeper.

The phone rang. 'I've got the school dates. Would you prefer me to book, I know what we need?' Anna offered.

'That would be a great relief,' Max replied.

The office was filled with silent animosity. Dinah stayed in her room and Max avoided giving her instructions. The very brief fling he had had with her had been a stupid mistake. Ever since then she'd thrust herself on him, finding reason after reason to come into his office and hover closely over him, refusing to accept that he did not want her any more. His great worry was that Anna might find out and he couldn't begin to imagine the distress that would cause, especially as she seemed to be happier now Barney was showing distinct signs of being able to function way beyond their expectations.

The realisation that he could lose Anna, damage the children and destroy the business, terrified him. He could hardly recall how he had got into such a mess and even though he wanted to blame Dinah, he knew he was more at fault. It had happened when he was at his most vulnerable, he was tired and had had a bit too much to drink. Anna was working day and night designing the special collection and he didn't have the heart to tell her how worrying was the drop in orders, especially as she was so obsessed with Barney. The trauma in Florida had left them all unnerved, particularly Anna whose realisation that Barney could be such easy prey to any predator had hugely increased her need to safeguard him. For a while it was as if Barney was the only one who mattered in the family and he and Oska had had to forgo their own needs.

It was during that time Dinah took on more responsibility in the business and enjoyed her new decision-making power. Max, too, appreciated and benefitted from the support and comradeship of colleagues working cooperatively together. Sharing sandwiches at lunchtime had developed into business lunches and late afternoon business discussions after everybody else had left had continued on into the evening. It was a special time when he could forget Barney. After one particularly late session, Max asked Dinah if he could give her a lift home. Once invited up to her apartment for a drink, exhausted and drunk, Max was hardly aware he was being seduced – until it was too late. It was a triumph for Dinah. Soon after this meaningless liaison, Max – trying to distance himself from Dinah – decided on the family holiday to Pondicherry.

27

The Family Holiday – 1992

Anna was especially excited about returning to Pondicherry with the family. She didn't have to worry about leaving Barney. It was still cold in London and two weeks in the sunshine was just what the family needed.

Narendra was waiting for them at the airport. 'So this is Barney and Oska! I've been waiting to meet you and want to show you around Pondicherry.'

'It is my pleasure to meet you, Mr Narendra. My brother Oska likes birds and nature and military history and I like everything except curry,' Barney announced.

'Then we should go straight to the hotel where they cater for your Western palate. I'm sure you'll be very happy there; the hotel is right on the beach and the sea is very calm at the moment.' The car moved slowly through the morning traffic, along a road lined with flowering trees.

'What an amazing red,' Oska observed.

'The tree is called "The Pride of India",' Narendra told them, 'And we have the French to thank for planting them all over Pondicherry.'

'The French?' Oska exclaimed.

'Yes, Pondicherry was a French colony until 1954 when they gave it back to us. The architecture and the rows of small painted houses makes you feel as if you're in France. And we still make very good French patisserie here,' Narendra told them.

'Can I see the factory? I want to see how they make Anna's designs.' Barney's unexpected request startled everyone.

'I'll take you there myself,' Narendra offered.

Anna realised that Barney was probably doing his best to show interest in Narendra, because it was something he had learned from one of his 'Teach Yourself' books on social etiquette. Anna couldn't imagine why Barney would want to see the factory.

Overlooking a turquoise sea and white sands, the hotel was beautiful; a white colonial building leading up from a path lined with jacaranda trees and surrounded by green lawns with borders of red hot pokers, sunflowers, gerbera and tiger lilies. A few stone steps led up to a wrap-around veranda with comfortable tables and rattan chairs littered with rose and gold chrysanthemum-design cushions.

'This is magical,' Anna exclaimed.

'Can I swim now?' Oska begged.

'I'll sort out the rooms and luggage. Why don't you and the boys sit on the veranda and order breakfast for all of us?' Max suggested

Anna appreciated the way Max took control of all the boring bits on holiday and his thoughtfulness in letting her sit back and take in the scene.

'I like Narendra,' Barney announced.

'And I like you, Barney,' Narendra replied.

When Max returned they all ate a full breakfast, Barney being particularly fond of the freshly baked white rolls. Anna didn't stop him but imagined him growing into quite a hefty teenager. He was twelve and looked like fourteen while Oska who was going on for eighteen looked like fifteen.

'Shouldn't we have a little rest? We've been flying all night,' Anna suggested.

'I can rest on the beach,' Oska insisted.

'Anna if you're tired, you have a rest, I'll watch the boys.'

'And I'll stay with you,' Narendra announced.

Anna went upstairs to inspect the rooms and was pleased with the arrangement of interconnecting rooms with a door between, large bathrooms and balconies with views across the bay. From the balcony she spotted Max, Narendra and the boys; Oska had taken off his shoes and socks and was paddling in the water, Barney stood at the edge.

Narendra discussed the business plans, Max was eager for Anna to see the new range of materials with all their colours and designs. Max reassured Narendra that the collection was selling well but he was concerned that prices were a little too proud for an increasingly competitive market. Unless the cost came down they would have to find cheaper materials.

'When Anna's rested, we can go over the figures and look at the new range of fabrics.'

It two o'clock when Anna came down, looking stunning in one of her cruise collection models. At forty-five her figure remained slim and shapely and Max was heartened to see people looking at her as she approached them.

'Is Barney still swimming? He must be starving,' Anna said, looking towards the ocean.

'This is going to be a perfect holiday. I haven't heard a peep out of the boys all morning. I think I'll go in for a swim,' Max said.

'Me too.' Anna took Max's hand as they walked towards the boys.

After lunch on the veranda, Max conceded, 'I've got to go and rest.'

'I'm tired too,' Oska added.

'Typical! I feel quite refreshed,' Anna laughed.

'Do you feel up to seeing the latest fabrics?' Narendra asked.

'Yes, I'd like that very much.'

'Can I come too? I'm not tired and you promised I could go to the factory,' Barney asked. He looked remarkably fresh and Anna thought it would give Max and Oska a rest if she took him with her.

When they arrived at the factory, Barney put his hands over his ears – the cacophony of machines, fans and seamstresses chattering was quite overpowering and Anna remembered his hypersensitivity to sounds. He asked if he could sit in the office while Anna and Narendra went to look at the rolls of new materials.

'You can sit at my desk and be the boss,' Narendra told him.

Laid out across the desk were account books and spreadsheets. Barney, with little else to do, glanced at the spreadsheets and became fascinated with the columns of numbers. Initially, without any conscious input, Barney's eyes raced across and up and down the columns of figures in pounds and rupees and couldn't help noticing various arithmetical errors. He could see that the total money at the bottom of the spreadsheet amounted to more than it should have.

Anna and Narendra returned and talked about the new fabrics. 'I think I can use at least four or five of those colour-ways but I'll have to get Max to take a look. The prices are a little too high for our market. We'll go through them again tomorrow, but I'd better get Barney back as he looks exhausted now.'

'I'll drive you,' Narendra offered.

In the car, to Narendra's astonishment, Barney instructed him on the route back to the hotel.

'You're a genius Barney,' he said as he dropped them back at the hotel.

That evening they decided on a quiet dinner together in the hotel restaurant and an early night to recover from their jetlag.

'Tell me about the new materials?' Max asked Anna as they sat around the table waiting for the waiter to take their orders.

'They are different; very good quality at ninety per-cent silk and ten per-cent dacron, quite beautiful with delicate designs. We could do a lot with them but I think the price is a little high.'

'The sums are also too high,' Barney piped up.

Anna laughed, 'What are you talking about Barney?' She looked at Max and shrugged her shoulders.

'When you and Narendra were in the factory I was looking at some of the numbers on Narendra's spreadsheet and they are wrong.'

'How are they wrong?' Oska, although amused, believed Barney.

'Narendra doesn't know how to multiply properly,' replied Barney.

'How are they wrong?' Max was now taking Barney very seriously.

'I am not wrong. There were twenty metres of fabric code number GCL12 which the cost column says cost 23.041 Rupiah per metre. Then, when that's multiplied by twenty the total cost column should show 460.82. But it didn't. It showed 520.82. And that's wrong. And there were lots of other wrong numbers like that.'

'You were only in the office for twenty minutes, Barney. How can you be sure you are right?' Anna asked.

'I added them up in my head and I did it three times and always got the same numbers. Don't tell Narendra I did it. I don't want to get into trouble but the papers were on the desk and I had nothing to do while I was waiting for you,' Barney said.

Anna and Max looked at each other.

'It's quite all right Barney, you've done nothing wrong, but none of us, not even you Oska, must breathe a word. Promise,' Anna said.

'Barney you are quite a clever-clogs,' Oska said, ruffling his brother's hair.

In their bedroom, Max, controlling his anxiety, tried to decide how to deal with the situation.

'I hope I'm wrong but first thing in the morning I am going to take Narendra by surprise and insist on seeing the invoices, spreadsheets and the bank accounts. If he and Agrim are peeling money off the top, we have some real problems.'

'What will you do?'

'There's no choice. I'll have to confront him. Perhaps this is the custom here, perhaps there is an explanation, perhaps it's something to do with local taxes – but without total transparency and trust we can't go on.'

'I agree. Trust and loyalty are fundamental to all dealings. I can't watch another business venture go down You know I'd rather go and work as a designer for someone else than put my heart and soul into anything when I can't trust my partner.'

Max was not surprised at the strength of Anna's integrity, his own behaviour breaking all the bonds of trust and good faith weighed on him heavily. He thought of Anna's hard work and dedication and how much she had helped Barney develop. He thought of Anna's talent, modesty and determination and how she was quite capable of giving up the business as a matter of principal and of just working for another fashion house. He also believed, now Barney was increasingly independent, that Anna would find the right school and convince them to take him. Her belief in Barney was unshakeable and he was beginning to agree with her that Barney could make something of his life. He was ashamed of his feelings about Barney, of how he had resented his intrusion into their lives and of how he would become thoroughly bored and irritated by his repetitive ranting and obsessive needs. For the first time, Max's heart opened to Barney's innocence and his courage in managing so many situations that must be frightening to him. There was something of Anna's kindness in his nature and Max was determined to make it up to him. He decided to spend more time with him in the water, and play ball on the beach with both boys. Depressed about his behaviour and deeply concerned about Narendra's trustworthiness, he went to bed.

Aware of his upset, Anna put her arm around him and kissed the back of his neck. He turned around and hugged her.

'Oh Anna, I do love you.'

It had been a long time since she had felt his body against hers and yielded, willing, helping him to continue. As every bit of tension left her body she fell into a deep sleep but he slept for an hour or two before waking to aching guilt. How could he have been so stupid, how could he not have foreseen the consequences of his actions? A damn stupid moment with Dinah could ruin the love and life he had with Anna, who had done nothing but love and trust him from the first moment they met.

The following morning they agreed that Anna and the boys would go on the beach and he would go to see Narendra. Arriving there just after nine, Narendra was more obsequious than Max expected but perhaps he hadn't noticed his pandering before. A tray of chai and Indian sweets were set out on a brass tray.

'I think Anna liked the new range of material yesterday.'

'She did, and I would also like to see . . .' Before Max could finish the sentence a young clerk brought in the rolls of material and laid them out on a table especially covered with a white sheet.

'They are quite stunning, Narendra.'

'I know you can't refuse this quality,' Narendra urged.

Max was genuinely impressed and couldn't hide his pleasure.

'Narendra, if we have time I wouldn't mind looking at the recent cost sheets and invoices. I need to compare prices before I make any decisions.' Max contrived to sound relaxed and at ease.

Narendra laid out the spreadsheet and Max, having studied them, said 'There's something I don't understand here.'

Narendra hovered over him. 'I can assure you our accountant went over the figures. Everything is correct.'

'I think there could be a mistake. You see here that fabric code number GCA14 costs 20.02 per metre but for 10 metres the total cost is 220.20! And there is a similar mistake down here. Also on the up side!'

'Oh I understand, the clerk has just made a mistake in multiplication.'

'Can I borrow your calculator Narendra?' Max made a point of sounding unhurried.

It took a lot of time as Max tapped in and checked all the multiplications over the last six months. Most of the results were correct but a significant number were not – and none had reduced the cost to the partnership, all had increased it. Max crossed out all the wrong figures put next to the corrected sums in red and totalled up the amended sum due in red on the spreadsheet. It came to quite a considerable sum of money.

He watched Narendra check all the figures. Again, this took some time then, calling in his clerk, Narendra began shouting and then raging at him in Hindi. Initially the clerk seemed to be protesting, looking at Max and trying to speak to him but in Hindi.

Narendra slapped his clerk violently in the face, who burst into tears. Narendra, now returning to English, shouted: 'Get out! Get out! If you ever come near here, the police will know and it's off to prison you'll go!' More rapid fire in Hindi followed. The clerk, now fallen to his knees, seemed to be begging but finally turned tail and fled.

'How long could this have been going on? All these errors, all one-way, are they just a matter of your clerk's arithmetic? Is this anything to do with a tradition here of a cash economy, of special presents for people or Indian tax?' Max stopped himself from saying a criminal offence.

'No, Max, believe me, I should have checked the books. I've been so overworked trying to get your deliveries on time, I never expected the business to expand so fast. I am dreadfully sorry, all I can do is go through all the books and wherever we find a shortfall, it will be paid back into the business, without question! I am horrified and deeply ashamed.'

'Perhaps you would let me have all the purchase and copy sales invoices and the spreadsheets and the ledgers for the last five years and I'll take them back to the hotel and work on them there. It's easier for me.'

'Of course, certainly, I'll pack them immediately and drive you straight back to the hotel.' Narendra couldn't have been more co-operative and to reassure himself that all would be all right, he added. 'What do you think of the new batch of material?'

'I told you, both Anna and I just love it.'

Max joined Anna and the boys on the beach, grateful to be out of Narendra's airless and untidy office.

Both Oska and Barney were playing in the water and Anna was particularly pleased to see how Oska had helped Barney overcome his fears.

'All I can say is Barney is a genius.' Max saw Anna's face break into a smile. 'In fact, I've brought the books home and I'd like him to check all the multiplications and additions. I can't believe he is capable of handling such a volume of arithmetic so quickly, almost instinctively.'

'If Narendra and Agrim are peeling money off the top what can we do?' Anna asked.

'He claims that it is his incompetent clerk and all the money will be paid back to the company.'

'When? How much? What choice do we have?' Anna asked.

'We could leave Barney here to check all the books.'

'Don't be silly Max, this is very serious.'

'The good news is that the company is expanding, making money and we've had no hassle with delivery dates or quality control.' Max sounded too accepting.

'But can you trust Narendra or Agrim or their clerks or whoever else in the chain is shaving off profits? You and I know once trust is gone in a relationship, something far more vital than profit is lost. It's like a marriage, you can't put it together again in the same way.'

Max looked horrified.

'Darling, you look exhausted. Go and have a swim, we'll talk about it later.' Lying next to him on the sand Anna put her hand over his.

At lunch, Max seemed preoccupied. The boys were starving after three hours of play in the sea. Oska laughed when, without being asked, the waiter brought Barney a large plate of hamburger and chips and said: 'No cheese'.

'Don't worry Max, we're on holiday, we'll work something out', said Anna reassuringly.

'Barney, will you help me check some numbers after lunch?' Max turned to Barney, who he wouldn't normally disturb while he was eating. Barney put the hamburger down.

'It will give me the greatest of pleasure, Max.'

They all suppressed a giggle whenever Barney became formal, another habit he'd acquired from an antiquated self-help book.

'But I must warn you, Max, I thought I liked Narendra, but I don't,' Barney announced, as if reading Max's mind.

'Why's that?' Max asked, surprised at the respect he felt for Barney's opinion.

'I can tell when people do things or could do things that aren't right. You remember at Disney world? I knew that Mickey Mouse wasn't going to come back with the balloons. I just know when things aren't right; that's why I get anxious sometimes.'

They were all astounded. Barney had gone up in their estimation and Max could see that he did have a future. He was different – but that didn't mean he was useless.

'Barney I'm so very proud of you, and thank you for all your advice.'

28

Broken Trust – 1992

That evening, Barney, with lightning speed and accuracy, arrived at the amount of money that had been skimmed off. Max then phoned Narendra asking for a meeting at the hotel in the morning.

Max and Anna sat on the hotel veranda keeping an eye on the boys on the beach. She felt her stomach tighten as she saw Narendra coming up the path and decided to leave all the talking to Max, who signalled a warm welcome as Narendra approached their table, which was filled with cold drinks, coffee and croissants. Narendra sat down.

'Isn't it wonderful to see the boys so happy playing in the sea,' he said.

Max kicked Anna under the table as if to say 'don't get redirected', then looked at Narendra.

'I don't know what to say except that a red line has been crossed. Narendra, I've known you since I was nineteen. I lived with you in my gap year, and I think of you as family, or at least as a trusted friend. What has happened? And no lies please – we both know that the truth will come out in the end.'

During what seemed like a long pause Anna looked across the white sands, seeing Oska and Barney fooling around in the clear turquoise sea. It meant far more than the missing money to witness this very normal scene of two brothers enjoying each other's company. Pondicherry had a magical quality – it was as if she couldn't be unhappy there. Everywhere she looked the jewel-like colours and light seemed to enter her being, giving her an overwhelming urge to paint.

'Max, I will admit that I was persuaded by Agrim to alter the prices in our favour. He came to me and explained he had originally quoted too low a figure but was desperate not to upset you and spoil a good business right at the beginning. He never held back on quality and we never let you down on a delivery date. Agrim was having trouble with the workers in the factory, he was under-capitalised and your business was expanding too fast. But I should have spoken to you, I really should have. I was going to repay the business as soon as I could, but things got out of hand and then somehow it was too late. We will give you back every penny. I am so very ashamed and want to continue working with you. Why break up a good business?'

Anna looked straight at him, ignoring Max's warning kick under the table. 'Narendra, it's true that we've built up a very good business. It's almost the perfect partnership where I can rely on you for quality control and to supply the best materials. But you must understand I have always had a problem with trust. I know people can make mistakes, but the question I ask is, what will stop you making the same mistake again?'

'I've learned my lesson, please believe me. I will sign any contract your lawyer produces to ensure I keep to my side of the contract. I will provide a bank guarantee. I will pay for your lawyer to come out from London. Please . . . ' he begged. 'Just give me a chance to show you how sorry I am and to repair the damage I have caused.'

Max intervened. 'In many ways I do believe you, Narendra. I also believe that a man should have a second chance to prove himself again. We can all make mistakes depending on our greed, stupidity and other weaknesses, but we have to be sure we really recognise the mistake before we can repair it.'

Max sounded as if he had gone off on a tangent, as if he was thinking of something else, which indeed he was. Anna had never heard him express those ideas before and was moved by his sensitivity.

'Max, I think we should hear more of Narendra's side of the

story.' Anna's sudden fear of losing Narendra surfaced. 'I suppose I'm more upset by the loss of trust. It's like everything you ever believed suddenly no longer makes any sense – and I end up not trusting my own judgement.'

'I see no point in killing the goose who lays the golden egg,' Max posited, only too aware that back home he had broken a far more sacred trust. He dreaded to think of the outcome if Dinah decided to get nasty.

Narendra was confused by their reaction. They both seemed to be going off on some sentimental tangent. It wasn't the way he did business. He had apologised, and had offered to put things right. Wasn't that enough?

'I suppose the way forward is for us to get our lawyers to draft a new contract to protect and secure your interests,' Narendra suggested.

They discussed the different kinds of checks they could implement, of all accounts and statements being copied to London and appointing new independent auditors with extended powers to be written into the new contract. But in the end Anna simply said:

'We wouldn't need all this if we trusted each other, would we?' She may have been wrong, but she thought she saw tears in Narendra's eyes, and the quiet sadness that swept over Max was apparent to them both.

'That didn't go too badly,' Max said as he too looked across the white sands and thought of his first visit to Pondicherry.

'Darling we can't afford to start another business again. We're doing quite well and, besides, I have great plans for Barney and we'll need every penny we can earn,' Anna said excitedly.

'What plans?'

'I'm going to try and enter him for a top school. I know of two public schools that have maths houses and Barney is a mathematical genius. Who knows, they might consider him. It'll cost a fortune but I'll write a letter to the headmaster and see what happens. You don't get anywhere if you don't try.' Anna sounded more confident than Max could remember.

On the way back to the airport Barney announced: 'May I thank everyone here for a most delightful holiday. The two weeks have gone by very quickly and I would like to come back one day. I would also like to inform the driver that he is taking the wrong route to the airport.'

Anna squeezed Max's hand and whispered, 'He's adorable sometimes.'

'Sometimes,' Max whispered.

29

Barney Moves On – 1992

Stepping out of Heathrow towards the taxi queue, the cold whipping through their coats, blotted out the memory of Pondicherry.

'You would think things would have changed after being away for two weeks, but the only thing that's changed is me.' Max didn't elaborate.

'We should travel more. I was feeling quite down before we left and now feel full of energy,' Anna added.

'I had a great time, I'd like to go back to Pondicherry,' Oska said.

'And I want to check more numbers for Max,' Barney announced.

At home Anna looked at the fridge of food that Bridget had supplied. There was also a note on the kitchen table saying there was a pot of Irish stew in the oven.

Anna went through the pile of post, opening first the brown envelope from the Local Education Authority. The educational psychologist would like to meet her next week and would Anna confirm the appointment at her office. Perhaps, she thought, they have a school place for Barney. His behaviour on holiday had given her hope. It was time to move on and she was not too surprised to feel herself ready to leave the support of Peeling Onions. She felt she needed to be rid of her dependence on Molly, no matter how indirect or well meant.

Suddenly, hearing screaming and shouting she rushed upstairs to Barney's room. He was pulling all his clothes and shoes out of the cupboard and rearranging them.

'Bridget changed the order, Bridget mustn't touch my cupboard!' he shouted.

'Calm down, Barney. Bridget tidied all the cupboards in the house. She always cleans everything when we are away.' Anna was distressed; she had forgotten how rapidly Barney could become agitated when anybody disturbed the systems that he needed to sustain himself. 'Barney, I came up to ask whether you want to go back to Peeling Onions, or whether you would prefer to stay at home until we find another school for you?'

'I'm much too old and it's very boring. I like Molly and I like Carol, but I need to do different things.'

Anna was delighted and rushed to tell Max about Barney's response.

'Sometimes I wonder whether we know anything that goes on in his head. He can be so profound and so maddening, all at the same time. Maybe if I spent more time talking to him I would learn more, instead of letting him slip into his world. His silence has become habitual and we have taken the lead from him. Maybe I'm wrong but I get the feeling he knows a lot more than we realise.'

Max seemed depressed.

'Max, it isn't your fault. There is so little guidance on what to do and I don't know if the professionals don't just make it up as they go along. I don't think we've done too badly with Barney. Why don't you go into the office for a couple of hours, then come home early and have a rest.' Anna felt he was at a loose end.

'Good idea, I'll be back in a couple of hours.'

There was no reason for Max to go into the office but he wanted to talk to Dinah. He had no prepared plan. All he knew was that his life depended on extricating himself from the consequences of a ridiculous and meaningless seduction. That's all it was and it would never be repeated. He had to get Dinah to agree that they had both been stupid, that it meant nothing and could never mean anything.

'You look wonderful,' Dinah said.

'Sun, sea and the best family holiday I can remember. Anything new happened since I've been away?' He walked past her desk into his office.

Dinah followed and sat opposite him. 'Yes, Max, there is some-thing very new you should know about.'

'I'm all ears.' Max didn't look up as he started going through the pile of post on his desk.

'I'm pregnant,' Dinah announced.

'How's that?' Max seemed both detached and numbed.

'I don't think I need go into the details, these things happen, and they've happened to happen with you.'

'I can't deal with this. You know it was unintended, we were a little tipsy, stupid and damn careless. I'm sorry, Dinah, I can't go along with this. We have never had anything more than a working relationship, nor do I have any feelings for you beyond loyalty and gratitude for your work. I have my family to consider. What are you going to do?' Max asked.

Triumphantly, she declared: 'I'm going to have our baby. Isn't that what most women of forty would consider a wonderful gift?'

The blood drained from Max's face and he heard the sound of his quickening heartbeat reverberating in his chest. He gave a deep sigh to catch his breath as his mind leapt to find words that might placate Dinah, that might induce her to consider not just hers but his situation, too.

'I'm truly sorry . . . ,' he began, only to be interrupted.

'I'm not. I'm overjoyed.'

'Well, that certainly puts me in my place. Is there any compro-mise?'

'I'm not getting rid of our baby,' she asserted.

'I understand and I wouldn't want you to do anything that in any way harmed you, but would you agree to keeping it away from my family? Of course I will do all I can to help but I can't let you destroy Anna and the children,' Max begged.

'Well, I can't hide it for long and Anna will soon see. What do you want me to say? I'm not a very good liar.'

'Are you sure it's mine?'

'I beg your pardon! I told you I'm not a very good liar.'

'Could you at least keep this to ourselves until I've got my head around it? Please, I beg you, not a hint.'

Dinah watched Max's face distort in anguish, his tan now faded to the colour of chewing gum. His eyes may be full of tears, but it was she who was abandoned. His rejection filled the air and despite a moment of pity for him she remained overwhelmingly angry and resolute.

'I know it's a shock, but you'll get used to it. I haven't even had the first scan and I probably won't show for a while, so we have time.' This was all she was prepared to concede.

'I'm going home now.' Max got up without looking at her and left.

At home, Anna and the boys had gone to lie down after the long flight. He joined Anna in their bedroom.

'Max, you look exhausted. Come and lie down.' Anna's caring reminded him of Dinah's selfishness. Lying beside her he put his arm around her relaxed, soft body.

'Relax, you feel so tense. I think you're overtired. I'll bring you a brandy.' Anna got up and went downstairs. Max sobbed into the pillow, wiping his eyes before Anna returned. He felt as if he was going to explode.

'Max, are you sure you aren't going down with something? You look quite ill.'

'Maybe I caught something on the flight.'

Anna closed the curtains. 'I'll go downstairs and let you sleep, I've had a good rest.'

Relieved to be alone in the darkened room, Max had a hundred and one ideas, not one of them making any sense; all he could hope for was for Dinah to have a miscarriage or to meet someone else. He couldn't trust her and it seemed obvious he had to get rid of her. He couldn't go into the office every day under the threat of her whims. She was like a time bomb ticking away, waiting to explode and destroy everything he held dear. Perhaps he could find a way for her to go abroad, maybe send her to Pondicherry with the new contracts. But he knew that she would not be so easily pushed aside.

Anna came into the room. 'It's six o'clock. You've slept for ages. Are you feeling any better? Will you join us for dinner or would you like a tray upstairs?' she asked.

'I'm coming down,' Max said momentarily feeling the need for the safety of his family.

Barney was on the edge of an explosion as Anna dished up the Irish stew.

'It's yukky, take it away!' he screamed and put his hand up to his mouth as if to retch.

'Barney there isn't anything else. We've been away and Anna hasn't had time to do the shopping.'

Oska took Barney's plate. 'Look Barney, I'm eating it.'

Max wanted to hit Barney but managed to control his anger; there were still moments when Barney's behaviour made him furious.

'What about baked beans on toast?' Anna feared a massive melt-down.

'Baked beans on toast,' Barney agreed, with a nervous grimace.

'Barney, if you eat all your dinner we can go and watch an Elvis film.' Oska too was sensitive to Max's black mood.

When the children left the room, Max got up to help Anna clear the table. 'I'm sorry for making our first evening home so miserable.'

'Barney's very sensitive and picks up things and I'm sure he knows something that you're not saying.'

'Are you telling me now that Barney is a mind reader as well?'

'I'm not sure but there are a lot of coincidences. Before we went on holiday, he said he didn't like Dinah. I told him he was being very silly because he hardly sees her. He said that he didn't want to see her and wished she would die now. I scolded him and told him he was being very cruel and you know what he said? "I'm scared of Dinah, she's got a bump on her nose and she won't tell us what she knows." He's suddenly become obsessed with her and was singing

"Dangerous Die, now, has a bump on her nose, Dangerous Die, now, won't tell us what she knows. Her eyes are made of glass and she wants to steal me with her eyes." Something must have happened when I took him to the office just before we went to Pondicherry, Dinah must have said something to him.'

'I don't think you should bring Barney to the office. It's incredible what goes on in his head.'

'I also felt a change in Dinah. I may be over-sensitive but I don't like the way she looks at me. I can't explain it.' Anna knew Max became irritated when she presented her fanciful notions.

'Barney really is affecting you. What the hell do you mean?' Max demanded.

'I think the only way I can explain it is that it's as if she wants to be me. It's as if she's envious of me. I don't know, she just makes me feel uncomfortable. She also talks to Barney as if she's patronising him, in a kind of babyish voice, as if he can't understand.'

While Max thought that Anna was imagining things, he also wondered whether he was transmitting his anxiety to Anna who, being naturally intuitive, was sensitive to his distress. She had been sensitive to Barney's thoughts and feelings for so long that she was capable of picking things up. Often she would say, 'Max, is something worrying you?' even before his anxiety had surfaced.

'Max, we really shouldn't be dependent on anybody. As soon as they realise we are, they start taking advantage. Get rid of Dinah.' Anna was insistent.

'How would I do that?' he asked.

'I was thinking, why don't you work from home? You have your office here and we have enough space for stock and samples. You can still go out to see our buyers. Narendra is running his side of the business more than efficiently and everybody nowadays seems to be using computers. We can buy a computer and tell Dinah that we are computerising the business. She'd run a mile. I even think Barney would be able to work a computer. Tell Dinah you need a computer expert.'

Max saw that Anna's creative mind never stopped. It all made sense – except for the one problem that would not go away and haunted him while Anna talked.

'Well, what do you think?' Anna asked, pleased with her suggestion.

'Let me think about it. I'll talk to Dinah in the morning,' Max said, thinking that he would be paying for much more than a computer if he could buy her silence.

At breakfast, Anna reminded him. 'Max don't leave it, talk to Dinah today. The longer you leave it, the harder it'll be.'

'Why if you leave something does it become hard?' Barney piped up. 'I think Dinah will become hard, so you must be careful when you talk to her.'

'That's very clever Barney,' Oska laughed.

'Don't talk in front of the children,' Max warned Anna.

'You can talk behind our back,' Barney said. 'We wouldn't become hard like Dinah. We can also talk behind Dinah's back because she's harder to talk to. I think Dinah tells lies because she's not up-front with us.'

'You're talking nonsense, Barney,' Max intervened.

'No, I'm not. I know Dinah doesn't like me because she pretends to like me. I know when people pretend and I have to be very careful because pretending is like telling a lie and Dinah might be a liar.'

'For goodness sake, Barney, you hardly know Dinah and you mustn't go around saying things you know nothing about. I don't want you talking about Dinah any more. Do you understand?' Anna could see Max getting irritated.

'Yes, I promise. Maybe she'll die now.' Barney was quite obsessed with her and Max, meeting Anna's eyes, began to believe that Barney might have telepathic ability.

Max arrived earlier than usual in the office and was surprised to see Dinah clearing her desk.

'I've decided to leave,' she said irately. Her eyes were full of tears and she looked tired and disconsolate.

'I appreciate your decision. It's for the best and you need not worry about managing, I will see you right.' Max knew this would not be the end of it and tried to stay calm.

'Don't think you can just get rid of me. You'll pay for this for the rest of your life.'

'I know . . . '

'I can tell you if I didn't think so highly of Anna, I would be around there now, and if I didn't feel sorry for Barney, I would have no compunction but to destroy the lot of you.'

'Dinah, you've helped me build up the business, I owe you a lot.' Seeing she was ready for a fight, Max was determined not to dig himself in deeper. 'Can I help you carry your things to the car?'

'Yes!' she replied, then dropping everything, threw her arms round him. 'You have no idea how difficult this is for me.'

He patted her back before extricating himself from her embrace and stepping aside.

'I'm truly sorry,' he said, picking up her box of things and walking ahead. Dinah's behaviour seemed very melodramatic and Max couldn't help but wonder whether in some strange way Barney was onto something. Then, driven by an inner force, Max heard himself say: 'I don't believe you're pregnant, I've worked out the timing of that terrible evening. It was the end of February.'

Dinah grimaced, as if half-laughing. Max felt as if he was being bullied. He recognised the same feelings he had had at school, of being teased and trying to defend himself.

'Why have you only told me now? You would surely be showing by now,' he challenged her.

'Let's wait and see, shall we?'

'Why are you punishing me?' Max asked.

'I'm so tired of your smug little wife who can do everything. I'm tired of seeing my life slip away and I have nothing.'

'You have a jolly nice apartment and financial security. You're attractive and clever, what more do you want?'

'I want what you and Anna have: a relationship and a family and a creative partnership. I'm tired of always being on the outside looking in.'

'Well, I'm sorry but we've both worked very hard to keep everything together and I can't see what you have to gain by trying to destroy us as a family.'

'I don't have to explain myself to you. It must be obvious that I've loved you ever since I started working here.'

Max was astounded and wondered if Dinah was serious.

'You can't go around behaving like this. I'll tell Anna everything,' Max challenged Dinah.

'You'd better tell her before I do, because my side of things is much more plausible. It's a simple choice: either you let me share you, or you lose Anna.'

Dinah seemed to have worked it all out. Max had no choice but to talk to Anna and time was not on his side. He realised that Barney was right, Dinah was capable of lies that had a ring of truth. The problem is that a lie once told is difficult to undo. Dinah had put him on the defensive and he was sure Anna would believe her. He would have to find the right time to talk to Anna but first he had to clear his head.

At home Anna asked, 'Did you speak to Dinah?'

'Yes, she was very angry and walked out.'

'Oh dear, do you want me to phone her? After all, she's been with us for a long time.'

'I think it's best to do nothing for now, let things calm down a bit. I've had the day from hell.' Max slumped onto a kitchen chair.

'Oh Max, I'm so sorry, I shouldn't have persuaded you. I don't know why I'm so impulsive. I think the moment I get an idea in my head, I have to act on it otherwise I might lose it or something

'Anna, you're right. I think Dinah is deranged, and harmful to our family. In some peculiar way, Barney seems to understand that. I must lie down now. We'll talk tomorrow.'

30

The Meeting – March 1992

'I'm sorry for keeping you waiting. Joan Kindle, the educational psychologist, came out to the corridor to usher Anna into her room.

Anna sat down in the dingy office and looked around at four other desks and a bank of filing cabinets while Joan Kindle cleared her desk of a dozen files and odd toys before putting a file marked 'Barney Elliott' in front of her.

'Sorry, our coffee machine has been stolen for the third time. This time they even managed to break the chain attached to it,' Joan Kindle remarked while opening her file.

'How extraordinary,' was all Anna could say.

'So you would think, but we have so many people using these offices. Almost everybody has to double up on space, so it's a bit hard to know whether it's the patients or staff with all the comings and goings. How's Barney getting on?' she asked.

Anna smiled. 'That's exactly what I came to find out from you.' She wasn't going to give anything away. She imagined reports circulating between various departments: 'Mother over-anxious, has an inflated view of her child's ability'.

After a pause, Joan Kindle spoke. 'Well, Barney presents as a mosaic picture. He is extremely high functioning in some areas. He also harbours some odd ideas. Even though he is quite articulate, I don't think he shares our understanding of language. I wonder if you've noticed how he distorts the meanings of words?' She waited as if expecting an agreement.

'I suppose we've got so used to Barney, we may have inadvertently encouraged him because he can be so clever.'

'Perhaps there is some truth in that but I'm concerned about the kind of educational setting that will suit Barney. By law he has to attend school.'

'What happens if you can't find him an appropriate placement?' Anna asked.

'There are many normal children who are not going to the most appropriate school for them. We may have to compromise,' she said, noticing Anna's face grow tense.

'I'm really not the sort of person that goes for compromise – it's not part of my vocabulary. If your department can't help me, I will have to look around myself. Perhaps there is a private school that might consider taking Barney.'

'Of course you are quite entitled to do that and it isn't a bad idea. Barney does have some phenomenal abilities. I am only able to look for places in a local authority school and I will make my recommendations. You can then visit the school and make your decision. I quite understand if you reject it but you realise that the local authority cannot fund a private school. I wish we could but at present it isn't our policy.'

Anna recalled how she had scorned Dawn Atkin, who had gone beyond the call of duty and found Peeling Onions, and suddenly felt ashamed of her attitude.

'I'm very grateful for all your help. I know Barney enjoyed doing the tests with you and of course I will visit any school you select for Barney.'

'Good, then I'll also look outside the borough. We mustn't give up just yet.'

Anna thought Joan Kindle more astute than she'd given her credit for. She must have dealt with hundreds of desperate mothers all wanting the best for their child, and she could hardly blame her if the local authority had little to offer.

'I'm sorry for appearing so contrary, especially as the local authority has supported Barney at Peeling Onions for nearly six years. I think I lost so much time in Barney's early years trying to get a diagnosis, fighting to keep him in his nursery school, and the

GP inferring I was neurotic, that I've become unreasonably suspicious of authority.'

'I understand. Unfortunately your experience is very common and I can imagine how the whole referral procedure exacerbates the emotional health of a family under extreme stress. I think Barney is a charming and most unusual child who does need an educational setting to help him realise his potential – but please don't quote me. I have to work within the constraints of my professional position.'

'Thank you for being so frank. You've been very helpful. I'll wait to hear from you.' Anna got up to go, then paused. 'May I ask you a question?'

'If I can help.'

'Barney seems more aware of what's going on nowadays but also gets more easily upset over little things. For instance, if anybody rearranges his books or our daily goes into his room without his permission, he'll suddenly flare up, become quite distressed and will go on and on complaining.'

'Yes, it's quite common, and when a child reaches thirteen we have the added problem of hormones. Plus he is going out more into all sorts of gatherings which could make him more anxious – especially if he doesn't always understand the context of the situation. Sometimes he might even become more moody.'

'How do you mean?' Anna asked.

'I'm not exactly sure, but it's hard to discern how much insight Barney has and he may at times feel depressed, seeing himself as different and lonely. Each child is an individual and I suppose you know Barney better than anybody so you'll notice changes before anybody else. My tests can only look at one dimension of behaviour: they tell us that Barney is extremely gifted but how he uses his gifts involves many more observations and interpretations. All I can say is if you are worried about his behaviour you should see a consultant who specialises in autism. They have much more experience than I do. I'm sorry I can't be more helpful.'

168

31

Anna's Mission – 1992

Anna was caught between hope and fear. If a suitable placement couldn't be found for Barney she might be forced to send him to a school for the mentally handicapped which took in a wide range of children with varying disabilities. She recalled Molly saying that inappropriate treatment could be more damaging than no treatment at all. Barney would not adapt and his behaviour would deteriorate. Over the years she had adjusted to Barney, and in turn he had shown her a way of thinking that she would never have known. His innocence had maintained all the family's integrity. He was capable of such loyalty and had a forgiving nature. His limited insight into his own condition and that of others often gave him a quite original understanding of the way people viewed him. He seemed to have an instinct for wanting to make things better and to help others. If he sensed the family was upset or in disagreement he would intervene with some universal truth, like 'people should love each other' or 'wars are dangerous and bad' and these statements delivered on cue would dissolve disaffection. Anna was convinced that Barney could go forward and she was determined to fight for his future even though Max didn't always agree with her when it came to valuing Barney.

She decided to research and write to private schools. She had to try and if she failed at least she had done her best; that's what every mother should be able to tell herself and she at least would be able to sleep at night, knowing she had tried. Sitting at her desk she composed a basic letter that could be tailored to meet the culture of different schools where she thought she might have a chance of finding a place for Barney.

Dear Head Teacher,

I realise that this isn't the usual channel by which to make an application for my twelve-year-old son Barney to enter your school. Barney suffers from autism. He has considerable talents and an IQ of 142 that puts him in the highly gifted range of functioning. His mathematical ability is phenomenal. He also has a photographic memory and can accurately draw representations from architecture and nature. However, he has a few problems. His social behaviour is somewhat stilted and appears highly mannered and we are not too sure to what extent he can read social situations. He has learned much from reading self-help books and has an encyclopaedic knowledge of geography, history and science but we have no idea how he applies this knowledge in real situations. You will find him at best eccentric but in no way a disruption to any group. On the contrary, he has a tendency to withdraw, although he does have some obsessive traits, food preferences and phobias when confronted with unfamiliar situations.

Autism is a condition that has multiple facets, although considerable research continues to be available without a specific answer as to cause or treatment. There are possibly more than 100,000 autistic children in England, many of them very high functioning and it is my belief that, with structured learning, they could contribute to society. I fully understand your priorities with regard to your students and if there is no place for Barney, I thank you for your time in reading this letter. I also wish to apologise for my unorthodox approach but as a mother who loves her son, I am forced to sacrifice my pride.

Yours sincerely
Anna Elliott

Anna went to the library to get information on all the possible public and private schools within a twenty mile radius of their home. She then selected those she thought shared some of her values. Buzzwords in their prospectus like 'caring, individual potential, wide range of ability, numbers of pupils etc.,' would give a hint of a chance. She decided to show the letter to Max this evening although she was aware that he might not be supportive.

Her enthusiasm for her scheme prompted her to go next door and show the draft letter to Madellaine, whose opinion she valued.

'How nice to see you, come in.' Madellaine's warm welcome reaffirmed their deepening friendship. 'How was the holiday?'

'Wonderful! We all benefitted, especially Barney. Everything all right here? You look a little tired,' Anna remarked.

'That's very perceptive of you.'

'Is it Rob?'

'It's Rob plus. Come into the lounge and I'll make some coffee.'

Anna went to sit on her favourite chair by the window looking onto the rose garden. She couldn't understand why Madellaine went on living in her large house. Perhaps she was unconsciously waiting for Doug to return even though there seemed little chance of that after so many years.

Madellaine returned with a tray carrying cups of coffee and a plate of chocolate-covered ginger biscuits. Anna took her coffee but declined the biscuits.

'Doug and Barbara are having a baby,' said Madellaine. 'It's a surprise – Barbara is forty-two. It is having a terrible effect on Rob. It's the final nail in the coffin. Rob won't even hear Doug's name being mentioned and he has totally rejected Doug's parents who are heartbroken.'

'Poor Rob, it's a terrible blow, not just losing a father but to be displaced. What happened at his school? Did you manage to talk them round?'

'I was pleasantly surprised, actually. They said Rob is very intelligent and they totally understand how he got into the wrong company. They half admitted they shouldn't have suspended him without first talking to me and they have recommended that he sees the school psychologist every fortnight to help him.'

'I'm impressed. It seems at least Rob's in the right school. Is he feeling better?'

'Not after this setback. I had hopes that one day he and Doug would reconcile but now it seems impossible.'

Anna found herself eating a biscuit although she couldn't recall taking one. 'I feel bad about coming to you with one of my ideas but I thought I could get the benefit of your wisdom before I rush into it.' She handed the letter to Madellaine, who put on her glasses.

'It's very good, honest and quite moving,' Madellaine commented, looking up.

'I haven't shown it to Max yet, nor have I selected any school to which I could send the letter.' Anna sounded uncertain.

'Send it to Dr Jarvis, Rob's headmaster. He must be quite extraordinary if he can deal with Rob!'

They both laughed. 'Madellaine you're a genius! I would never have thought of it and what's more, Rob is probably the only boy in the school who would protect Barney.'

32

Barney's Practice Interview – 1992

Anna was surprised at the prompt reply she received from Dr Jarvis, the headmaster of Hillside School. A preliminary meeting with John Dutch, the head of the mathematics department, was arranged for the following week. Anna rushed to tell Max, who was now working upstairs in his study at home.

'You're amazing, Anna. I must admit when you showed me the letter I didn't think you had a chance and was more worried about your disappointment.'

'Oh ye of little faith! I must phone Madellaine as it was her idea. I feel so blessed, Max. You are a wonderful husband and father to the boys. How many women can work with the man they love? No matter what, you've always been there for us and I don't know what I would do without you. I don't know how Madellaine manages. Did I tell you the latest insult? Doug and Barbara are having a baby. Can you imagine what that's doing to Rob? I do wish you would be a little nicer to him, he's had a bad deal.'

Max felt the heat rise in his cheeks. 'You're right, I will be nicer to Rob. I think I had better start preparing Barney for the interview. How to behave and all that. I certainly can't help him with maths.'

'I'll tell you one thing I can't do. I can't take Barney to the interview. I'll be so nervous, and knowing Barney he'll pick it up. You'll have to take him Max, he really is better with you.'

'Of course I'll take him, and in the meantime, we'll do practice interviews every day.'

'Max I know he has a chance, I'm so excited.' She was bursting to tell Madellaine.

Just then, Barney came into Max's study and sat down.

'Barney, something very important has happened. You've been invited to meet the head of the maths department at a very good school next week. If you say and do all the right things there's a good chance that they will allow you to join the school. It is a great opportunity because you will learn all the things that interest you. I am going with you to the interview and I am going to help you prepare, so they will see what a nice chap you are.'

'Can I take Hoorah Hippo with me?'

'We can take him with us but he'll have to wait for you in the car. The interview is at midday next Wednesday. So, I'll pretend to be the master. Go outside and knock at the door.' Barney did as he was told.

'Come in! Good morning Barney, I am pleased to meet you.' Max got up to shake Barney's hand. 'Please sit down.'

'Sir, it is four minutes past twelve, so I would like to say good afternoon.'

Max scratched his head. 'I've been told that you enjoy mathematics. Who has been teaching you?'

'I teach myself, from books.'

'Where do you get the books?'

'My friend Rob lends them to me and I get others from the library. I read them and answer all the questions. Sometimes I make up my own questions just for fun.'

'Can you tell me about that?' Max was beginning to find Barney quite fascinating.

'For example, when we went by plane to Pondicherry, they give us an "in flight" book to read and in it there was a map of the world and lines connecting all the flights. I made up this game in my head. I read the number of miles between each major city or airport that went the straightest way all round the world and added them all up. Sometimes I had to guess. Then I worked out how long it would take if I had to walk around the world at about three miles an hour, and some days if I was tired, like if I was going uphill, I could only do two miles an hour. Then I also had to cross the sea and I'm not such a good swimmer. I worked out that it would take me about fifteen years, three months, four days and six hours to go round the whole world.'

Barney's serious expression combined with his distinct, monotonous voice and quaint mannerisms as he moved his fingers had a mesmerising effect on Max, who had completely forgotten the question.

'That's very good Barney, but I think the maths teacher will give you his own questions to answer.'

'I am very grateful to you for spending the time with me, sir.' Barney got up and left the room.

'We'll have another go later,' Max shouted after him, deciding that Barney was a lot more extreme than he let on, but he couldn't tell Anna.

'How was he?' Anna came into the room and sat down.

'I suppose it all depends on the day. He certainly has an extraordinary mind. All I can do is try to train him how to behave,' Max told her.

33

Anna's Impulsive Idea – 1992

Anna sat on the edge of her chair in the kitchen, waiting for the right moment to try out her new idea on Max.

'I was thinking . . . we haven't behaved well towards Dinah, and I feel responsible. It isn't the right way for her to leave after all these years. I know we will give her severance pay and all that but it feels wrong. I thought of phoning her and asking her over for lunch or tea or something.'

'I agree,' he lied.

'Perhaps you should do it, because I really don't know how she feels and your description of her walking out sounded somewhat dramatic. There must be something more to it,' Anna mused.

'I'll phone her this morning and see what's happening,' Max said, contriving to be casual.

'Good, then that's another thing I don't have to worry about. It's good having you home. In less than two hours you've agreed to go along with Barney to the interview and to deal with Dinah. I'd better go to the studio and start on the new collection, the materials are quite inspiring.'

'Yes, and if by some miracle Barney is accepted in the school, I can't imagine the fees being less than Oska's school fees. With two children at private schools we are going to have to make more money.'

Max was thinking of how much money Dinah would demand and how he would have to do some creative accountancy to hide the payments to her. While Anna was working in the studio and Barney was watching an Elvis video he closed the door of his study and phoned Dinah.

'How are you feeling? I'm sorry we parted on such an unhappy note and wanted to discuss how best to handle this predicament.'

'I'm at home, it's best to talk here.'

Max detected a softening of her tone. 'Would tomorrow morning be all right?'

'Come at eleven,' she replied abruptly, perhaps suspecting Max was phoning within earshot of the family.

Max went upstairs to the studio. 'I phoned Dinah and she suggested I meet her tomorrow. I avoided inviting her to lunch because she still seemed angry.'

He was getting so good with his lies of omission that there were moments when he believed himself. He was relieved when Anna didn't question where he was meeting Dinah. Having achieved some respite, Max called Barney up to his studio for another practice interview.

Barney knocked on the study door.

'Come in,' Max shouted from behind his desk. 'Good afternoon, Barney', he said, standing up to shake his hand.

'Good afternoon, sir.' Barney sat down.

'I see from a copy of a test you did with the educational psychologist that you are very good at maths. I've prepared a few maths questions and I would like you to answer them. Don't worry if you don't understand them, just do what you can.'

'I would be very happy to oblige,' Barney answered.

'That's excellent Barney, but this is just a practice interview so I don't really have any tests for you. But this is the kind of thing that could happen when you go for your real interview.' Max hoped Barney understood.

'Yes, sir', Barney replied. 'Can I go and watch Elvis now, please sir.'

'Of course, you've done very well.'

Max thought that short spurts of practice was about all Barney and certainly he could take. He was too preoccupied with seeing Dinah tomorrow.

34

Max Digs in Deeper – Feb. 1992

Dinah lived in a three-bedroom apartment in an 1930's mansion block in Maida Vale. Max walked up the path to the front door and rang the polished brass bell. 'Come up,' he heard Dinah say, as a buzzer unlocked the door. His anxiety intensified as the lift rose to the fourth floor.

Dinah had obviously gone to some trouble. She had made herself up, had her hair done and wore a pair of beige silk trousers with a pale pink blouse. Her unblinking eyes scrutinised him closely as she ushered him into the lounge. On the coffee table sat a plate of croissants and a pot of coffee. He sat back on one of a pair of green armchairs and she perched on the edge of the other. She poured his coffee just as he liked it.

'How are you feeling?' he asked.

'I'm fine at the moment – it's more of an emotional and practical problem.'

Max could see demands were coming and stopped himself from making any offers. He knew it was a matter of money but had no idea how much. He also knew he must not offer any support that Dinah could misinterpret.

'I can imagine,' he replied.

'Can you? Can you possibly know what it feels like to be alone and have only a limited amount of money?'

'What about your parents, will you tell them?'

'I think I have to wait for the first scan, don't you? Will you tell Anna?'

'I will have to but perhaps, as you say, we should wait until after the scan.' Max knew that no time would be opportune. 'There is one aspect that worries me. I read that a sibling of an autistic child has a fifty per cent greater chance of having autism. The research didn't specify whether it was with the same partner.'

'Are you trying to frighten me, or encourage me to have an abortion? Why are you telling me this?'

'It's been worrying me, that's all. You have no idea what it's like living with Barney. Anna's moods are totally dependent on the sort of day she's had with Barney and I am also deeply affected.'

'I know, but even if our child turns out to be autistic, I still want our child,' Dinah declared.

'I don't want to upset you or make things worse, but tell me honestly, Dinah, how and when should I tell Anna? Because there are four other people involved and all of us will suffer. You have always been sensible and reasonable. I don't blame you for wanting the baby, I just want to know what you think I should do?'

'You could leave Anna and come and live with me.'

'I'll never do that. Never! You can't expect it of me. I will do what I can to help you but I will never leave my family.' Max saw the disappointment on her face accompanied by a hot flush of anger but was pleased that he had said it.

'You can start by giving me a monthly salary to live on,' Dinah snarled.

'Of course – there is no question of that. I have no intention of making you suffer and we should both respect each other's situation. I just can't see what good will come out of telling Anna.'

'She might kick you out,' Dinah replied, suddenly falsely calm.

'I'm sure she would, and I daren't think what that would do to my two sons. Nor would you benefit, except from some perverted sense of revenge, because your action wouldn't bring me closer to you – quite the opposite.'

'Get out!' Dinah shrieked, 'Get out! Get out!'

Max was trembling and his legs felt weak as he lifted himself out of the chair and walked towards the door, leaving without looking back.

It was lunchtime when Max arrived home and Anna was in the kitchen.

'I've made Spaghetti Bolognese – would you like some?' Barney was sitting at the table twisting a single strand of spaghetti onto a fork and neatly putting it into his mouth.

'I couldn't eat a thing, I'm sorry. I must go and lie down.'

Anna looked at his pale tense face. She didn't want to comment but thought he might have been crying.

'Can I bring you up a cup of tea?'

'Thanks Anna.'

Max closed the curtains and lying in the darkened room saw his life unravel. Dinah, who for six years had been nothing but reliable and supportive, had turned out to be a bully. He should have recognised this from his experience at school. How the bully at first seemed friendly then teased his victim, then struck. Max realised that he had always been slightly wary of Dinah. Her contrived caring had merely been a ruse to seduce him. He couldn't think of how to tell Anna, especially with Barney's interview hanging over them. But he knew he had to tell her because Dinah might decide on a whim to destroy him.

Anna came into the room, 'I gather it didn't go too well.'

'You gather right! She wants and is entitled to severance pay and I'll speak to our accountant.'

'So, that doesn't seem too complicated', Anna reassured Max.

'It's her anger, she's a bitter woman. I'm amazed I didn't notice before.'

'I think when woman reach forty they become broody. They see their life slipping away. Her job was her life and she's bound to have a reaction. She'll find another job and will settle down again. I'm more concerned about how this is affecting you.'

Anna's decency floored him. 'I'll be all right. I haven't been feeling well lately, maybe I caught some bug in India. I'll come down later.' Anna left and turning away from the door he broke down and cried.

35

Barney's Real Interview – June 1992

The day of the interview arrived. Anna had Barney's brand new shirt unwrapped on the chair in his bedroom. She had tossed and turned all night worrying about how he would cope with the interview and whether she could trust Max not to upset him. She was preparing breakfast in the kitchen when she heard Barney screaming. 'No! No! No! I don't like new shirts, I don't like new trousers.'

Anna rushed upstairs. Barney had thrown his new clothes in the waste paper basket. 'It's OK, Barney. I'm taking them away. I just thought you wanted to look smart for your interview.'

'I don't like the smell, the new smell,' Barney protested.

Anna rummaged through his cupboard and handed him an old pair of jeans, a T-shirt and a sweater. She worried that Barney had grown out of the jeans and they would be too short but she couldn't risk another tantrum. She also needed to protect Max, who still seemed unsettled.

Barney did indeed look odd in trousers that stopped short at the top of his ankles. Barely hiding her anxiety, she said goodbye to him and Max and then phoned Madellaine to tell her about the disastrous morning. She was surprised when Madellaine laughed.

'It's hilarious; the teachers know what they're looking for and anyway there is nothing you can do now. So relax, or you'll be sending a telepathic panic message to Barney.'

'You're right. Barney is what he is and I can't change him even for an interview.'

'Pop round for a coffee; it'll help the time pass,' Madellaine suggested.

'Would you come round here? I don't want to leave the house in case Max phones.'

Max found parking round the corner from the school. 'How are you feeling?' he asked Barney.

'I like tests because I'm clever, but I don't like talking to strange people,' Barney replied.

'I understand, but don't worry, they will be very kind to you. Just try to remember what I told you.'

The secretary welcomed them, took them along a long corridor to the maths department and knocked on the door.

'Come in! Good morning Barney, I'm Mr John Dutch. I've been looking forward to meeting you. Perhaps the secretary will show your father around the school while we have a chat.'

'See you soon, Barney,' said Max. He patted Barney on the shoulder and followed the secretary.

In the wood panelled room with two large Georgian windows, Barney sat opposite Mr Dutch, separated by a large desk.

'Can you tell me something about yourself, Barney?'

'Yes, sir, thank you for asking me. I have a few problems and many interests.'

'Can you tell me what you like doing?'

'I like mathematics, space travel, geography, science, drawing, reading encyclopaedias and Elvis Presley.'

'Tell me about the things you don't like.'

'It's kind of you to ask, sir. I sometimes don't like brown food, I don't like the smell of the polish in your school, I don't like being with a lot of people, I don't like new clothes. There are lots of other things but I am trying to be more sensible. My brother Oska helps me a lot and Rob who lives next door also helps me. And Molly who used to be my teacher has helped me a lot, and . . . '

Mr Dutch interrupted. 'Perhaps we should proceed to the maths tests now. Here are some papers for you to read, if you don't understand the questions, just ask me. Here is a pencil and paper. Are you ready to start?'

'Yes, sir.' Barney focused on the work and after fifteen minutes he had written down the answers and handed the papers back to Mr Dutch.

'Have you finished already?' Mr Dutch was astounded. He had given Barney a two-hour GCSE exam paper. 'Have you checked your answers, Barney?'

'I don't have to, but thank you for asking.'

Mr Dutch scrutinised Barney's almost unreadable writing and was amazed to find he hadn't made one mistake.

'Very good – but tell me, Barney, how did you work out your answers?'

'I don't know, sir. They just arrive in my head.'

'Could you write down each stage of your mathematical progression? Let's try with this question here.' Mr Dutch handed Barney a question.

Barney looked up and told him the answer.

'I see, um, thanks Barney. While we're waiting for your father, could you do a quick sketch of this room?' He handed Barney some paper and a pencil and watched him as he drew without looking up an accurate representation, in perspective, of the panelled room, without including any human figures.

Mr Dutch then phoned the secretary to tell her that Mr Elliott could return.

Max immediately thought the worst; he hadn't expected to be called back so soon.

'Ah, Mr Elliott, Barney has done well, very well. Perhaps when I retire next year he might want to apply for my post as head of mathematics!'

Max gave a nervous smile. He didn't respond well to public school humour, recalling how he had suffered as much from the sarcasm of the teachers as from the bullying of the pupils.

'I would like the headmaster to meet Barney but I'm sorry we can't arrange it for today. Could you bring Barney back at the same time next Monday?'

'Of course. Thank you for seeing us.' Max signalled to Barney, who jumped up.

'Sir, may I thank you very much indeed. I enjoyed the test and I'm sorry I couldn't tell you how I worked out the answers. Perhaps you know how the brain works and I would be very grateful if you told me.' Barney stretched out across the desk to shake his hand.

'Not today Barney, not today.' He got up and ushered them to the door.

Anna heard them come through the front door and rushed to meet them. Max made a thumbs-up sign and told her they had to go back next week.

'I'm so proud of you Barney,' Anna said.

'Can I go and watch Elvis?' Barney went into the television room while Anna ushered Max out of earshot to find out the details of what happened.

Her face melted into a warm smile. 'Oh Max, do you think we have a chance?'

'I think I've become as anxious as you. I can't be objective.' But Max knew his disquiet came from another source.

'Max, I've been thinking, why don't we see if we can employ Dinah part-time, say three mornings a week? She could take away some of your load and you would be freer to visit our buyers. She could work from her home, and you have to admit she does have a lot to offer.' The idea came to her like so many of her other ideas and she needed to act on it straight away.

'How does that work with severance pay?' Max needed time to think.

'Does it matter? We are doing well. When you feel better, come up and see my new designs.' Anna wanting to make Max feel better and, believing his obvious stress had something to do with Dinah, phoned her.

'Hello Dinah, it's Anna. Have I caught you at a bad moment?'

'No, it's fine.' Dinah waited.

'I want to apologise for not making contact earlier. I feel bad about your abrupt leaving after we returned from Pondicherry but we've decided on an entire change in our business plan. It was my idea that Max should work from home as Narendra is doing all the production and distribution side of things.'

'I understand,' Dinah said, not having a clue what Anna was getting at.

'Anyway, you know I'm a bit impulsive and I suggested to Max that we computerise the business. To cut a long story short, I've now changed my mind and wonder whether you would consider working part-time from home. After all, no one knows the business better than you and it isn't right that after six years you should leave without proper consideration. I just want you to know it wasn't Max's idea, and I want to put things right.'

'I very much appreciate your call. We have always got on well and I feel so much better now that you've cleared things up.'

'What a relief! I thought you would be furious with me. Perhaps you'll come over for dinner one evening?' Anna suggested.

'Thank you, I'd like that,' Dinah responded.

Anna didn't think to tell Max about her conversation with Dinah. She knew he would be pleased with her and maybe it would help him feel better. He had seemed depressed after that tiff with Dinah.

36

Rob Knows – June 1992

Anna was so excited about the possibility of Barney being accepted by the school that she phoned Madellaine immediately to tell her about the interview.

Madellaine laughed. 'He'll do it; there's something quite charming about Barney.'

'Do you really think so? Do you think he has a chance?'

'I'm sure he has. At the moment I'm more worried about Rob. You wouldn't believe the reaction he's had to Doug's news. He said if Doug came near him, he'd kill him.'

'I think it's good he's expressing his feelings. Perhaps the psychologist is helping him. By the way, I hope you haven't told Rob about our application to the school.' Anna couldn't account for why she said that and hoped she hadn't offended Madellaine.

'No, I think Rob has enough to contend with, but if Barney gets into the school we'll have to tell him.'

'I agree. I can't thank you enough for all your support,' Anna said appreciatively.

Later that day, after school, Rob rushed home.

'Mum!' he shouted. 'Guess what?' Madellaine waited. 'I saw Max and Barney in the corridor with Mr Dutch. Is Barney coming to my school?'

Madellaine couldn't tell whether he thought it a good thing or not.

'I really don't know. You'll have to ask Anna, but don't go in just yet.'

Rob dropped his school bag on the kitchen floor and ran out

before Madellaine could stop him. Anna opened the door to Rob who told her that he had seen Barney and Max at his school. 'Is Barney coming to my school?' Rob asked excitedly.

Anna told him the truth and that Barney would be going back next week to meet the headmaster.

'Promise me that you will keep it a secret and I'll promise to let you know before anybody else what happens.' Anna knew she had to include Rob and still couldn't understand why she felt conflicted about Rob's motives and his relationship with Barney. Rob felt gratified by the respect and trust Anna bestowed on him.

'I do hope Barney gets in, and you can be sure, if he does, that I'll look after him.'

Anna was moved by Rob's kindness and thought how much more she could have done for Rob by making him feel more welcome. She also felt ashamed she hadn't understood the extent of Madellaine's suffering; Rob's potential was under as much threat as Barney's. He, too, was just as much a victim of circumstances.

'Would you like to join Barney? He's in the TV room and I'll bring you in something to eat.'

'Thank you, Anna.'

After giving Rob and Barney their tea picnic-style on the floor, she went to see Madellaine and told her what Rob said.

'I swear I never said a word,' Madellaine protested.

'I know you didn't and I'm pleased it happened because I found out that Rob is such a nice person. The poor boy is quite courageous considering Doug's unwarranted and cruel rejection. I really don't blame him for saying he felt like killing Doug. I do too, on his behalf.' Anna sounded resolute.

'Thank you Anna, your words mean a lot to me. It's so easy to judge a child unfairly because once you feel they are a disappointment it becomes harder to help them. I'm so grateful to the headmaster who has taken Rob under his wing instead of kicking him out.'

Anna's only thought was that perhaps the headmaster might also give Barney a chance.

37

Max and Dinah – 1992

Max was always astonished at the way Anna seemed tuned into his thoughts. It wasn't the first time when he was thinking of Dinah that Anna would suddenly express some idea connected to her. If this was true, and he believed it to be so, he had little chance of containing the nightmare. If he didn't do something soon it was possible that Anna, in an attempt to patch up the problem with Dinah after her abrupt departure, would make contact with her. Knowing Anna, he might come home one day and find them both happily chatting over a coffee in the kitchen. Anna didn't like leaving things unsettled; she would work away at repairing unresolved situations until all parties were happy. He could see that Anna was building up to some idea: the part-time work scheme was only the beginning. He had to go and see Dinah to try to contain the situation and warn her of Anna's intentions.

When Dinah opened her front door to greet Max with a seemingly warm smile, he was quite bewildered. He followed her into the lounge and sat down.

'Guess who phoned me?'

Max shrugged his shoulders.

'Anna,' she said, pausing to see his reaction. 'I realised that you didn't know and I can tell you I had to think on my feet. Really, Max, she's such a decent person.'

Max didn't answer and Dinah relished his impatience to know what transpired. Relenting, Dinah related much of the conversation and added, 'I wouldn't mind working part-time, actually. Of course, that mustn't exclude getting my severance pay. Nor will it prevent Anna from knowing about our baby.'

Shock registered all over Max's face. 'What do you suggest?' he asked.

'I don't know. I don't want to hurt Anna but she's bound to find out, isn't she?'

'I don't think it's inevitable. It all depends on you. Of course she will eventually see that you are pregnant but why does she have to connect it to me? If I could rely on you never to declare who the father is, it would work to all our benefit,' Max pleaded. According to his calculations, which he had gone over many times, he doubted that Dinah's baby was his, nevertheless he was guilty of the one night seduction, and if Anna knew it would destroy the family

'What have I got to gain?' Dinah challenged Max.

'You would have a baby which I don't believe is ours.'

'What if the baby turned out to be the image of you?'

'We would have to face that when the time comes. I can't think beyond what I've proposed that Anna must never know. In fact I can't think much about anything these days and Anna has noticed that.'

In a fleeting moment of sympathy, Dinah relented. 'OK, let's leave it like that for the moment.'

'Thank you! I need time to think and can't when I'm under so much pressure.' Max could barely get out the words. He felt Dinah was punishing him, and yet he couldn't be sure. He knew he was at her mercy and she was relishing his weakness. It was as if he was back at school and being bullied. He recalled when he had plucked up enough courage to tell his mother how unhappy he was in the playground. She had been so kind: 'Max, darling, in every bully there is a very big coward hiding inside, and the more you let them bully you, the more they can hide the coward. You have to fight back and you can be sure both the bully and the coward will run away.' He had tried that. But the bully did not run away and he had got beaten up badly. It's odd that he thought of it now.

Max thanked her and left. In his car he felt an overwhelming desire to drive away, to escape. He couldn't go home, he was feeling so contaminated and confused. Driving aimlessly around, he found himself by Regent's Park and an empty parking space appeared by the Rose Garden gate. He sat on a bench under a canopy of climbing white roses, breathing in their delicate scent. If she was capable of being ruthless enough to threaten him and blackmail him once, she could do it time and time again and again. How could he trust her? The thought that those few minutes of folly could destroy his life was agony, especially as he couldn't actually recall how it happened. He tried to understand what had led up to his downfall. He had never needed another woman. Perhaps if he could understand what had taken place on that evening, how he had been seduced into the meaningless liaison, he could in time explain it to Anna.

It had happened at the time when intimacy had disappeared from their marriage. It seemed as though Barney was sleeping in-between them. Anna was distant and preoccupied. But that was no excuse and they had gone through similar periods before. He knew above all, that Anna was guided by trust and loyalty.

He had taken Dinah out for a coffee after work to explore any ideas to boost the business. She adopted what seemed to be a natural and companionable manner, putting her hand on his arm. He had seen this as caring. Her suggestions about selling the business while Anna's name was so respected in fashion seemed a good idea. He was grateful for her advice, and it seemed she had quite a head for business. When she'd talked about her unhappy childhood and how she had hated her father, he should have been alerted to her need to win, for the implication was that she had been victorious and in the end her father had left her sufficient funds to enable her to purchase her elegant apartment. Max thought her lack of gratitude odd but then he knew only part of the story. He recalled feeling some sympathy for her lonely life and had offered to drive her home. She asked him up to see her apartment and, wanting to show interest and praise for her good taste, had accepted the invitation.

Now he realised he had been duped. She had offered him a size-able drink in the lounge, and offered to show him around the other spacious, high-ceilinged rooms. He had duly admired the mod-ernised kitchen, the state-of-the-art bathroom and all the furnishings and fabrics straight out of designer magazines. He followed her into her bedroom and was pretending to admire the fashionable fabrics when she suddenly turned round and burst into tears.

'I have all this and I'm so lonely. I envy you and Anna, I even envy you having a child like Barney. Anna's commitment to Barney makes her complete. Barney will always need her. I haven't got any-thing.' She stood close to Max, who was aware of her need for comfort. As she cried, he put his arm around her. Her perfume was exotic. Now as she snuggled up against him, he heard her say, 'Oh Max, you're so kind and good. I've always loved you.' He remem-bered thinking 'What am I doing?' as she put his hand to her breast. One action led to another and within minutes he had succumbed.

Dinah was the first to get off the bed while he was still half asleep. She came back into the room dressed in a pink silk dressing gown holding a silver tray. 'Would you like some coffee?'

'Thanks,' he said, adding, 'I must rush.' He leapt out of bed, dressed and sitting on one of the chairs in the lounge, drank his coffee.

'This never happened,' he said, filled with remorse.

'Don't be such a prude,' she teased.

'I can think of many other words, but prude isn't one of them,' Max responded determined to extricate himself. He drank the coffee and said he would see her at work tomorrow.

Like many women whose biological clock was beginning to tick faster, it seemed to him that Dinah craved a child and he had been duped into possibly providing one. This could be the only explana-tion for his stupidity, because he had no feelings for her; he hadn't even enjoyed their intimacy, which had been a coupling that was anything but intimate. He argued with himself that it was one of those thoughtless acts of kindness where no good deed goes un-punished. She may get what she wanted: a baby. If anything, she owed him a debt of gratitude. But why him? There were many men around more available than him. Why was she pretending that there was more to it, and why was she emotionally and financially blackmailing him? He could only think that she had some mad fantasy of playing happy families.

He decided to wait until she'd calmed down and then he would confront her and get her to agree to just forget about the whole thing. He felt a sense of relief, having cleared up, in his mind at least, the way it had all happened. However, he couldn't explain even to himself why he had participated. This was far from the first time in the fashion business he had been propositioned by younger, beautiful women. Why now, after all these years, had he succumbed and cheated on Anna? He recalled Dinah's power, there was a moment when he knew what was happening and yet rather than reject her in her distress it seemed easier, kinder even, to go along with it, although he had no feelings for her. He had no way of explaining his aberration to Anna and the more he looked into himself the more he knew that it was all wrong. And that made him feel worse.

Dinah's apparent sudden change of heart did not put an end to Max's fear of losing Anna. He thought of Anna's creativity, her artistic talent and her need to explore and be in tune with her world. He also understood how Anna was fascinated by Barney's unique personality, whereas he became easily irritated and bored by his son's repetitious behaviour. Anna's imagination enabled her to gain insight into Barney's bizarre thoughts and to find a nugget of gold.

He paced round the Rose Garden, then, with a heavy heart, he made his way back to his car, knowing that Anna would be worrying where he was. He still hadn't worked out a way to tell her about his stupidity without destroying her love.

38

Anna's New Collection – 1992

'Where have you been?' Anna asked with concern.

'I needed some fresh air so I stopped off at the Rose Garden in Regent's Park.'

'How did it go with Dinah?'

'Oh that . . . Yes, she agreed to work part-time but still insists on her severance pay.'

'I think that's fair enough. Do you feel up to coming upstairs? I want to show you my new collection.'

'That sounds interesting.' Max followed Anna up into her studio. Her sketch-book with the new designs beautifully illustrated and delicately painted in watercolour depicted mix-and-match combinations of the plain and floral silks made up into long tunics, trousers, wrap-around skirts and long scarves, creating shapes with flowing long lines.

'The collection is called "Any Age". What do you think?'

'I think it walks and talks. I love the concept of any age, any time – and any size.' Max sounded enthusiastic.

'That's why I suggested we needed Dinah. There's so much paperwork to be done and you'll be liberated to do more selling.'

'Anna, it's a brilliant concept and I'm ready to start work tomorrow,' Max said convincingly.

'Not tomorrow,' Anna said with a lilt in her voice. Max looked at her. 'Surely you haven't forgotten; you have to take Barney to his second interview. You are his lucky charm. He feels safe with you, we all do. I don't know what it is but you inspire confidence. I might be the creative partner but I can assure you I would be nothing without you. You're like Barney's Hoorah Hippo to me!'

'I think I'd better call Barney for another rehearsal, although he seems to have got the hang of it now.'

Max sat in his study, he thought of Anna's enthusiasm for the new collection, her anxiety about Barney's interview and the restructuring of the business. It was hardly the time to talk.

Barney knocked on the door. 'Come in,' Max called.

'Good afternoon, headmaster.' Barney put out his arm to shake hands.

'Very good Barney, that makes a good first impression,' Max encouraged. 'Do you have any friends, Barney?'

'Oh yes, sir. I have Rob, who lives next door. He is also a student at your school and is very kind to me. I also have Hoorah Hippo who isn't really a person but I regard him as a friend because he helps me whenever I feel anxious. I left him in the car because my father said it isn't appropriate for a thirteen-year-old boy to bring him to an interview.'

'What do you do when Rob comes to visit you?'

'We talk about Elvis or maps of England. Sometimes Rob tells me about how unhappy his mother is because his father went away with her best friend. He hates his father for making his mother so unhappy and one day when he is big enough he will tell him.'

'Why would you like to come to this school?' Max asked.

'I would like to come to your school so that I can learn more. I like books and I am very intelligent and want to be a scientist one day.'

'Is there anything that worries you about coming to such a big school?'

'Oh yes, sir. I will have to have a lot of courage because I don't like crowds, I'm different to other boys and I'm worried they won't like me. They may call me names and say things like "Hi, Mental". I don't know what they mean sometimes. If they leave me alone, I will be all right because I can read my books and Rob says that he will look after me.'

Max felt tears welling in his eyes. He had never even thought

about how Barney felt and understood now why Anna had protected him so fiercely. Even Oska had more insight than him. Max
was as humbled by Barney's innocence as he was ashamed of his
own insensitivity. These mock interviews had shamed Max, for they
showed Barney had more courage than he had himself. How could
he have been so irritated with his son?

'Thank you very much, Barney, I appreciate you being so honest
with me.'

Barney got up and stretched out his arm. 'Thank you very much,
sir, it has been a pleasure to talk to you.'

Alone in the study Max broke down. Barney might be autistic
but he wasn't cruel, he wasn't a drug addict or a bully. He was just
Barney – and Max couldn't understand why he had found it so
difficult to value him.

39

Another Practice Interview

Anna managed to give Barney's new clothes a double wash to ensure that there was no trace of their new smell. 'Hurry up, Barney,' she said as she came into his bedroom to find him sniffing every surface of his clothes, including his socks. She knew better than to mention that everything was fine because that would spark off a series of questions as to when they were washed, who had touched them and why were they on his bed instead of being on the top shelf in his cupboard.

'I'll be downstairs. Max and Oska are having breakfast,' she said, as a way of motivating him to move. Barney could take an hour to dress, going through his latest ritual, or he might suddenly decide to study a map and work out the distances from one country to another.

'You look worried,' she said to Max, who seemed a little withdrawn.

'No, just thinking,' he replied.

'Wouldn't it be great if Barney gets into Hillfield? Then I could tell everybody how clever he is and they would have to believe me. They say they can't visit me because we have a no-brain living in our attic,' Oska told them.

'Which boys say that?' Anna fumed.

'Oh, not all the time, just when they want to tease me, usually in the playground. I don't mind because I love Barney,' Oska said.

'Should we complain to the head?' Anna asked Max.

'I think it might do more harm than good. I think bullying is part of the school culture. Believe me, I know!'

They heard Barney thumping down the stairs; he seemed to be so heavy on his feet. 'I think Barney has your flat feet, Max,' Anna remarked.

'I think he's a replica of dad,' Oska added.

'Well, Barney, how do you feel about the interview?' Max asked, wanting to change the subject.

'I think I shall do very well because you have been very kind and helped me. Even though it was a pretend interview, it wasn't exactly a lie because we both knew it was a pretend interview. It's only a lie when one person doesn't know the truth,' Barney stated.

'How did dad help you?' Oska asked.

'When we finished the pretend interview, Max reminded me to shake hands and look straight into the headmaster's eyes and not look away when I'm spoken to. I must not interrupt the headmaster, I must address him as sir and I can't take Hoorah Hippo into the interview.'

'Have you got a clean handkerchief?' Oska asked.

Barney checked his trouser pocket. 'I even have a spare pen and pencil in case I need to write a story, and Rob says that Dr Jarvis is a very nice man who talks straight. That means he doesn't talk in circles, which means he keeps on saying the thing over and over like a record going round and round.'

When they left Anna poured herself a cup of coffee and went into the lounge. The conversation at breakfast had unnerved her. Barney was definitely odd, whatever the diagnosis. She would never get used to his way of looking at the world and only hoped that he didn't appear too unconventional in the interview.

The phone rang and she recognised Dinah's voice.

'How's the new collection going?' Dinah asked.

'It's really turned out much better than I expected. Would you like to come over and see it?'

'Very much. When is a good time?'

'Well, if it's not too much of a rush, this morning would be good because Max has taken Barney for his second interview and we are all crossing our fingers. I don't know what I would have done without Max, he seems so calm and is much better with Barney than me.'

'I'll be round in about an hour and I'm also keeping my fingers crossed. He's a great kid and deserves to get in,' Dinah said.

'Thanks Dinah, I really appreciate your support. See you soon.' Anna put the phone down.

Barney was taken into the headmaster's room while Max was invited to sit in the library and have a coffee.

'Good morning Barney, I've heard a lot about you,' said Dr Jarvis, shaking Barney's hand.

'Good morning, sir, and I've heard a lot about you.'

'Have you now?'

'Oh yes, Rob told me that you are a real gentleman, fair, strict and kind and I appreciate straight talking.'

Dr Jarvis, quite captivated by Barney, suppressed a smile. 'Why would you like to come to this school Barney?'

'To learn more, sir. I love to learn about facts and I noticed you have a large library. I wouldn't be any bother if I could sit and read many of your books.'

'What facts interest you?'

'I'm interested in the universe, I know all the planets and stars, I'm interested in space travel although I wouldn't like to be an astronaut because I would need to work in a team and I don't think I could do that.'

'Why not?' The headmaster found himself drawn into Barney's conversation without realising it.

'Well, you see even if I have enough knowledge about the universe, I don't like small spaces and I wouldn't like being confined in a rocket. I suppose I could work as a space scientist because I like physics and mathematics.'

'I see . . . I believe you also like drawing.'

'Oh yes, sir. Would you like me to draw a map of outer space with a rocket, or perhaps this room?' Barney took out his pencil from his inside pocket. 'Please may I have some paper, sir?'

The headmaster handed him a piece of paper and watched

Barney draw the interior of his room with speed and precision. He had forgotten the questions he had in mind to ask Barney. Impressed by the maths teacher's report, and now by Barney's conversation, he decided the boy wouldn't be any trouble and might make an interesting contribution to the school and its academic results. He also thought of Rob, and felt that looking after Barney would give Rob a role and increase his self-esteem.

'This is very good, Barney.' The headmaster studied the detailed drawing. 'What else are you interested in?'

'History, sir. I know all the kings and queens of England and the dates and names of battles, although I don't understand why people should fight and kill each other so I suppose I wouldn't make a good historian.'

'Thank you for coming to see me. The secretary will take you to the library while I talk to your father.'

'Thank you very much for spending time with me, sir.' Barney got up to shake his hand.

The secretary came in to take Barney to the library and also brought Max to see Dr Jarvis.

'Good morning, Mr Elliott, please sit down. I found Barney a courageous young man. I imagine it can't be easy for you and Mrs Elliott to deal with him, but I must say you've done a splendid job.'

'It's not what I expected in a son but Barney has proved to be quite marvellous in many ways,' Max heard himself say.

'I can tell you, we have far worse boys here than Barney and I can't even give them a label as an excuse.' Dr Jarvis smiled. 'I am going to offer Barney a place, Mr Elliott. He is obviously extremely intelligent but we both know the problems and we'll have to see how we all cope. We've never had a lad like Barney before and I'm sure you too feel concerned. I think the fact that he knows and trusts Rob might help him integrate into our system. In some ways it may also help Rob, but that's not why I'm offering Barney a place.'

Max could hardly believe it; he thought of what it would do for

Anna and Oska. 'I deeply appreciate your offer and we'll do all we can to support Barney and your school.'

'The secretary will give you all the information and if you fill in the application form and return it as soon as possible, Barney can join the school next term. I will also write to you with the curriculum, so that you can spend the next month preparing him.' The headmaster stood up. 'Perhaps we should go and find Barney.'

40

Anna's Confusion – 1992

When Max arrived home, he was shocked to see Anna and Dinah sitting in the kitchen drinking coffee. Anna leapt up. 'How did it go?'

'Good. We'll talk later. Excuse me – I must go upstairs,' he said, without greeting Dinah.

Anna was surprised and embarrassed by his obvious rudeness in snubbing Dinah. She asked Barney how it went.

'Dad said I did well and now I'm very hungry, if you don't mind.'

'I'd better be going.' Dinah got up while Anna rushed around the kitchen making a sandwich for Barney.

'Thank you so much for coming, Dinah. I really like your idea about the buttons, we'll talk soon. Sorry about the rush but I have to put on my domestic goddess hat!' Anna smiled.

While Barney tucked into his sandwich, Anna ran upstairs to see Max.

'What the hell is going on? Why did you ignore Dinah?'

'I was just surprised to see her here.'

'I had no idea that Dinah wasn't welcome. I think she's being very helpful and we enjoy each other's company. We spend most of the time discussing the business so I can't see what your problem is.' Anna could see that Max's mind was on other things.

'I've had quite a morning with Barney, and although it's turned out better than we could have hoped, there's still a lot to think about.' He watched Anna's face melt into sheer joy as he told her the good news.

'You looked so down when you came in I thought the worst,' Anna said, smiling.

'I suppose I wanted to rush in and share it with you and felt irritated when you weren't alone.'

'I think Dinah got the message, she shot off immediately. When I think about it, she is phoning more often these days. I thought you wanted me to encourage it after her hasty resignation and I assumed she wanted to come back; she as good as said so. But let's forget about her. I want to know everything that happened at Hillside this morning. I can't believe it! Max, you've been wonderful with Barney, he has really improved since your coaching – even Bridget notices it.'

Max handed her the envelope with the application form. 'Did you see the school fees?' he remarked.

'Oh Max, who cares? It's only money and we'll just have to work harder. I've had a good morning with Dinah who has some clever ideas to expand the business, so you see we're already one step ahead.'

Max was horrified that Dinah had wormed her way into their home and charmed Anna into believing she could be the dedicated help that she needed. It was all part of Dinah's hidden agenda to be near him and then to blackmail him, emotionally and financially.

'Dinah is really smart. She's bought a computer and is doing a course and says that she will soon be able to scan our designs and send them to Narendra. She's also told me that Narendra's accounts are looking healthy and the business is ready to take-off.'

'I didn't know that Narendra was sending her copies of our accounts. They are all meant to come directly to me, here.'

'I thought you knew! She said ever since you told her about all those mistakes in his spreadsheets, she thought it would be sensible to check the figures every month.'

'How come she never mentioned all this to me? She's supposed to be my PA and I don't like her taking the initiative on business decisions. Narendra could be insulted by her interference. And why didn't she discuss this with me?'

'To be honest, Max, you haven't been very accessible lately. Even I feel you've become rather preoccupied and distant, so I haven't wanted to disturb you. Maybe you are doing too much and we need Dinah's help. She's offered to work four mornings a week to help me organise the collection.'

'I thought Madellaine was helping you and was shaping up to be a real Girl Friday.'

'She is, and I certainly wouldn't want to get rid of her. Dinah's idea to computerise the business is going to take some time but in the end will save a lot of time and money.' Anna's enthusiasm couldn't be dampened.

'Well how long will all this computerising take? Wouldn't it be better to find somebody who is already computer literate?' Max was obviously resistant.

'I've thought of that but Dinah knows the business inside out and so would create a more user-friendly system for us. She's a quick learner. I think she's even prepared to work full-time again. I must say she looks terrific; she's lost quite a bit of weight and looked pretty good in tight jeans and a pale blue cashmere sweater. She also loves Barney and was so supportive to me this morning when I worried about the interview.'

'I'll go and see her and try to work out a new agreement. I don't like this vague approach. We must have a proper job description which makes it clear whether her role is full-time or part-time.' Max felt trapped between Anna's naivety and Dinah's malevolence. Anna's description of Dinah's new-found figure, confirmed his belief that she never was pregnant. She had told one lie after the other and he was so distraught that even though he had calculated the dates of their liaison, Dinah had so unnerved him that he couldn't be sure of anything. How could he have been so stupid? He thought of Barney, who only this morning had said it takes two people to agree to pretend – but only one to tell a lie. What else had he missed? He was going over to see Dinah, determined to have it out with her.

It seemed as if she was expecting his call.

'Sure, I'm in all afternoon.' Dinah sounded triumphant.

He told Anna he was going to see Dinah to discuss their arrangement, which further fuelled Anna's enthusiasm for her plan.

'Thanks, Max, I know you must be tired but the sooner we sort out Dinah's working contract the better. I'm so excited about Barney. I must go and tell Madellaine and phone Molly. We are so lucky to have good people around us. You know, at the beginning I didn't really like Dinah; I felt scared of her although she interviewed very well. It's funny it's taken me all these years to get used to her. It's as if she knows too much and is trying to hide it. I just can't explain it except that we are getting along so well now, it's fun working with her.' Anna sounded convincing.

Max was more fearful than irate. Dinah had managed to charm Anna. Anna was right, he had let things slip in the office. God knows what else Dinah was planning. He didn't believe anything she said and felt very threatened. All that talk about her father, then seeing her extravagant apartment and her lunch-time designer shopping jaunts. It just didn't make sense. How much money did her father leave her? And if that was the case, why did she have to work?

He thought about finding a private detective to have a look into her affairs, but it was too urgent. He had to act now before she did any damage. He was the target of a bully, of a blackmailer and a liar. All he knew was that he had to get rid of her. But as he rang her bell he realised he hadn't thought through how to do it . . .

Dinah opened her front door.

'That was quick! You must have driven at a hundred miles an hour.'

Max stayed standing in the hall and, suffused with anger, shouted: 'I want you to leave my family alone, leave your job and stay away for good. I don't believe you are pregnant, nor do I see your amazing new computer. What I see is a confidence trickster, a liar and a blackmailer who will be dealt with by my lawyer, who you will be hearing from.'

'What's brought all this on?' Dinah looked shocked. As he

slammed the front door she shouted after him: 'I don't think Anna will agree with you.'

Feeling weak and quivering inside, Max managed to get back to his car and sat for ten minutes to give himself a chance to calm down. He felt some relief in that he had started to take back control of the situation and knew that he had no choice but to tell Anna everything immediately.

Opening his front door he heard the sound of crying coming from the kitchen. Rushing in, he found Anna red-faced and shaking.

'I've been so stupid,' he said.

She took one look at him and cried out, 'Oh, have you? It's me who's been stupid all these years!'

'What do you mean?'

'So you've been lovers for years and you forced Dinah to have an abortion last month. That's why she resigned. She's just rung and told me everything: how you were going to leave me and go and live with her. Well, you can go now! Please leave! I can't believe you would do this to me. I want you to go.' Anna was shaking and looked on the verge of collapse.

Oska came into the room. 'What's going on?' he demanded.

'Ask your father,' she yelled.

'Please, mum, you're upsetting Barney.'

Anna ignored Oska. 'I'll take care of the boys and you can see them every Sunday. What concerns me is how Barney will take this; it may put him back and he won't be able to go to school. I hope you're satisfied.' Anna wiped her face with a wad of tissues.

'How can you believe her? She's a pathological liar!'

'Get out! Please leave before I do something terrible.'

'What about the boys? They need me,' Max pleaded.

'Don't pretend to be concerned, just get out! Pack your things and go!' Anna screamed. 'Go! Go! Go!'

Max had never seen Anna in such a state and was scared that she might have a heart attack or a stroke. He had heard of shock causing such things and had to stop her getting more upset.

Running upstairs he packed a few things in a holdall and rushed down again.

'I'll see you on Sunday, Barney. It'll be all right, Oska,' he shouted out before shutting the front door, knowing an explanation would only add fuel to the fire. He had to get out, to do whatever Anna wanted. His presence was only causing her unbearable hurt.

He drove round the streets of London for hours, relieved whenever he found himself in a traffic jam for it gave him moments to think. When the car moved his mind went blank. His body felt like a dead weight and he wondered if he would be able to stand or walk. He wished he could cry to release the tension in his chest and stomach but it was as if a slow paralysis was enveloping him. Later that evening, while waiting at the traffic lights in Russell Square, he saw a sign saying 'Bed & Breakfast'. He parked and, leaving his holdall in the car, rang the bell. A pleasant woman of about seventy opened the door and in a well-spoken voice invited him in. The hall was spotless and welcoming.

'Yes, we do have one double on the second floor,' she said, in answer to his enquiry. 'How long do you intend staying?'

'I don't know, but could I book in for two weeks?'

She seemed to recognise Max's state of shock: it probably wasn't the first time that her home had become a refuge for one half of a marriage break-up.

'Stay as long as necessary. A cooked breakfast is served downstairs in the dining room between seven and nine. We only have four other guests here so you'll find it very quiet. There are no rules, except I don't allow any uninvited guests.'

'I understand,' Max said.

The room was quite pleasant, and Max thought he was lucky to find such a relaxing place to stay. He noticed a kettle and tea bags on a tray in the alcove but was too tired to get up, or even take off his shoes as he waited for sleep to rescue him.

It was two days before Anna realised what she had done. Barney kept on saying, 'I need Max to help me prepare for Hillside.

Where's he gone?' Barney had also gone back to needing his food cut up in little bits. Oska in the middle of his A-level exams, was clearly affected by the added stress. She had told him the whole story and he'd reacted by becoming even more of a second father to Barney.

'I just don't believe it!' Oska had said emphatically. 'And in any case, I think you are being a little hasty. Barney's behaviour has obviously regressed. He won't even let me into his room or come down to the kitchen. He says he needs to talk to Rob because he knows about fathers who leave. He also said that Rob's father went away by himself but you made dad leave, and I can't explain it to him, nor do I understand it myself.'

Anna recalled what Madellaine had once said when she questioned her about contacting Doug; that when it came to your child, there is no such thing as pride.

Impulsively, she phoned Dinah. 'May I speak to Max?'

'What makes you think he's here?' Dinah replied, knowing the havoc she'd caused.

'Where is he?' Anna demanded.

'I have no idea, nor do I care,' replied Dinah, and banged down the phone.

'Well, if he was so involved with Dinah, wouldn't he have gone there?' Oska reasoned.

Anna couldn't answer but it was obvious she had caused irreparable damage to the family. The thought of not knowing where Max was living created a more frightening anxiety. What if she needed him? She had always felt safe because she'd always known where to get hold of him, but now for the first time she was totally alone.

She and Oska were having lunch downstairs, but they couldn't get Barney to come and join them. Anna was preparing a tray for Barney, which Oska was going to take upstairs, when suddenly they heard thumping and banging coming from Barney's room. They both rushed upstairs and pushed hard to open the door, which had been barricaded with a desk and a chair. Barney was on the floor, jerking and shaking. The convulsions soon subsided as his breathing quieted and he fell into a deep sleep. Anna saw he had wet himself. This was the first time he had had an epileptic fit. Oska screamed at Anna.

'You see what you've done?' Tears were streaming down his face.

'Should I call an ambulance?' Anna was sobbing as she examined Barney's head.

'I think he'll be all right. There's a guy in my class that has fits regularly and unless he's hurt, he recovers by himself,' Oska told her, calming down a bit.

'I'm phoning the doctor. Please stay with him.' Anna tried to control herself in the face of Oska's fury.

She came back to say that the doctor would be round soon and that they mustn't move Barney. She didn't tell Oska that the doctor had initially wanted her to call an ambulance but she had refused, as she didn't want to subject Barney to a strange place or have to deal with the hectic goings on in Accident and Emergency.

Anna and Oska rapidly tidied the bedroom, placing the desk and chair in their usual position by the window.

'Look at this!' Oska picked up a sheet of paper that had fallen from the desk and handed it to her without saying anything. She could hardly read Barney's scribble.

BARNEY NEEDS ELVIS
JINGLES JUMP IN MY MIND,
A HUBBUB TO BLUNT THE BUZZ OF BLUES,
ELVIS IS MY ROCK MY SOUL,
ROLLING IN HIS BLUE SUEDE SHOES,
I HEAR A TUNE ON THE WING,
A CHORD TO MAKE ANGELS SING,
MY SKIN TINGLES, TAUT AS A GUITAR,
AT NIGHT MY TAPE STAYS, BETWEEN CHEEK AND PILLOW,
A HARD AND SOFT SENSATION,
WAITING FOR MY MOTHER,

RUB-A-DUB INTO ETERNITY,
LUB-A-DUB I CAN TRACK IT BACK,
LYING ON YOUR BREAST, OUR HEARTS IN FUSION,
AGAINST YOUR SILKY SKIN, MY CHEEK WOULD REST,
DRINKING FROM YOUR VELVET CUSHION,
WHEN DID I BUILD THE WALL?
TIME SLIPPED BY, REPEAT, REWIND,
WILL YOU FIND ME? WILL YOU CALL?
STOP THE REVOLUTION IN MY MIND.

'He must have written it just before he had the fit,' Oska guessed.

Tears rolled down Anna's cheeks. 'I don't think we can ever know what goes on in his mind, nor his suffering.'

'I think it's a damn good poem,' Oska said, trying to lighten Anna's mood.

It was crystal clear to her that she had caused irreparable damage to Barney and, even if everything Dinah said was true, which she now doubted, forcing Max to leave had been a critical mistake. If she'd known where he was staying, she would have gone to see him.

When Barney woke up, Anna helped him wash and change. The doctor arrived and after examining Barney said he couldn't find any thing wrong but advised that Barney see a neurologist. He gave Anna a prescription for a sedative to be taken every morning. Barney seemed less hungry than usual and Anna was further worried when he left most of his food on the plate.

'Would you like to come downstairs and watch an Elvis film?' Anna asked.

'No, because last time I was watching my Elvis film you shouted at Dad and told him to leave. It's got something to do with that.'

'What would you like to do?' Anna asked.

'I would like Rob to come over and stay with me in my room.'

'I'll go and see if he's at home,' Oska offered.

41

Anna's Dilemma – May 1992

Consumed with guilt, Anna was desperate to find Max. She had to know the truth, her inability to resolve matters just added to her conflict and stress. Overtaken with anxiety, she had no choice but to telephone Dinah again.

'Dinah, are you sure you don't know where Max is? There's been an emergency with Barney and I need to get hold of him.'

'I told you, I have no idea.' Dinah sounded flat and disinterested.

'I need to know whether everything you told me is true.'

'Anna, you can believe what you like, but please leave me alone,' Dinah said, putting down the phone.

Two days had gone by and Anna hadn't heard from Max. Barney still wouldn't come downstairs. Still shocked and ashamed at the breakdown of her family, Anna phoned Madellaine and asked her to come over. Madellaine sat and listened to everything that Anna told her about Dinah and Max.

'First of all, Anna, if you and Max have such a good marriage you would know whether he was having an affair or not. And even if he was, which sounds unlikely to me, it's possible that you've over-reacted. I can tell you, there are many marriages with the odd blip but couples move on, often for the better. I'm no expert but I always thought your marriage was unbreakable. Why do you think you reacted so violently?'

'I think I've been so tense about Barney getting into Hillside and when Max came home and told me the good news I thought that finally everything was going to be OK. Then two hours later Dinah phones me with that incredible story. Everything, my faith and trust in Max, my whole life, was taken away from me. One minute I was in heaven and the next in hell. I couldn't look at Max and didn't want him near me. I just wanted to get shot of him.'

Perhaps because of, or despite, her own experience, Madellaine understood how Anna's response had been both so natural and yet so hasty.

'But didn't you think of letting Max give you his side of the story before kicking him out, with the children hearing every word?'

'I didn't think. I've just always believed in love and loyalty and honesty.'

'Life isn't a fairytale where everything white is good and everything black is bad. You have to be pragmatic. I really am surprised at you. You seem so insightful yet you couldn't see further than some dreamlike ideal when the reality of life is adaptation and compromise. I told you I didn't kick Doug out. He left, but if he had come back and explained himself I would have taken him back for Rob's sake. I even wish we could just be friends.'

'Oh Madellaine, I feel so ashamed! I've behaved like some prissy idiot and I don't know how to repair it.'

'Well, I can tell you! Rob has been telling me some of the odd things that Barney is saying. Barney asked Rob how to make you happy, because even though you told Max to leave, if you really wanted him to go you would be happy now but he hears you cry every night. He asked Rob if he would help him find Max.'

'What did Rob say?'

'Rob laughed and said he had enough trouble with his own father and one day he would look him straight in the eye and tell him that he had ruined his life. Barney said that Max hadn't ruined his life as he had helped him get into Hillside and he didn't understand how he had ruined your life. He knows it has something to do with Dinah and he often told you that he didn't like Dinah even though she kept on buying him presents.'

Anna sobbed, 'Oh! How we hurt our children without even

knowing. But I certainly know what I've done and God knows if they will ever forgive me.'

'Will you forgive Max?' Madellaine asked.

'In principle,' Anna replied.

'And what principle is that?'

'That nothing is perfect. And I've been very stupid always trying to make everything perfect. That's how I trained myself at work: the inside of every garment should be as good as the outside. But no relationship can be perfect.'

'Well, that sounds like a good enough start,' Madellaine said gently, putting her arm round the stricken Anna.

42

Max Fights Back – June 1992

Mrs McCloughlan, Max's landlady, served his breakfast just the way he liked it. He was the last to come down to breakfast and was pleased to be alone. Mrs McCloughlan reminded him of his mother, a valiant woman who had struggled with arthritis for years and never complained.

'Your breakfasts are excellent,' Max said, enjoying her homemade marmalade.

'Thank you. Not many of my guests appreciate the difference between bought and homemade. I haven't always been a landlady. When my husband died he hadn't sorted out our financial affairs, but fortunately by then the children had all left home, so I converted my home into a bed and breakfast. It's not so different from looking after my four children.'

'It's very well run and I certainly appreciate being here,' Max told her.

'Life never works out the way you expect it, but pride isn't an option when something terrible happens. You just have to go out and fix it the best way you can.' Mrs McCloughlan spoke from the heart.

Her words resonated with Max. He had been wallowing in self-pity, but Mrs McCloughlan's simple statement had shown him what had to be done if he was ever to be free. He rushed up to his bedroom to phone his solicitor and made an appointment for eleven that morning.

Charles Devon, his solicitor, was a man of about sixty, rather chubby with a kindly expression and two large dimples in his

213

cheeks, which gave the impression he wasn't taking one seriously but concealed a sharp analytical mind. Max spoke quietly and succinctly while Charles made notes. Having clarified some points, he reviewed his notes, sat thinking for a moment or two then spoke briefly and to the point.

'I think we need a pincer movement here. Firstly I know a good detective who can look into Dinah Deedes' background. Seduction followed by blackmail is often part of a history of other transgressions. Secondly, we need to send her a letter by hand informing her that we will be seeking an injunction at the High Court ordering her not to make contact by any means, with you, your family, friends and business associates and neighbours, or any other person connected to you in any way. If in the meantime the lady tries to make contact, you must not respond in any way at all. Under no circumstances should Anna have any contact with Dinah and you must also ensure your children reject any approaches from her.'

'Charles, it's such a relief to be able to share this with you. I've been an absolute idiot and I shouldn't have waited until things got so out of hand.'

'It's quite understandable, Max. Look, my advice is that we put your indiscretion to one side. It's her word against yours. You never loved her, and nothing meaningful has happened. My hunch is that she has probably done this sort of thing before and will scarper after our letter. As to your business, I suggest you have your auditors in to check that nothing untoward has occurred. I know she walked out on you but you still may be liable to pay her a statutory minimum amount and after your auditors have checked out the books and found all is in order, I'll attend to all that. We'll probably find something incriminating in the investigation, which may put things into perspective for Anna.

'Max, I've known you and Anna for years. You have too much love and respect for each other to let one silly blip blow it all to smithereens. If there is one thing that gets me going, it's a destructive woman undermining a vulnerable family.'

Charles Devon stood up and they shook hands. 'I'll get the

affidavits drafted. You'll have to come in to sign them and I'll send you copies of all my correspondence. Please let me know if anything, however seemingly insignificant, crops up.'

Max, profoundly relieved, thanked him profusely, then left. He drove back to his room by Russell Square to phone home. As soon as he heard Anna's voice he said, 'I'll be home to pick up Barney at eleven on Sunday,' and put the phone down, even though he heard Anna shout 'Max! Where are you?'

He felt angry. It served her right after the way she had believed everything Dinah had told her and had thrown him out of their home without giving him a chance to reply. In his despair, he had wanted to die, to escape from the nightmare that he had so stupidly caused. Nor did he know how to deal either with her obstinate blindness or his own and Oska's sacrifice any longer. She refused to talk about Barney's future and what would happen to him when they died. Did she expect Oska to look after him? Even though Barney seemed highly intelligent, he couldn't fit into the real world. It would take a saint like Dr Jarvis to give him a chance. Max remembered he hadn't yet filled in the application form for Hillside. In overprotecting Barney at home Anna had failed to prepare him for the real world. Barney would just have to have one or two tantrums to lose his place at Hillside. They had made a rod for their own backs but she couldn't see it.

He thought of the silences and tension between them – recalling an argument not long after Barney was diagnosed with autism and Anna had wanted another child. He had been absolutely against it. Probably the news that Dinah was pregnant with his baby and that he had forced her to have an abortion had pushed Anna over the edge.

Bombarded and flooded with all these thoughts, he felt exploited. It was as if for Anna and Barney to survive, he and Oska had had to be the sponge to absorb Anna and Barney's excessive feelings. He hadn't had a moment to consider himself and when Dinah was so attentive, perhaps it was his deep frustration that had led to his terrible mistake. That's all it was: an aberration, a bid to break out

215

of the strait jacket that he had worn ever since Barney had taken over the household and controlled all their behaviour. He had not been allowed to breathe without deferring to the hundreds of rules that Barney imposed. Year by year he had felt more restricted. It wasn't in his nature to live an increasingly narrow life. The whole household was living under a dictatorship from which there was no escape. Perhaps, too, Anna's breakdown was also the result of Barney's oppressive tyranny adding to what she thought to be Max's betrayal of all they believed in having an affair.

Whilst he could understand Anna's turmoil, he couldn't forgive her for upsetting the boys. It was Anna more than he who had broken every principle by which they had lived; each one of them had given up enough of their own needs to accommodate Barney. Anna had destroyed that unspoken principle of individual sacrifice for the good of all. Max knew he couldn't go back to that life.

Well it would have to stop. He could no longer live as a shadow of his true self with his daily frustrations, and although these past six days away had been hell, they had also broken the spell. He had regained some perspective. He hoped that the detective would find something to support the lawyer's hunch and if he did, he would feel partly vindicated although he couldn't shake off his guilt and shame.

43

After Barney's Best Shot – June 1992

Five days later, lying in the hospital bed waiting for the nurse to dress his shoulder wound, Max tried to piece together the events before Barney shot him. He recalled resisting using his key and ringing the doorbell. His sense of foreboding was amply reinforced by Anna's cold disaffection as hardly greeting him, she shouted for Barney to come down. Then she left him alone in the hall and went into the garden. He had felt nervous, hearing Barney's heavy foot-steps, worrying how Barney would greet him. Barney seemed detached as he came down the stairs, avoiding eye contact. Max didn't notice the gun because he was used to Barney's manner of holding his arms stiffly at his side. Barney lifted his arm and shot him, then walked out to the garden. It all now seemed surreal.

Whilst desperately wanting to leave the hospital he worried how Barney and Oska would accept him. They had never before experi-enced the family in tatters. Anna, who had created all the rules, and who had practically purified the air Barney breathed had broken every one.

It was nine-thirty in the morning when Max phoned Anna.

'I've just been discharged and I want to come home but I think it would be best if the boys weren't there until we've had a chance to settle things.'

'I agree. Oska has gone to school and I'll ask Madellaine if she would take Barney out or have him at home. Fortunately Bridget isn't coming in this morning so we'll have the house to ourselves. Max, I'm so sorry.'

'Anna, we're both very bruised but we have to move on for the sake of the boys.' Max felt he was regaining his confidence and getting back in charge.

Above all he could never tell Anna the truth about his one-night stand with Dinah. It would serve no good purpose. Charles Devon wasn't just a good lawyer; he had the wisdom of a man of the world. He even managed to play down the gunshot that could incriminate Barney, but Max knew they were still not sure that Barney would be free of the consequences of shooting his father.

'I'll order a taxi, see you soon,' Max said in a hollow-sounding voice.

Anna rushed upstairs and made some effort to look good. She slipped on a long, navy dress, neatly tucked from shoulder to waist and one of the samples Max liked from her last collection, pulled her hair back in a chignon and gently applied make-up to her face to try to hide her pallor and suffering. Soon after she heard the taxi arrive, she went to open the door to see Max walking slowly and gingerly up the path. He was obviously in some discomfort.

Their mutual restraint reminded them that the pain of the last week lingered between them.

'Sit in the lounge and put your feet up, I'll bring in some coffee,' Anna suggested.

'Thanks,' Max said and meant it.

Anna, sitting opposite him, looked tired and drawn and had obviously lost weight.

'How are the boys?' Max asked, breaking the silence.

'It's been bad Max, and it's my fault. After our row, Barney had an epileptic fit. It was frightening to see him lying on the floor, his twisted face clenching his teeth, his arms flailing and legs jerking in different directions. It might have lasted less than a minute but it was so frightening. If it wasn't for Oska, I don't know what I would have done. I realise I've put too much responsibility on Oska and now he's rebelling. I can feel his anger the moment he walks into the room. As though it isn't bad enough, he has one more A-level exam to do.'

'Didn't you think of the boys when you went into that rage and ordered me out?'

'I didn't think of anything. I just felt catastrophically let down and abandoned by you, the last straw was when Dinah said that you had forced her to have an abortion. I was in shock, especially when she had been with me all morning and we had got on so well. I just can't understand people like that. I'm far too honest, I would never do anything like that, pretending to be a loving part of the family.

'Didn't it occur to you even for one second that she could be telling lies?'

'Not until Oska suggested it. I know it's no excuse but I've been so anxious about Barney's interviews, the new collection and your health. You haven't been yourself since we came back from Pondicherry and I was frightened. When Dinah was crying her heart out on the phone I was ready to believe her. Part of me must have known she was lying because I was also shocked by my own re-action. But I couldn't stop myself. It was as if some deep, pent-up feelings inside me exploded and had to come out. It's like a beautiful vase – once you break it you can't put all the pieces together again.' Anna burst into tears.

Max was distressed and felt burdened with his own guilt, but was still angry about the effect her outburst had had on the children. 'I don't think we can go back. We all feel broken in different ways.'

'Do you remember when Barney used to want to cover up the lines in his hands with Scotch tape? I used to get so impatient with him. Well now I know how he feels, I think all the tape in the world can't put our family together again,' Anna lamented.

'Let's not be so melodramatic. It's up to us. We're the adults here and we have to make some hard decisions.'

'Like what?' she asked nervously. 'Last night I woke up to the sound of a gunshot – I can't recall the dream, only my anxiety about Barney being locked up somewhere.'

'I don't think that Barney will cope at Hillside, and now that this has happened, God knows how he'll be assessed.'

Anna interrupted Max. 'Surely they can't hold him responsible.'

'I don't know if a twelve-year-old is criminally responsible. Even if they decide that Barney didn't know what he was doing, which is clearly the case, he still might be subject to some sort of supervision order. I don't know.'

Anna burst into tears. 'It's all my fault.'

'Now's not the time to give up, we have a big fight on our hands. The children, our marriage and the business are all at stake, so I've hired a detective to investigate Dinah. Charles Devon suspects there is more to her than just talk.'

'Where do we start?' Anna sobbed.

'We have started – this morning. When the boys come home we'll talk to them together so that we stress unity and let Barney ask as many bizarre questions as he likes. More importantly, we'll give Oska an opportunity to be frank with us. All his goody-two-shoes behaviour isn't appropriate or healthy for him.'

'What about us?' Anna asked nervously.

'We've both been deeply hurt and I'm afraid I'm still too vulnerable to support you, and you're still too mistrusting of me – so we will have to wait. The boys come first.'

The last five days had shown her how incompetent she was without Max, and made her reflect on how she had subjected Max and Oska to her obsessive preoccupation with Barney. She felt particularly bad about Oska. 'Max, I wouldn't blame you if you wanted to leave me.'

'Why would you think that?' Max asked, his annoyance apparent at her naivety.

'Because of what I've done to you. I accused you wrongly about Dinah and didn't trust you or give you a chance to explain yourself. Poor Oska . . . in the middle of his A-levels, on the only day he had planned to go out with a friend, I called him back to look after Barney. He blames me for the shooting and he is right. God knows, he's probably right about not wanting Rob to come to the house. I'm sure he had something to do with the gun.'

Max was relieved to hear Anna's more realistic understanding of what had happened. He also wanted to avoid mentioning Dinah.

'I agree with everything you say and we can't expect things to go back to what they were. Oska is entitled to a life. Barney is entitled to having the optimum opportunity but we can't go on pretending he is some kind of genius. In many ways he is, but what use is his mind if he can only use it in a uniquely tailored environment? How long do you think he'll last at Hillside? I admit he made a startling impression but both you and I would be plagued with anxiety waiting for the day when we were told that he couldn't continue there. I don't say I have any answers but I know I felt as though Barney got into Hillside under false pretences. I am as thrilled as you that Barney was accepted but I didn't realise the extent of our vulnerability. Scratch the surface and we all collapse. Then God knows what would happen next. I want a simple life, I can't live any longer on a rollercoaster of risk, with you working all hours of the day and night to meet your collection deadlines and me trying to control a business over which Narendra, despite everything, has more and more control. Perhaps we should sell him the whole business and you should take a back seat for a while.'

'And what do we live on?' Anna asked.

'We'll have to downsize. This house is worth a great deal more than it cost and we have a small mortgage. We could live more simply, have financial security, and freedom. I don't know – I'm just tossing ideas around. All I know is something has to give, or perhaps I should say that something very fundamental has changed and we have to recognise it, otherwise there might not be a next time.' Max looked as exhausted as he felt. Anna put a cushion under his head.

'Max, have a little sleep. We'll talk later.' She kissed him on the forehead as he shut his eyes. It felt natural and reassuring, as if in that small gesture, like waving a magic wand, all their problems would melt away.

44

Barney and Oska – 1992

'Oska! Max's home, come quickly,' Barney shouted from the kitchen, as if Max might leave any minute. 'We're going to have a pretend interview with Anna and Max, and this time we're going to pretend to be the headmaster.'

Oska half-sneering, half-smiling, dropped his heavy rucksack on the kitchen floor. Anna said: 'Of course I'll speak to you separately, but we wanted you to know how Barney responds.'

'As long as we don't have to have a group hug. I'm in no mood for nursery school games.' Oska deigned to follow them up to Max's study.

'First, I want to apologise for going away and not coming back sooner.' Max looked directly at Barney.

'Anna kicked you out! Why? I'd really like to know?' Oska demanded. 'I think I'm also entitled to know, as I've been totally thrown in the middle of my exams. I don't think either of you care whether I pass or not – so why should I worry about you two?'

'Anna wanted to get shot of him,' Barney asserted.

'It was all a terrible mistake. Dinah told Anna some terrible lies about me and Anna believed her and became very angry without asking me if they were true,' Max explained.

'I was incredibly stupid and I'm very sorry that I behaved so badly and asked Max to leave. It was very wrong.' Anna tried to keep it simple but Oska wasn't having it.

'Was Dad having an affair with Dinah?'

Oska looked Max straight in the eye, demanding an answer.

Max was beginning to think this group discussion was a bad idea when Barney piped up.

'He's like Doug, only Madellaine didn't want to be shot of Doug. And Rob is very angry, just like Oska.'

'No, Oska, I am in no way involved with Dinah. Dinah is a dangerous liar and I have asked our lawyer to take out an injunction against her.'

'What's that?' Oska asked.

'It's a court order forbidding her from any contact with our family or with anybody connected to us.'

'I've never liked her,' Barney piped up.

'Nor I,' Oska agreed.

'Well, you were both right. Unfortunately Anna liked her and trusted her and didn't realise that she was a liar and a troublemaker and got very upset.'

Anna felt her face flush with embarrassment as she thought of her naivety. She could not have envisaged that anybody could be so cruel. She had trusted Dinah. She had welcomed and encouraged their friendship. She recalled how Dinah would walk into the kitchen, flop onto a chair and gasp 'You've just saved my life,' in her Yorkshire accent as she watched Anna leap to make her fresh coffee. Anna was grateful for Dinah's constant show of responsibility. That her interest in Barney was feigned went unnoticed. Her attention to every detail of the business was invaluable to Max and in helping Anna keep abreast of developments, gave purpose to their own informal get-togethers. She was totally unaware that Dinah was stalking Max and that her little treats for Oska and Barney were but another tactic to ensure her welcome into the family – and so to be near Max. Anna didn't notice the way Dinah held onto him just that second too long after a greeting kiss, especially after she had hugged and kissed the rest of the family when arriving for a birthday with her thoughtful presents.

Still, sometimes she had felt uncomfortable with Dinah. It was as if she had to placate her or compensate her and Anna often found herself less than sincerely complimenting her. The more

Anna thought about Dinah the more she felt she had been contaminated. She had allowed herself to be conned. And now more than ever she needed to shift her priorities. Oska had matured in the last few weeks. It was as if the family trauma had forced him to become more independent and perhaps less trusting. Max was right that Barney shouldn't take priority over the whole family. Her reverie was interrupted.

'What's going to happen to Barney now that he shot you and won't tell us where he got the gun?' asked Oska, hoping to get an answer in the presence of Max.

'Who gave you the gun, Barney?' Max asked.

'Is this still a pretend interview?' Barney asked.

'Yes,' Oska said, hoping that it could persuade Barney to tell the truth.

'Nobody actually gave me the gun but somebody hid it in my cupboard and told me not to touch it.'

'Who hid it in your cupboard?' Max persisted.

'Rob. I was keeping it for him for another two years until he was big enough to shoot Doug, who is a terrible man and deserves to be killed. Not like Max who is a good father and doesn't deserve to hear Anna say that she would like to be shot of him. You see, it's a good thing that I was keeping it safe because today when I was with Madellaine, Doug phoned and she said that Doug now wants to visit Rob. So I will have to tell Rob that the police have the gun.'

'Where did Rob get the gun?' Max asked.

'He told me he bought it from someone at school. You can also buy drugs or anything you want at Hillside,' Barney said, as if he was giving them advice.

'You've been very helpful, Barney. If you like, you can go and Oska can stay with me if he wishes.'

'No, thank you. I think I've had enough as well,' said Oska, storming out.

Max and Anna followed them down to the kitchen where Anna had prepared Barney's favourite foods.

'And you want Barney to go to Hillside!' Oska shouted.

'Just as well – the disaster changes everything,' Max told Anna.

'The last thing I want to do is get Rob into trouble. Madellaine told me he's doing so well now and she's been so helpful to us,' Anna whispered to Max.

'Do you want to be done for being an accessory?' Oska demanded. 'It would be fun, wouldn't it, having both of you in prison and Barney in some school for maladjusted children. Wow! I'll be the coolest kid on the block.' His nervous laugh was followed by a silence which marked the tension between them.

That evening, when Barney asked if he could watch an Elvis movie, Oska didn't volunteer to help. 'I think you can watch it by yourself, Barney, Oska is in the middle of exams and needs to rest,' Anna told him.

'I think I'll go up as well.' Max got up from the table, having hardly eaten anything.

'I'll bring you up a cup of tea when I've cleared up,' Anna offered.

'Thanks, but I just need to sleep.'

The family were hanging together by a thread. It wasn't like the calm after the storm; Anna felt everybody was still raging inside except for Barney, who now seemed more dependent than ever on his rituals of watching Elvis and only eating cut-up food. She could rely on Barney to go to bed once the film finished and left him to go upstairs. Exhausted, she climbed into bed next to Max, who was either asleep or pretending to be asleep. Either way, she felt the animosity radiating from his inert body. She turned on her side away from him, trying to control the salty tears dampening her face.

The next morning, Max was up early having a cup of coffee.

'How's your shoulder, any pain?' Anna asked.

'I'll get over it,' Max said.

Oska came running in. 'I'm late. It's physics today.'

'Have a proper breakfast, then. Anna can run you into school. I'd do it but I can't drive with my shoulder.'

'Of course I'll drive you there,' Anna said, pleased to do something positive for Oska.

'Really, I can manage, the exam doesn't start until two.' Anna caught Max's look as he shrugged his shoulders. It was obvious to them that Oska couldn't help punishing them, even if he was harming himself.

'I'll have to get a taxi to collect my things from Russell Square and pay the landlady,' Max told Anna.

'I'll drive you,' Anna replied.

'And who'll look after Barney?' he said accusingly. 'We aren't allowed to leave him alone.'

'I forgot. Perhaps you should phone the landlady? I don't think you're well enough to go on your own. We could send Bridget by taxi.'

'Yes, we could,' Max agreed.

The phone rang and Anna rushed to answer it. 'It's for you.' She handed Max the phone and he gestured for her to get a pen and paper.

'What? I suppose when I look back it seems so obvious. Yes of course, I'll take a taxi. I'll be with you at midday.' Max put the phone down.

'What's happened?' Anna asked.

'It appears that Dinah has left her flat and gone up north to her parents.'

'I thought her father was dead.'

'It appears not; nor are both her ex husbands, who she seems to have conned out of money.'

'Oh my God! What next? I don't think I can take any more.' Anna sounded defeated.

'Anna, now's the time to think, not to be impulsive. We've already gone down that route and look where it's got us. I want you to give as much attention as you can to Oska and Barney; leave me to deal with the lawyers. Ask Bridget to work extra hours if need be. Don't mention anything about the gun to Madellaine. In fact, if you must, just tell her that I'm working things out with our lawyers. And try and keep Barney away from Rob for the moment.'

'I understand Max, I won't let the family down again,' Anna

sobbed. Max knew he was punishing Anna but couldn't stop himself, all this needn't have happened. He also knew that he, too, was to blame but knowing Anna's frailty had decided never to tell her the truth.

'We'll get through this.' It was all he felt able to say, but he didn't really believe it.

Later that day sitting in Charles Devon's office, Max was surprised when another man knocked and came into the room.

'I'd like to introduce you to James Madden, the detective. He's made quite a contribution to our dealings.'

Max shook hands with James Madden, who placed a thick file on the desk.

'We'll start with Ms Dinah Deedes and then go on to other matters. The subject has quite a history. She met her first husband in Spain and married him when she was 18. After two years she divorced him and under Spanish law was entitled to half of their house. She returned to Newcastle and stayed with her parents where she met Deedes, a much older man, who she married at the age of twenty-two, getting divorced eighteen months later with a sizeable settlement. She then came down to London, bought an apartment in Brixton and held various jobs in Liberty and Harrods. Starting as a sales assistant, she worked her way up to being a buyer. During this time she acquired secretarial and administrative skills. Unusually, and most significantly, we have not been able to obtain much information as to the reasons for leaving her employers. Some six years ago she joined your company as your personal assistant, and, so far as you are aware, she was an excellent PA. I don't know whether proper references were obtained at this time and I can't comment on the emotional aspects of her behaviour. Mr Elliott claims that she had a crush on him and he felt as if he was being pursued, as Ms Deedes insinuated her way into his family. Charles Devon is attending to these matters.

'There is another aspect to this case. We are still working on it but there is a pattern of monies from your company being paid into Ms Deedes' personal bank account, monies far in excess of her salary. I am sorry to tell you there is quite a possibility she has been defrauding the company, I would suggest you advise your auditors.'

'Good God, man!' Max burst in. 'How on earth did you uncover all this? What's the evidence? How did you get to see her bank account?'

Madden smiled at Max. 'Well, sir, there are some things in our work that are best left unsaid. Suffice to say, the porter at her block of flats was very accommodating. I have taken photographs of her bank statements and various invoices and correspondence. Charles may well advise you of any difficulties in directly using such information in any court proceedings but I think it may be useful in his handling of the case.'

Max was shaken but on second thoughts not surprised. He was now in a more powerful position so far as Dinah was concerned and she still had her apartment, on which he might have some claim. This new light cast on Dinah showed her to be an amoral and manipulative person and that meant that Anna and Oska would now believe him. Thank God he had not rushed to tell Anna everything, as he knew that she would never have been capable of forgiving him. He would have to learn to live with his lie. Dinah had duped and deceived him and was a thief. She had fooled him into feeling sorry for her, and then used him. He could not get over what a fool he had been. It was only right that Charles report her to the police.

Max told Charles what a relief it was and how wise he had been to stop him from mentioning his encounter with Dinah to anybody.

'May I move onto another matter? It's about Barney.'

Charles listened to Max, whose concern was Barney's legal position and whether there was a chance of protecting Rob from prosecution. Charles thought there was a reasonable chance of nothing happening so far as Barney was concerned but he would have to think about Rob. The police would want to know who gave Barney the gun.

'I think Barney just found it at the back of his cupboard. Anyone could have put it there. So many people could have gone into Barney's room – we've had odd workman in the house, so who knows when it was put there,' Max said unconvincingly. He wondered for a moment about telling Madellaine or the police about Rob's gun and dismissed the thought, He had too many immediate problems to deal with and needed to support Anna who had begged him to protect Madellaine and Rob.

'I'll have another talk with Sergeant Murray.' Charles gave a little smile conveying a sense of 'leave it to me, perhaps we can sort something out'.

It had been an extraordinary meeting; full of surprises and of hope. Tears came to Max's eyes. He felt exhausted and his shoulder ached. They shook hands and Charles said.

'Go home, Max, it's enough for one day. I'll be in touch.'

45

Walking on Eggshells – June 1992

Anna took one look at Max as he walked in and suggested he go straight to bed.

'Thanks,' he said, went upstairs and dropped onto the bed. Anna followed him up and drew the curtains. She didn't tell him that Hillside School had phoned to enquire if they had returned the application form, as they hadn't received it. Anna had apologised profusely, saying there had been a family crisis as Max was ill and they would be sending off the form within the week. She surprised herself by still harbouring the fantasy that Barney would go to Hillside.

It seemed she had to keep everything as planned, finding it difficult to think of more than one thing at the same time, and Max's suggestion that they have a complete rethink of their life had only added to her anxiety.

Barney seemed much calmer since Max had returned. He'd been watching all his Elvis films since breakfast. Oska arrived home looking a little more relaxed.

'How did the exam go?' Anna asked.

'OK,' he said.

'Well, at least it was your last one, you can relax now.'

'Oh sure, in this mad-house.'

'Would you like some lunch? I've made a cottage pie. Max is asleep.'

'Sure,' Oska said.

Oska ate ravenously, pleasing Anna when he asked for a second helping. She would have to cook something else for Max and

Barney, who hadn't eaten for a few hours. It seemed that the whole household was upside down. Bridget was still away getting Max's things from Russell Square, and she needed to go shopping as they were running out of food. She found some potatoes and put them in the oven. It seemed that the uncertainty of their future was reflected in their home that was falling apart. The phone rang. What next? she thought as she anxiously picked it up.

'Is that Mrs Elliott? This is Joan Kindle, the educational psychologist. I'm phoning about Barney.'

It took Anna a moment to make the connection, and she heard, 'Are you there?'

'Oh yes! I'm just surprised, that's all.'

'I wanted to let you know that we've had a case conference about Barney's educational placement. A place has come up at Hollybush Village. It's near Brighton and is run on Rudolph Steiner principles. It's a wonderful place for many reasons and we wondered whether you and your husband would like to visit it.'

'Where is it? Isn't it a bit far to go to Brighton every day?' Anna asked.

'I'm sorry, I forgot to mention that it's a boarding school – but a remarkable environment. I would like you to visit it before you make up your mind. Just a visit, that's all. I should also mention that our education department would subsidise up to fifty per cent of the fees. We do this every so often when we can't find a suitable placement in our area. Almost everybody at the case conference agreed that Barney is an exceptional boy who needs the optimum education and we think Hollybush Village can provide it.'

'I am most grateful to you. My husband and I would like to visit whenever you can make an appointment,' Anna heard herself saying.

'Good, I'll be in touch soon,' Joan Kindle replied.

Anna wanted to do some food shopping but felt unable to ask Oska to look after Barney. It was as if Oska had read her mind.

'I'm going to lie down,' he said, walking out of the kitchen. It was unlike him not to help clear up the dishes or say thanks for lunch.

231

It seemed to Anna that the whole family was punishing her. She cleared up the dishes and waited for Barney to come charging into the kitchen demanding his lunch.

She fought against her sadness and could see no way forward. She'd been trying to repair the damage but everyone in the family was resisting her attempts. Just then, Max appeared in the kitchen; she hadn't heard him coming down the stairs.

'I'm afraid there isn't much to eat: a couple of baked potatoes with cheese or I can make an omelette, Oska was ravenous and ate the whole cottage pie. I haven't been able to go out shopping.'

She put together a tray with Barney's lunch and was heading into the TV room just as he was about to come into the kitchen.

'I want to eat in the kitchen, I've had enough of Elvis.'

Anna followed him back to the kitchen and sat at the table, knowing he would take forever and wouldn't talk until he had finished.

'Baked potatoes are fine,' Max replied. Suddenly flooded by guilty feelings, he watched Anna slowly drag herself up from the table. Pain was written over her face, with dark rings under her swollen, tear-filled eyes and patches of pink dotted on her pale complexion. She looked moments away from collapse.

'Sit down, I'll get them.' Max went to the oven now feeling deeply ashamed. Suddenly he realised what he was doing in continuing to punish Anna. He recalled how she had stood by him and realised that in many ways she was as innocent as Barney. Anna was always the first to forgive and make up after a spat and he could rely on her coming round . . .

Realising his unwarranted cruelty added to his remorse.

'Why don't you go and lie down? Barney will be all right.'

'Oska's lying down,' she told him.

'I know. Don't worry about food, we'll go out for dinner tonight.'

'Hamburger and chips!' Barney shouted.

'Are you sure?' she asked.

'Anna, please go and lie down. I'll bring you up some tea.'

When Max went up with the tray, he stood outside the closed door and heard her sobbing. He went in and, putting the tray on the bedside table, sat on the edge of the bed. He put his arm round her and felt her body quivering.

'Anna, it will be all right.' He bent down to kiss her damp face.

'Oh Max, I want to die. I've been so stupid and I'm deeply ashamed. I'll never forgive myself. The only thing that stops me killing myself is that I can't leave you with the boys. I couldn't be that selfish.' She swallowed but a lump in her throat made her choke and she rushed to the bathroom to throw up, although she hadn't eaten all day.

Oska came in. 'What's going on?' he demanded to know.

'Anna is ill!' Max couldn't look him in the eye.

'I'm not surprised. For God's sake, how much more can we all take?'

'You're right, Oska, absolutely right.' Max went to help Anna as she came out of the bathroom.

'I'm sorry,' she said and climbed back onto the bed.

'You have nothing to be sorry about,' Max said tenderly. 'Everything is going to be OK, I just want you to rest.'

'I'm going back to bed,' Oska announced.

'Good,' Max said supportively, wondering if some sort of balance in the family might be returning.

He went downstairs and found that Barney had almost finished eating.

'Do you want to go to Hillside School?' Max asked him.

'I know I'll learn a lot but I don't think they will let me bring Hurrah Hippo into school and I don't think I would like to share all those books in the library with the other boys. I'm worried that when I'm not there, they might rearrange the books or take one out for themselves.'

'I see,' Max said, relieved that Barney wouldn't be too disappointed with a change of plan. 'Would you like to help me clear up the kitchen so when Anna comes down it will be a nice surprise for her?'

'Yes, and Anna won't have to cook tonight because we are going out for dinner.' Barney started clearing the table.

The phone rang and Max went to answer it.

'Hello this is Joan Kindle, from the Department of Education, is Mrs Elliott available?'

'She's resting. May I take a message? I'm her husband.'

'Oh Mr Elliott, I'm pleased to talk to you. I've made an appointment for next Thursday for you and your wife to visit the Hollybush Village. I'll be sending you all the particulars in the post, but I wanted you to know immediately.'

'Thank you very much,' Max replied, even though he had no idea what it was all about.

46

The Fragile Family Dinner – July 1992

It was six o'clock when Oska came down the stairs. Max was sitting with Barney in the playroom, watching a cartoon.

'Where's Mum?' Oska asked.

'She's still resting,' Max answered.

'Should I take her up some tea?'

'I think she would really appreciate that, Oska,' Max replied.

Anna heard the door open and saw Oska standing next to her with the tray of tea.

'Oh darling, thank you, I really could do with that.'

'Are you feeling better?' Oska asked.

'Much better, I'll get up soon and come down.'

'Good. Max says we're all going out for dinner this evening.'

'Well, you deserve it after finishing all your exams, and I'm not worried about the results because I believe in you Oska. I always have and I know you've done your best. I also know we didn't make it easy for you, and I'm sorry.'

'It's OK, Mum, let's just move on. I'll see you downstairs.' Oska wanted to hug Anna but hesitated, and went downstairs.

Anna had a quick shower and dressed in one of the samples from her latest 'Anytime Anywear' collection. Max looked at her as she walked downstairs, admiring her outfit. Wearing a khaki silk wrap-round skirt to the ankles, a papaya-coloured loose tunic and a brown silk scarf arranged round her shoulders, with bright pink pumps on her feet, she looked elegant and exotic. Her hair, now streaked with platinum grey, was pulled back in a loose chignon and added to her svelte and haunting beauty, but her liveliness was now spent, replaced by a sort of serene surrender to her fate. She struggled to smile.

'Is everybody ready?' she asked, with forced enthusiasm.

'What do you think boys, doesn't Anna look stunning?' Max said, appreciating the effort she was making.

'You look great, Mum,' Oska agreed.

'I think Hoorah Hippo needs to come to our special celebration for Oska,' Barney added.

'I didn't realise it was a special celebration for me,' Oska said

The only reason he wanted to get good A-levels was so that he could leave home and go to university. It seemed to him that something fundamental had changed in the family. It was as if each person was moving on in different, obscure directions and there was no return to what was.

'I just hope my results are OK.' Oska sounded disheartened.

Max had to say something positive. 'Well, I've got a surprise for all of us tonight, so I hope you can wait until after dinner.' He had yet to think what it was, but hopefully something would occur to him.

Their conversation during the dinner at one of their favourite restaurants was forced but superficially congenial. They noticed Barney uncharacteristically speeding through his hamburger and chips.

'Barney, you don't have to rush, we've hardly started eating,' Anna reminded him.

'Max is going to tell us about the surprise,' he reminded them.

'OK, I'll tell you now.' Max couldn't stand watching Barney stuffing the chips into his mouth.

'I know we've all had a difficult time lately, and especially Oska who has worked so hard and finished his A-levels. I think we should all go away on holiday for two weeks.' Max waited to see their reaction.

'I think that's a very good idea,' Anna said immediately.

'I haven't any objections,' Oska added.

'Can I take Hoorah Hippo?' Barney demanded.

'Does anybody have any objections to going to Pondicherry?' Max asked.

The silence showed that some explanation was required, so Max continued. 'We have some serious problems to sort out, which have been the reason for the difficulties we are having in the family.' Max looked at Anna.

'I hope this isn't just an excuse,' Oska said.

'No, Oska, it's way beyond that and you are old enough to participate in the decision. We are all exhausted and need to get away in order to return refreshed and fit to confront the problems that face us. Dinah has been stealing from the business. I haven't trusted her for some time and couldn't understand her behaviour, but even so, I really am shocked. The last straw was when she told Anna the most terrible lies about me and almost destroyed your mother. That's when our lawyer advised getting a detective. Well, it seems that she has been married twice before, has fleeced both of her ex husbands and has wilfully tried to destroy my marriage.' Max looked at Anna and stretched out and held her hand. 'There is a lot more to it but I've told you the essentials. I want to go to Pondicherry and try to sell our part of the business to Narendra while it is still a going concern. We want to downsize here, but he mustn't know the reason for the sale. I will put it to him that Anna is not well and we need to sell out and I felt it only fair that I give him the first offer. I won't write to him but just pretend to be going on a family holiday and then at the right moment suggest selling our half of the business there to him. It makes sense because he owns 49 per cent, he's running a smooth operation and can continue. I just want out.' Max sounded determined.

'Well, I don't mind going to Pondicherry to that hotel on the beach,' Oska said.

'I think you're absolutely right, Max. I don't think I can go on, the problems are getting ever more serious and I can't face this emotional and financial rollercoaster. We've come to a natural end of our business.' Anna sounded quite calm and relieved.

'We have, but it doesn't mean that Narendra is going to get the business at a fire sale price. We need all the capital we can get and I must be one step ahead of him.'

'What about Dinah?' Oska asked.

'She's left her flat in Maida Vale and has gone back to Newcastle. She knows she's in trouble and we mustn't have anything at all to do with her. The detective is still in the middle of his investigation and our solicitor is in charge of the case against her. Our main task is to sell the business to Narendra and leave the legal matters to unfold. After we've made the sale we will be better placed to decide on our next steps.'

'Wow!' Oska exclaimed. 'I had no idea what you've been going through.'

'It's not your fault, Oska. It took me some time to realise what Dinah was up to and I know it looked like something else was going on but she certainly made an idiot out of me. I even felt sorry for her. That's the genius of a confidence trickster.'

'I didn't want to be shot of you, Max, but I had to help Anna,' Barney explained.

'It's OK, Barney, but you must never, never touch a gun again, do you understand?' Oska said.

'Only if I get a licence, because I don't know how to use one. I didn't like the gun hidden at the back of my cupboard,' Barney said.

'We still have that to clear up.' Max looked at Oska to warn him not to discuss it with Barney.

It seemed as if the oxygen had returned to the air and they all breathed more lightly.

'So are we agreed about a holiday in Pondicherry?' Max asked.

'I think it's a brilliant plan and I just hope Narendra will buy the business,' Oska said, seeming to want to take responsibility again.

There was an air of excitement and relaxation as they arrived home. Max suggested Anna go straight to bed. Oska and Barney went into the TV room. When Max came up, Anna was sitting up in bed.

'I forgot to mention about the phone call from the educational psychologist.' She told Max about the possibility of Barney boarding at the school and then he told her that he had agreed to going to see it with her next Thursday.

'It's only a visit, but I really don't think he'll survive at Hillside and I also think he needs, we need, an alternative lifestyle for all of us.'

'I think I'm ready for that,' Anna replied.

'We'll book for Pondicherry after the visit,' Max suggested.

'Oh Max, I feel things are going to get better.' Anna turned over and fell into a deep sleep.

47

Game Changer – July 1992

It was a sunny day when they set out on their journey to visit Hollybush Village. Oska, concerned about Barney's future, decided to join them. Anna did the driving to give Max a chance to rest his injured shoulder. They were due at the school at eleven and were expecting to be shown around by a Mrs Jane Masters, have lunch in the communal dining room and meet some members of staff.

'It seems very well organised,' said Max, as he read the brochure and looked at pictures of the grounds, music room and hall. 'I'm totally happy with their philosophy that each child is an individual and will be helped according to his needs and his nature.'

Oska kept an eye on the map and navigated them to the gates of the school. The tree-lined path bordered by white oleander leading onto mowed lawns welcomed them as they parked in front of a large, ivy-covered Victorian house. Anna rang the brass bell on the panelled oak door and was greeted by Jane Masters. 'This must be Barney,' she said, as Barney clutched Hurrah Hippo.

'Who have you brought with you, Barney?' she asked.

'My parents, my mother Anna, my father Max and my elder brother Oska,' he replied.

'Would you all like a cup of coffee after your long journey?'

'That would be most welcome, although I'm not tired because Anna did all the driving because Max has an injured shoulder and Oska is tired because he has just finished his A-levels,' Barney replied.

In the sitting room, with each wall painted in a different shade of the same hue, they sat on comfortable armchairs covered in cream linen loose covers. The large windows looked out onto acres of green fields, a copse of trees and then open farmland.

'I don't know if you know anything about our work here?' Jane asked.

'Very little,' Anna said.

'Of course you'll understand more as we take you round the different departments and see the children at work. Please feel free to ask as many questions as you like. We are guided by the work of Rudolph Steiner, the nineteenth-century Austrian philosopher and educator, who believed in the spiritual nature and wisdom of every human being. We try to address the latent possibilities in each individual. The pupils can sit GCSEs and A-levels, but they can also do hands-on activities like gardening, woodwork, cooking and our essential eurhythmy, which is basically stylised movement in response to music and speech. We find it relaxes and centres the mind and body. We see ourselves as a community of individuals.'

'I very much like the way this room is painted in such delicate colours,' Anna remarked.

'We use vegetable dyes to provide the most natural response and we grow our own produce on the farm.'

They walked round the different departments. Each room was impressive, the children all quietly focused on their work. In each room there were a few children with Down's Syndrome and perhaps one or two autistic children displaying classic repetitive movements. Anna was surprised that each child slept in their own room painted in various pastel shades.

They were taken around the farm and saw older children milking cows. Some, Jane told them, decide to stay on and work on the farm full-time. Barney wanted to stay and watch the sheep being brought in. He seemed riveted by the wealth of activities, especially the music room where the school orchestra was having a rehearsal.

At lunch they sat with some staff members who talked with them as if they were part of the community. Everybody was on first name terms and no one seemed to mind when a child came up to them with a problem. Max and Anna knew without saying that

Barney would be fulfilled as they took in the calm and deeply meaningful experience.

On the way home, Oska offered to drive and they stopped for tea in a small village to reflect on the day's experience.

'Did you like that school, Barney?' Anna asked.

'I like the smell. It's not like Hillside, which smells of piss and polish. I like the music and everybody seems very kind.'

'I think it's a wonderful environment for you, but you know you have to sleep there during the week and can come home at the weekend,' Oska told Barney, seeing that as possibly the most worrying part for Barney.

'I will have my own room and I can take all my books and Hurrah Hippo and I can see the sheep from my window.' Barney seemed less anxious than Max.

'We can visit you as often as you like,' Max said, although he had no idea about the visiting rules or home visits on the weekend.

'Would you like to go there?' Oska asked.

'I think it would be a very interesting experience and my family will visit and I can phone you every day and I won't get Rob into trouble if the police can't find me,' Barney pronounced.

Max had no idea that Barney was so worried about the gun, and decided that he should talk to Charles Devon.

'What do you think, Anna?' Max asked.

'I think we would have to move near the school so that we could see Barney often,' Anna insisted.

'Well, as you know, Sussex University have offered me a place if I get reasonable A-levels. I'll be able to see Grandma and Uncle Harold more often. Rottingdean is also fairly close,' Oska enthused.

'One day at a time,' Max said, warmed by the thought that the family were coming together again. It was serendipitous that this was the part of England where he felt most at home. He had always liked living near the sea and as a child had lived in an Edwardian house a block away from the shore. He thought of the tea shop his mother opened fifteen years ago which had become part of the village landscape. She had done well to sell the house, and buy the shop with a flat above. It had kept her busier than she liked but also less lonely.

Max felt that life was working out. There seemed to be a place and a purpose for his sons and, best of all, Anna seemed less fragile.

48

Full Circle – July 1992

The next morning Joan Kindle, the educational psychologist, phoned to ask what they thought of the school.

'We all think it's marvellous and it's just a matter of the boarding part,' said Anna. 'We are considering moving down south to be near the school, but that might not happen that speedily.'

Dawn was impressed by their commitment and wanted to be helpful. 'Perhaps I could persuade Jane Masters to accept Barney as a day pupil from September and he could start boarding from January. Would that give you enough time? It does mean a long day for him and taking a train each way but at least he'll have a full day of activity. Perhaps you could find someone who could accompany him on the train. It would be such a pity to lose the place, as there is a waiting list.'

'We'll take it and do all we can to make it work.' Anna sounded determined.

'Good, then I suggest you come and see me tomorrow at ten o'clock and we can do all the paperwork. I feel so pleased we've managed to find something for Barney, I know he'll do well.' Dawn couldn't hide her enthusiasm.

'Thank you so much,' Anna replied.

Anna rushed to tell Max about the conversation. 'It all feels right, doesn't it?'

'Yes, I don't have any of the doubts I had about Hillside. And I think it fits nicely into our plan to downsize and move away from London. We can probably find a lovely home near Brighton for half the price of London and will have time and capital to think again. I don't want you working yourself to a frazzle. And if Oska gets into Sussex there will be a lot to be thankful for.'

'Do you still want to go to Pondicherry?' Anna asked.

'Yes, especially now we have to get Narendra to buy us out.'

'I'd better get on and book tickets for the flight,' Anna replied.

'Don't mention anything to Madellaine though,' Max reminded Anna.

At lunch, Anna told Max she had got tickets for the following Thursday and had also managed to get rooms in the same hotel, which would be familiar to Barney.

The week flew by. Max had two more meetings with Charles Devon, who had managed to persuade Sergeant Murray that none of them had any idea how the gun had got into Barney's cupboard. Charles had got Sergeant Murray and his superintendent to agree that nothing on which they could rely would come from taking a formal statement from Barney. He explained that the education authority had advised that Barney should become a boarder in a special school that would provide appropriate help and security. Barney was suffering extreme stress, he had had his first epileptic fit after the incident and the family and all the professionals were pro-foundly concerned to relieve him from any additional anxiety. The police had finally agreed; they would retain the gun and no further action would be taken.

The last few months had taught Max never to give up until the job was done, no matter how long it takes. It was his tendency to give up, that had led him into more trouble and he saw that Anna, with her principles to persist and her nature to endure, was the better person. He would never put her through such chaos and trauma again. When he thought how he had all but destroyed her, he promised himself he would make it up to her, starting with the holiday in Pondicherry.

Sitting on the veranda in the hotel, watching Oska and Barney fooling around in the turquoise sea, felt like heaven to Max and Anna drinking their citrons pressés.

'It was a brilliant idea of yours to come here,' Anna told him.

He stretched across and cupped his hand over hers. 'This is where another new life for us will begin.'

'When are you going to see Narendra?' Anna asked.

'We have to think, Anna. We can't afford to make a single mistake. I'm determined to get this right, everything depends on it.'

Anna suggested that Max phone Narendra before their presence was discovered and they lost the advantage.

'You're right. I'll go to our room.' Anna stayed to watch the boys although she knew Oska was quite capable of looking after Barney. She wanted Max to be in control as that was when he was at his best.

'Hello, Narendra.'

'Max! Where are you? How nice to hear from you.'

'I'm in Pondicherry, at our old hotel. Last-minute decision, both the boys are on holiday, Oska just finished his A-levels, Anna hasn't been too well, so we just got on a plane, arrived this morning and the boys are in the sea.'

'Wonderful! How long are you here for?'

'About ten days or so. It all depends on Oska's results and applications to university and that sort of thing.' Max gave no hint of any business dealings.

'When can I see you?' Narendra asked.

'Anytime you like. We're just relaxing here.'

'I'll come round at tea time after you've all had a rest,' Narendra suggested.

'Look forward to seeing you.' Max put the phone down and went to tell Anna about the conversation.

'It must have been quite difficult – talking, but not talking.'

'I think he was probably doing the same. He's no fool. Anna, do you think you can keep the boys away this afternoon? The last thing we need is Barney coming out with one of his jewels.'

'I can take them to the zoo.'

'Good, and if you see us deep in conversation, let them go into the sea and you sit on the beach where you can see them. I'll be at this table and I'll take my hat off to signal you to come over.' Max made notes.

'Have you any idea of the figures, how much he should pay?'

'It depends how much he wants our share. I'll just mention that you're not well and I'd like to get out at some time. I'll just have to take my cue from him. Think on my feet, something like that.'

'Max, that's what you're really good at.'

'I have to be in the right frame of mind and believe me, after all we've all been through, I'm lucky to have a mind.'

Anna smiled. 'We've been through worse. Remember Disney-world!'

'You know, I think that Barney could be happy at the Steiner School, and if it all works out we could open a small boutique on the coast. We'll think of something, Anna.'

'I know. I've always believed that a crisis is also an opportunity.'

49

Max Calls His Bluff – July 1992

Max saw Narendra wave as he came up the path. They hugged each other.

'Where's the family?' Narendra asked.

'Barney wanted to go to the zoo and Anna wanted to tire him out so that he would sleep tonight.'

'It must be very difficult for Anna, worrying about Barney's future.'

'It is, that's why we came on holiday. Barney has now become epileptic and this has affected Anna very badly. She's absolutely exhausted and her health isn't so good either. I'm really worried about her. You know her mother has multiple sclerosis.' Max felt he had prepared the field for Narendra.

'I didn't know. How worrying for you.' Narendra sounded genuinely concerned. 'Is she still able to work on the collections?'

'Fortunately Anna is usually ahead of herself. But between you and me, I'm really very worried.'

'Would you like to sell out?'

Max felt that Narendra had shown his hand far too soon. 'I was thinking about it, but nobody wants to kill the goose that lays the golden eggs. We've had a lot more interest from abroad lately, Australia, Canada, Milan, Geneva and even Berlin.'

'What sort of interest?' Narendra asked, his eyes blinking like a cash machine.

'To tell the truth, what with all the problems we're having with Barney, I just took the calls. They want me to send them catalogues of our collections, prices and delivery. The problem is, I need to get someone who can use a computer. I think we could make a fortune if we restructured and, quite frankly, I don't know where to start with my family problems. Thanks to Anna we have enough designs to go on producing for years and thanks to you we are maintaining our quality and meeting our delivery dates.'

'Max, how can I help? You know you are like family to me and I haven't seen you so down before.'

'With all my family problems, I think it wouldn't be a bad idea to sell out now that the business is so successful and on the brink of expansion. Thanks to you doing your part. But I must put Anna and the boys first. Would you consider buying me out, or do you think I should look for another partner in London?' Max said in a matter-of-fact voice.

'I would, but of course it depends on the price,' Narendra replied.

'Well, make me an offer, I'll consider it, no harm done.'

'There's a lot to think about, can we leave it for a couple days?' Narendra asked.

'As long as you like, of course I have to get Anna's agreement.'

'Of course!' Narendra replied.

Max looked across the beach. Anna and the boys hadn't returned. 'I think I must go and lie down now. Will you excuse me?' Max winced and held onto his shoulder.

'What's wrong with your arm?'

'That was another bit of bad luck I forgot to mention. An accident, so no more tennis and golf,' Max said, although he had never played either before. They embraced each other carefully and Max went up to his room.

When Anna returned she looked exhausted. 'We had a good time but I think the boys have collapsed. They're both in their room. What happened with Narendra?' she asked, but before Max had finished telling her she was fast asleep.

Later on Barney came into their room. 'Can we have room service?'

'Sure.' Max was pleased that he and Anna could have some time together and suggested they also have room service. It was the first opportunity they'd had to talk without the boys hovering over them.

'Do you think Narendra will come back with an offer?' Anna asked after hearing the details from Max.

'We can only try. I know he will make a pretty low offer as he controls the production side of the business, he has us in a bit of a tight corner.'

'I think I'd better stay well away. I'm not up to negotiating, I've lost my confidence and feel far too anxious. We mustn't fail, I want to leave everything to you. I was right to depend on you taking Barney for his interview at Hillside and I feel the same way now.

'Come here, you silly old thing.' She came towards Max and he grabbed her and pulled her down onto the bed.

50

Leaving Pondicherry – August 1992

Max hadn't heard from Narendra for three days, and was beginning to wonder whether he'd had his bluff called when the phone rang.

'Sorry I haven't been in contact but the way you talked I really didn't want to disturb your family holiday. My accountant and I have worked out a proposition and wondered when it would be convenient to meet?' Narendra asked.

'We're going out for the day. Are you free first thing tomorrow morning, because the boys want to go out in the afternoon?' Max continued to play hard to get.

'That's fine. I'll be with you at nine o'clock tomorrow morning.' Narendra sounded impatient.

The following morning, Anna and the boys went to the beach and Max waited for Narendra, who turned up exactly on time. Max had worked out the figures with the help of Barney, his human calculator, and had analysed the value of the business including Anna's designs. He was helped by their latest certified accounts, which he and Narendra had recently agreed. He had included values of all the assets then added something extra to give him a figure from which he could allow himself, with every appearance of reluctance, to be negotiated down.

Narendra handed Max a paper with his offer written down. It was less than Max was aiming at but left enough wiggle room for a deal. Max sat back and thought. He thought of the time Barney had caught Narendra falsifying the figures and of Narendra's copious apologies and excuses; he thought of the detective indicating pretty clearly that Dinah had been stealing money from the company and his seemingly passing comment that Dinah had a lot of faxes to and from India. Then it came to him.

Leaning forward 'Narendra' he said quietly, 'I must of course tell you that Dinah has suddenly left the company and on my return I will be having her financial affairs investigated by the authorities.'

Narendra, his mind racing, looked unblinkingly at Max. If Dinah's affairs were investigated his private arrangement with her would be revealed and he too could face criminal charges.

In the silence between them they both knew they had to make a deal.

Finally Narendra leaned forward. 'Max, add fifteen percent to my asking price and I'll shake on it.'

Max pretended to wait a minute or two before replying. 'It's much lower than I wanted, but if we can conclude contracts in the next two days, and let me have a certified cheque I'll go for it. Anna and I will resign as Directors and it will be a straightforward sale to you of all our shares in the company. For the sake of friendship, and for the sake of the family's health, I'm happy.' Max felt drained.

'You are a true gentleman, Max,' Narendra stood up to shake hands with him.

When he told Anna about the deal, she said: 'Max! Haven't we undersold?'

'Darling, we've actually done very well. You still have your talent and with the money from the business and if we sell the house we should have quite a lot of capital to rebuild our lives. For the first time Barney's future is secure, hopefully Oska will get into Sussex University and we can live a stress-free life near the family.' His voice sounded flat.

Anna relaxed and while thoughts and worries surged in her mind, she determined to trust and rely on Max.

Max reflected that whatever had happened between Narendra and Dinah and whatever their future together or separately might be – thankfully it would no longer be his concern. His concern was how Barney would adapt to boarding school, remembering past arguments about wanting to send Barney away. Once again it seemed that Anna was reading his mind.

'Max, do you really think that Barney will adapt to leaving us?'

'I do, because Barney doesn't see things in their entirety. He liked the sheep, the music, the colour of the walls in his room and those things seem to sustain him. If people are kind to him and let him be, he will adapt and if he doesn't, we'll think again.'

'I would like to go home.' Anna sounded determined. Max knew that while he had saved the family financially, he couldn't save Anna from her feelings of loss with Barney and Oska away and no creative deadlines to meet. He knew he would have to live not only with the guilt of his stupidity in having let Dinah seduce him but with the burden of having lied to the most precious people in his life.

It was as if it had all come full circle. Twenty-three years ago, they had started their life together in Pondicherry. Now they would return to London to begin a different life.

Sitting on the hotel terrace looking onto the ocean, Anna saw Barney and Oska splashing each other. Feelings of sadness and gratitude swept over her. She couldn't explain her exhaustion – it was as if her heart was breaking into pieces and she had to keep very still and quiet waiting for it to pump life back into her. She was drifting into a limbo, and she recalled those same feelings in Disneyworld, where only the present existed and the past seemed as remote as the future.

Waterford City & County Council
RECEIVED
DEC 2015
Library and Arts Department

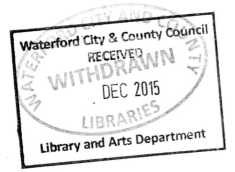